SHARAI TOOK ANOTHER SIP OF WINE AS THOUGH TO PUT OUT A CONCEALED FIRE.

Her facade was firmly back in place. She was a very controlled person, despite her passion. Or perhaps because of it. Was that what haunted her? Had she taken her passionate nature and hammered it into the cold shape of hatred?

The Israeli secret service is spread more thinly than any spook stable in the world. This woman conducted herself professionally, but she was just too damn beautiful and therefore too memorable to be much use in the field except as a Mata Hari. Despite Sharai's obvious commitment to Israel, I didn't see her turning tricks in the name of national security.

I looked up suddenly, catching an entirely different expression on Sharai's face. I knew then that she was wondering how my hands would feel on her body, and whether I would be half as careful of her as I was of the wineglass I was holding.

"Look Sharai—" I began, but she spoke quickly, as though she knew what I was going to say.

"The four Palestinians—what did they look like?" she asked.

Bantam Books offers the finest in classic and modern American murder mysteries. Ask your bookseller for the books you have missed.

A. E. Maxwell

The Frog and the Scorpion

BANTAM BOOKS
TORONTO · NEW YORK · LONDON · SYDNEY · AUCKLAND

THE FROG AND THE SCORPION

A Bantam Book / published by arrangement with
Doubleday & Company

PRINTING HISTORY
Doubleday edition published May 1986
Bantam edition / August 1987

ISBN 0-553-26876-7

Published simultaneously in the United States and Canada

Bantam Books are published by Bantam Books, Inc. Its trademark, consisting of the words ''Bantam Books'' and the por-
trayal of a rooster, is Registered in U.S. Patent and Trademark
Office and in other countries. Marca Registrada. Bantam Books,
Inc., 666 Fifth Avenue, New York, New York 10103.

PRINTED IN THE UNITED STATES OF AMERICA

O   0 9 8 7 6 5 4 3 2 1

1

It was the bomb that really ticked me off. That was the sound it made, too. *Tick, tick, tick,* just like it had been hoked up on a George Lucas special-effects assembly line. I remember looking at the bomb, recognizing what it was, and wondering whether the Timex sitting on top of those three sticks of dynamite was shock-resistant.

But the story really began well before that, back in 1978, when the Ayatollah left Paris and flew back to Teheran in triumph. Or maybe it was in 1948, when the Brits left the Arabs and the Jews to fight it out in what was at that moment Palestine and soon became the bloody Middle East.

Oh hell, it was probably two hundred or six hundred years ago. Or a thousand or two hundred thousand, or a million, before men were men, back when they were renegade apes.

Or maybe it all began with hummingbirds.

I say this because I remember sitting on the deck in my backyard, face turned up to the sensuous July sunlight, when the first phone call came in. I was watching the hummingbirds at play around the hummingbird feeder Fiora had given me for my birthday just before she took off for five weeks at Harvard, a midsummer seminar on leverage deals and silver bullion futures trading. Rigor mortis set into my soul at the thought of sitting through a few learned lectures on how to screw thy neighbor while preserving every legal nicety. Fiora didn't see finances that way. The thought of money manipulations brought a light to her eyes that could only be equaled by the prospect of a prolonged romp in bed.

Unfortunately, a romp was not why she had dropped in on me that morning. When I reached for her, she kissed me just enough to get my full attention, smiled beautifully and handed me a package.

"I wouldn't want you to be bored while I'm away," she said, "so I brought along some world-class warfare for you to watch."

My relationship with this honey-haired, hazel-green-eyed woman is a complicated one. We are still married in a lot of

1

ways, although we try to keep the natural friction of two strong wills and two different natures at manageable levels by the polite paper pretense of divorce. Life isn't that easy, of course. Society can make a union legal or illegal, but it can't do a damn thing about unruly hearts. Fiora and I still care for one another in extraordinary and sometimes painful ways.

Fiora knows that one of the biggest problems in my life is boredom. She even feels a bit responsible. After all, she's the one who took the steamer trunk full of currency that my uncle Jake left me and turned it into a small fortune with some shrewd manipulations of the sort taught at Harvard during the summer doldrums. So when Fiora takes off on business junkets, as she regularly does, she tries to leave me with something amusing.

That afternoon I took the package from her and began pulling off bright ribbons when I sensed her watching my hands. The scars don't show too much anymore; only small, vaguely shiny little circles remain to mark the places where nails from the Oxy-Con packing crate slammed through flesh and bone. But the hole left in Fiora's life was considerably larger and didn't show at all on the outside. We rarely talk about her twin brother's death and our own encounter with his murderer. The memories are there, though; they show in Fiora's eyes when she watches my hands; they show in the sad gentleness with which she touches the scars, giving me silent apologies that I never asked for and certainly don't deserve.

Fiora brushed the corner of my mustache and traced my mouth with an elegant, smooth fingertip. "This present is to keep you out of trouble while I'm gone," she said in a husky voice.

"I'm perfectly capable of amusing myself," I said, deliberately misunderstanding her. I ripped the gift paper with more force than necessary.

"That's what I am trying to prevent," she retorted.

"Then this had better be a hell of a lot sexier than the square box suggests," I muttered.

Fiora slid a nail into the crease between my lips and I opened my teeth to catch it. Like I say, we have a very complicated relationship with a pretty simple core.

"Sex is a part of this," she said, tapping the package. "But it has a lot of other things you like, too. Power and competition, courage and cowardice. All the bloody absolutes that fascinate you."

With that introduction I was not expecting a bird feeder. I gave her a look that had become familiar after years of marriage and separation.

"Love," she whispered, bending over, ruffling my hair and nerve endings, "have I ever misled you?"

There was an obvious answer to that, but pinpointing the specifics was as elusive a task as identifying the fragrance Fiora wore.

"On second thought," she said, "don't answer. It's such a beautiful day."

As she reached for the cardboard carton, she gave me that special smile, the one that crushes hearts—or makes them whole. She was right. It was a beautiful day. I smiled in return, admiring the way her hair and body shimmered beneath sunlight and pale green silk. I saw her hesitate and knew that she was thinking about chucking the bird feeder in the koi pond and dragging me off to bed. Then she sighed and began prying at the stubborn package.

"No?" I asked softly.

"No," she said, regret clear in her tone.

I watched her slender fingers moving over pictures of soft little hummingbirds and reminded myself that where Fiora was concerned, patience was the only virtue that mattered. She had an unusual amount of trouble opening that box but I didn't offer to help. If I touched her again right away, it would take more than a lovely smile to make me let her go.

Finally a brash red-and-yellow plastic feeder emerged from the shambles Fiora made of the innocent cardboard box. The more I looked at the feeder the uglier it got. I tried to hide my reaction to her present. I shouldn't have bothered. That woman can read me like a ledger sheet. She shot me an amused glance and turned the feeder in a complete circle for my greater aesthetic appreciation.

"Yeah, I know," she said. "These things look like whore's Christmas, but they're more fun than a seat on the Grain Exchange."

With what I hoped was a polite expression of disbelief I eyed the contraption dangling from her hand. There was a clear glass bottle that ended in four red plastic bugles which I assume were intended to look like big flowers whose unlikely centers were a chrome-yellow mesh. I have a feeling, now that I know a bit more about it, that the flower likeness is for the humans rather than the hummingbirds. Hummers have very little of what I would call an aesthetic sense, but their olfactory equipment more than compensates. They could scope out a drop of nectar in a parking lot the size of Kansas. They sure as hell don't need phony stamens and pistils to point the way.

Fiora reached into her Gucci bag and produced a pint bottle full of a transparent scarlet fluid. "You can make this stuff yourself," she said. "Don't bother to buy the prepared nectar. They price it like it's something special, but it's just sugar and water and a little food coloring."

Her motto is: Watch the pennies and the dollars take care of themselves. A true Scot. I, on the other hand, am a true son of Uncle Jake, who loved adrenaline more than he loved dollars but spent both with equal abandon.

"Fiora, I don't like to seem ungrateful," I said, trying to be tactful, "but you're in the wrong place. This may be California's Gold Coast, but I've never seen a hummingbird in my yard. Maybe the salt air doesn't agree with them." I added, waving toward the endless sapphire ocean that was my backyard. "Or maybe the rent's too high."

"That's what I thought about Beverly Hills," she said. "C'mon. I'll show you where to put the feeder."

She filled the feeder and hung it on a nail sticking out of an overhead beam in the middle of the patio deck. Then we sat in the brilliant afternoon sunlight, drinking a bottle of crisp Fumé Blanc from Rutherford and watching the world's ugliest imitation flower.

After fifteen minutes I said, "Better than most television, I have to agree."

Fiora lifted one honey eyebrow at me. "Patience, Fiddler." So we watched the damn thing for a while.

I was about to suggest that we adjourn to the bedroom for our second glass of wine when I heard a low, thrumming roar about three feet from my ear. My head snapped around. For an instant I saw something hanging in midair, staring at the unlikely flower dangling from the nail over the deck. The "something" appeared to be a cross between a redheaded bumblebee and a green Gambel's quail.

So help me God, at first glance that's what the hummingbird looked like. And a glance was all I got. The sudden movement of my head startled him and he darted off so quickly I wasn't even sure I had seen him in the first place.

"Don't worry," Fiora smiled. "He'll be back."

Fifteen seconds later the hummingbird reappeared as though he had teleported into position six inches from the feeder. This time I clamped down on my reflexes and watched without so much as moving an eyelash. The hummer wasn't much bigger than my thumb. His tiny wings beat so rapidly that they were nearly invisible. He was shiny and soft and cute—a tiny Disney character—until I noticed that he was equipped with a beak that looked as long as a darning needle and about as sharp.

As I watched, he hovered, inspecting the garish feeder. Then he snapped forward like he was on an invisible rubber band and thrust his sharp bill into the heart of one of the plastic flowers. After a moment he withdrew, then thrust again. A little bubble boiled up through the red fluid, indicating the bird's success at solving the minor mystery of the feeder.

"No hummers around, huh?" said Fiora, licking a bit of the wine with a quick pink tongue. "If you get one this fast, you're going to have a swarm before long."

She was on a plane for Boston when her prophecy came true. I had dropped her off at LAX, kissed her until I had her full attention and reminded her that I cared a great deal for her. By the time I got back to the house on Crystal Cove, between Newport Beach and Laguna, it was evening. I tucked the Cobra into the garage and walked along the deck to the back door. Before I reached the back patio I heard a harsh, metallic squirring and caught sight of a pair of hummers circling and darting and slashing around the feeder. I stopped and stared, fascinated by the most dazzling and bloodthirsty aerial display I'd seen since the Harriers and the Pucaras traded insults over the Falklands on the CBS news.

Like most modern battles, this one lasted for about fifteen seconds. There was a king on the ocean bluff—I assumed he was the original discoverer of the world's ugliest flower—and a pretender to the plastic throne. The two hummers flew directly at one another, stopped to hover in midair a few inches apart, darted sideways a foot and hovered again. Then the franchise holder thrust with the speed and grace of an Olympic duelist. The interloper fled. His dominance successfully enforced, the king darted off to perch in my lemon tree.

Five seconds later the interloper reappeared, facing the intrepid defender and challenging him with a sound like a fingernail on a blackboard. They darted side to side, then clashed and locked, hanging in midair for a moment before falling with a soft thump onto the redwood deck. They lay there almost at my feet, oblivious to anything but each other and their war.

In an odd way the battle was all the more vicious for the badminton heft of the combatants. You expect lions or eagles to go at one another talon and claw, but hummingbirds? They're so small. How can those little bodies hold so much courage and hatred?

There was no answer and the birds knew it. They untangled beaks and claws and scrambled back into the air. One hummer fled and the other zipped off to the lemon tree, which was about ten feet from the feeder. With the bad sportsmanship I have come to associate with hummers, the winner jeered metallically at his vanquished opponent and then sat preening his minute feathers with his warrior's beak. I walked onto the deck. That silly bird *screed* at me, warning me off the ugly flower.

"You must have heard about David and Goliath," I said politely. "You know, the boy with more guts than brains."

The hummer sat and cursed me nonstop.

"Right, Davy. I can take a hint."

Five minutes after I went inside I heard another battle, and it went on that way for the rest of the summer. As long as I kept the feeder primed there were about a dozen fierce hummers doing battle for their positions around the ever-blooming flower. Hummers are hyperkinetic. They can go through several times their own weight in food every day, so a constant source of energy was worth fighting for.

And fight they did.

At first it was entertaining to watch them. Their patterns of behavior were so erratic and yet so predictable. The head son of a bitch was King David, a little greenish guy with a ruby throat that extended almost to his eyes. He spent hours on guard, driving away any and all comers. Maybe once an hour he would let a small, soft-gray-green female drink but he would terrify any male who appeared.

And then, for reasons I still have not been able to explain, at the close of day the flower warden would declare a twilight amnesty. For a few minutes it would be free-for-all, with four or five hummers at a time lined up to refuel under the head hummer's baleful screeing. King David would squirr and curse up a storm, but he wouldn't defend the flower. After a seemly amount of time, he would take to the air again and clear the skies, a miniature Von Richthoven in a blood-red scarf.

For a while I thought that it was nice of King David to share the wealth of the bottomless flower. But then I found myself wondering whether he let the others drink simply to keep them from losing heart and flying off to other flower kingdoms where they might have a chance of becoming the head hummer. That kind of perverse generosity isn't a comforting or comfortable thought, I suppose, but then life isn't always comforting or comfortable.

I had reason to reflect on such matters over the next few weeks. And these reflections began and ended with the hummingbirds, the phone call I got from Shahpour on a bright July morning, and the bomb that had started ticking long, long before.

The sharp-beaked warriors were in full flight when the phone rang, the sunlight was molten gold on the back deck, and the Pacific was a blue so bright it burned. I had finished the newspaper and was glancing about for something to do to amuse myself. That's the price you pay for not having to work for a living, for being what Fiora calls "independently well-heeled." Ultimately, you have to invent your own way of proving self-worth and social value.

Well, self-worth, anyway. Social value is a matter of organized opinion, like the number of angels that can do unseemly acts on the head of a pin, or whether the United States is the Great Satan and Khomeini is the Third Coming. Some people go to the office every day to reinforce their sense of self-worth. Me, I fiddle around in other people's business, lending a hand where I can and deviling the comfortable in behalf of the uncomfortable. But I had no special projects at that moment, so I was in precisely the proper frame of mind when the phone rang and a secretary on the other end asked me to hold for Shahpour Zahedi.

Shahpour was a shrewd, handsome Middle Easterner who owned controlling interest in a little bank down the Gold Coast from me. I knew he was Iranian, and that his father had been finance minister under the late, lamented and lamentable Shah, but I tried not to hold that against Shahpour. I figured the sins of the sons are bad enough without stacking on holdovers from the previous generation.

Fiora and Shahpour met a few years ago when they collaborated on financing a small business park near Los Angeles International Airport. Since he knew Fiora was playing the game with my money, I was included in the obligatory business lunches. That was the first test and Shahpour passed it with all flags flying. You see, besides having a tangled personal life, Fiora and I present some unusual challenges to modern business sensibilities. When it comes to money, she is the heavy. I'm not a fiscal dummy, but I have sense enough to recognize genius and to give it—or rather *her*—the power of attorney.

Cops, Latinos and Middle Eastern types are baffled by the power structure of my relationship with Fiora. They have a hell of a time figuring out just who does what and with which and to whom. There is usually a fair amount of thrashing around and some minor bloodshed at Spago or Jimmy's where the high-powered male executive we're lunching condescends to Fiora and flatters me. Then he gets totally confused trying to figure out why she is feeding him his lunch and I'm sitting there smiling at my beautiful mate and applauding every slice and slash.

Middle Easterners can be overweening, particularly in their disdain for women. But Shahpour was different from the outset. For one thing, he talked to both of us as intelligent adults; I don't think Fiora had to zing him once to get his attention. Shahpour had been educated in the West—Paris and the Wharton School of Finance—and he carried in those dark eyes a shrewd self-assurance that both accepted the intricacies of American culture and acknowledged importance wherever it was found. Fiora was one of those important intricacies. I was another. Shahpour enjoyed us both.

"Fiddler, how are you?" he asked as he picked up the receiver.

There was not a trace of accent, neither French nor Farsi. His voice was like his mind, endlessly flexible and enormously quick. The tone was different from what I had remembered, though. There was an edge to it that was more than worry and less than fear.

"I'm fine, Shahpour. How are things in the banking business?"

"I'm afraid my family picked the wrong time to get into the American market," he said. "We bought our shares at the Gold Coast Bank for the right price, but the returns aren't as strong as we had expected."

I knew enough about reading bank prospectuses and profit-loss statements to know that the returns on the four million dollars Shahpour had pumped into Gold Coast Bank were substantial. I also knew that bankers were never satisfied.

"Well, you could always find a spot on your board for Fiora," I said. "She has a few ideas about how to run banks."

There was a low chuckle. "She does indeed. But I have a different kind of problem, one that you're, ah, better equipped to handle than she is."

I felt like a hummingbird that has just scented nectar. It was unusual for Shahpour to get to the bottom line so quickly. Whatever his problem was, it was just slightly less urgent than a heart attack.

"I would prefer not to discuss my, ah, difficulty on the phone," continued Shahpour. "I know it's an imposition, but could I ask you to have lunch with me? Today?"

Like I said, I was bored. Besides, it's nice to encounter someone who appreciates your talents, particularly the kind of limited talents I seem to possess.

"Where and when?" I asked.

"The Ritz-Carlton. One o'clock. But, Fiddler . . ." He paused, as though unsure of his words.

"Yes?" I said, wondering what had left the eloquent Shahpour speechless.

"I'll be at a table alone. If I don't greet you, ignore me and leave. I know that sounds unusual, but there may be a certain element of, ah, risk in being seen with me. My precautions are for your own safety."

I almost hummed with pleasure. With every word my incipient boredom faded. "I'm a big boy, Shahpour," I said carelessly, "but I won't say hello if you don't."

There are days when I'm as arrogant as a hummingbird with a full feeder. I never know which days those are until it's too late to apologize to anyone who might be kind enough to still be speaking to me. This turned out to be one of those days. Shahpour really was worried about my neck. And with good reason. King David and his darning-needle beak wouldn't have anything on the men Shahpour led me to, men who possessed courage, stupidity and hatred in equal, ever-blooming measures.

I didn't know what I was getting into then. I only knew later, when I was counting my wounds and my losses—those shiny new scars across my self-esteem.

2

The Ritz-Carlton is one hotel chain's effort at bestowing instant class on the Gold Coast. Like nearly everything else on that strip of land between Malibu and San Diego, the jury is still out on the result. Only time will tell whether the $41 million invested in Mediterranean cream stucco and sixty-foot palm trees will pay off. Right now the palm trees still look like they grew to that height a hundred miles away and were trucked in. Which they were. And the cream paint needs a little more time in the sun and salt air to acquire the proper patina. But then, the hotel is only six weeks old. Give it a few months before you start talking about historical landmarks.

The hotel does one thing right: there are four valets at the front door, each one of them eager to be at my service. It might be that all four salivate to get their hands on the Cobra, with its big Ford V-8 shoehorned into an English Bristol roadster body. My Shelby Cobra is the one material object I truly value, and the only one I own that can go from zero to one hundred to zero in fourteen seconds. It's the kind of car that adds excitement to anyone's life, even a parking lot attendant's.

"Sorry, guys," I said over the muscular ticking of the big engine. "I park myself. I just wanted to memorize your faces so I would know who to come looking for when I find a big white Olds parked in close, and white paint on the dinged bodywork of my friend here."

The valet who was trying to tug open my door was a teenaged surfer with a twenty-five-dollar haircut. He looked puzzled for a moment, then he lit up. "I get it. You're saying you don't want anybody parked close to you."

I rewarded him with the smaller half of a ten-dollar bill and stuffed the larger half into my shirt pocket. Sometimes material possessions are a pain in the ass, but the Cobra repays the trouble. The day it doesn't, I'll probably take up Volkswagen Rabbit diesels. Zero to fifty to zero in fourteen days.

The Ritz-Carlton was laid out along the sandy bluff that led into Dana Point, where Richard Henry Dana threw cow hides down to sailing ships during his two years before the mast. But the hotel was not interested in some minor mid-19th Century novelist. The decor didn't allude to Dana or to the Spaniards and Mexicans who preceded him along California's golden coast. The interior was Italian marble and stainless steel and flawless mirrors. The main dining room was full of natives drinking white wine and lunching on plates of expensive seafood.

Shahpour was sitting alone in the mirrored dining room. He sprang to his feet when he saw me. I was glad to know that I wouldn't have to sit and stare at one of the many reflections of myself while I waited for Shahpour to make up his mind about whether we could safely eat lunch together. While there's nothing inherently wrong with my dark hair, mustache and gray eyes, there's nothing inherently fascinating about them either.

Shahpour shook my hand firmly before graciously indicating my chair. I shot a glance around the room.

"It's all right, Fiddler," he said in soft, discreet tones. "I've been here for forty-five minutes. I'm quite sure I wasn't followed."

Unlike most Middle Easterners, Shahpour was entirely clean-shaven. Not even a mustache. It was probably a studied move to reduce the intimidation level. With his smooth cheeks and light gray Brooks Brothers suit, he could have passed for Italian or Greek, or perhaps even a gringo with nothing better to do than lie in the sun.

Shahpour's lean face was relaxed and his voice confident, but his eyes were very busy as I sat down. He was continually—and discreetly—watching all the comings and goings of the patrons, an easy task at our perfectly situated table. I doubted that the seating arrangements had been left to the maître d'.

Shahpour poured me a glass of wine from the bottle of Chardonnay in the ice bucket beside his chair, a gesture which told me he had asked that the waiter keep his distance until signaled. Only one glass of wine had been poured before I arrived, and half of that glass was still catching light in the crystal tulip in front of Shahpour. This was a controlled man, able to stretch a half glass of good wine for forty-five minutes. Shahpour might have been uneasy, even afraid, but he wasn't looking for a bottle of courage or instant oblivion.

"You're very kind to come to me under such, ah, inauspicious circumstances," Shahpour said, pouring himself a bit more Chardonnay to cool the half glass before him. "I thought my family had left behind all need for conspiracy and circumspection when we came to this country but—" He shrugged elegantly and left his sentence unfinished.

I shrugged, but it was more massive than elegant. It's one of the disadvantages of being six two and a touch meaty about the shoulders; people rarely accuse you of finesse or elegance. "You've never struck me as the kind of man who frets over small things. If you're worried, there's a good reason."

Shahpour sighed slowly, like a man who had just negotiated a tight turn and could see the home stretch. "Thank you," he said simply. "Americans have led a sheltered life in comparison to others in the world. Sometimes it's hard for them to understand the need for caution." He closed his eyes for an instant, as though hearing his own words echo. "That sounded very arrogant. I'm sorry."

"You don't have a corner on arrogance, and besides, you're right. Most Americans are sheltered. That's why people are standing twelve deep at our borders trying to get in."

Shahpour smiled rather grimly and saluted me with his glass of wine. He took a small sip of the Chardonnay and I did likewise. It was a 1981 Spring Mountain and somebody had taken good care of it.

I could have made polite conversation, but I didn't. Shahpour hadn't called me to talk about certificates of deposit or IRA versus Keogh. After another sip Shahpour looked beyond my shoulder at the doorway, then turned to weigh me silently. I wondered what was hidden behind those shrewd black eyes. I didn't ask. I just waited. The first thing a reporter or an interrogator learns is that most people are terrified of silence and will natter on to fill it up. Shahpour proved the principle; he took a final small sip, met my eyes, and spoke.

"Do you know anything about how the American immigration service works?" he asked quietly.

"A bit," I said. "It's a small, understaffed bureaucracy barely capable of answering the phone, to say nothing of keeping order on the U.S. borders."

He smiled slightly, as though recalling something. "Yes," he said, "that's what I've heard."

"Heard?" I asked carelessly, but I was watching him like King David watched the pretender to the plastic throne. "Surely you had some experience with INS when you immigrated here."

Shahpour's smile became smaller, more ironic, almost cruel.

He ignored my conversational bait. "Tell me," he murmured, gently swirling the pale gold wine in his glass, "are these men who can't enforce the immigration laws . . . corrupt?"

It was my turn to sip wine and look at the golden currents curling against crystal. I didn't know where this conversation was going, but the orchestra in my head was stretching its multiple arms, flexing its hands and tuning up its many-voiced instruments. I'd heard the opening strains of the overture called *Trouble* often enough to recognize it.

"I assume that some are corrupt," I said finally, watching for a reaction from Shahpour. There wasn't any. "But," I added, "you've been around long enough to know that bureaucratic corruption isn't a national hobby here like it is in some other parts of the world."

Shahpour sighed softly. "That's what I thought, too, but I wanted an opinion from someone who, ah, knows the ropes. Is that the correct idiom?"

I nodded and waited. He waited too, studying his wine as though the future were written in the enigmatic swirls. I decided to see what would happen if I applied a bit of friendly pressure.

"Shahpour, if you don't trust me, why don't we just order lunch and get together the next time Fiora has a hot industrial park to build?"

The Iranian banker studied me for a moment over the rim of his wineglass. I couldn't tell whether pride or fear made him reluctant to speak. Both, probably. In the male of the species, it's sometimes hard to tell one from the other.

Shahpour raised his hand. The waiter appeared long enough to take our order for spinach salad and fresh local swordfish. When he departed, I could see that Shahpour had made up his mind. Anticipation went through me like a ripple of discordant notes, setting me on edge.

"I don't wish to burden a friend, but I do need advice." Shahpour drew a deep breath and his face flushed slightly, as though he were embarrassed. "You see, Fiddler, I'm an illegal alien."

He paused, waiting for some reaction, and I realized that his embarrassment was deeper than I could begin to understand. There are maybe a million people in Southern California whose immigration status isn't kosher. Whether Mexican field hands or Middle Eastern millionaires, they live in uncertainty, constantly fearing discovery and deportation.

"So, for that matter, are the other members of my family, twenty of us in all," Shahpour continued. "Someone has discovered this. Our secret will be kept, though."

"For a price," I said.

He nodded tiredly, looking ten years older.

I chewed on that, along with a piece of warm dill bread the waiter had brought. The irony of the millionaire banker cum illegal alien was sharp enough, but I had met some of the other members of Shahpour's family. I particularly recalled his younger sister, a glowing beauty who was studying for a master's degree in fine arts. Then there was his father, a cultured Iranian gentleman who spoke French and English flawlessly, lived in a four-bedroom house below the Boulevard in Encino and read *The Wall Street Journal* every day.

In all, the Zahedis were a modern Southern California immigrant clan. They had money, position, sophistication and the ambition needed to scramble to the top. I had always suspected that the Zahedis had a fascinating history, and I was damn sure that they were not your average huddled masses yearning to be free and rich.

It was as though Shahpour had read my thoughts.

"Yes, my whole family is at risk," he said. "My parents and my sister, my wife, even my two sons, who are in the Newport Beach Little League and the Corona del Mar Elementary School. We're no safer here than the busloads of Mexicans who are rounded up every day in the garment district and driven south to Tijuana."

"How did you get in?" I asked.

"When the Shah fell, we all managed to flee to Paris," said Shahpour, shrugging and smiling sadly. "But the French, who are always looking for a chance to cultivate trade in the Middle East, decided it would be unseemly to accept too many refugees from the Ayatollah's tyranny."

Shahpour smiled ironically again. This time there was no doubt about the cruelty implicit in the gesture.

"Poor France," he murmured with distinct satisfaction. "They didn't know that the new imam would let his people stone each other to death in the dark rather than strike a single Western match in the name of light." The smile vanished as quickly as it had appeared. "But that is, as you say, history. What mattered to my family was that the French refused to extend our visas. We applied to visit the United States. The State Department was delighted to give us thirty-day visas. So we came to America quite openly, as ordinary tourists, temporary visitors."

Shahpour looked up from the wine. His eyes were dark and calm, the eyes of a man who made decisions and never looked back in anger or regret. "That was years ago. The visas were never renewed."

He didn't say anything more. He didn't need to. I knew enough about the U.S. immigration system to know that it had been overwhelmed by the hundreds of thousands of people whose native lands had little to offer but poverty, political turmoil and a high birth rate. It wasn't just the masses of poor Latinos—Mexicans, Guatemalans, Salvadorans, Nicaraguans and the like—who walked across the deserts and filtered into the barrios of Boyle Heights and Santa Ana and Guasti. There were also Chinese and Italians and Irish by the thousands who had taken exactly the same path to Los Angeles that Shahpour was describing. For every Vietnamese who came legally as a refugee, another came through the illegal pipeline.

In Los Angeles, newspapers are printed in twenty languages.

One of them is Farsi.

"You've been safe for a long time, Shahpour. What went wrong?"

He shook his head. "I don't know. Someone called my office yesterday and demanded that I pay five thousand dollars a month or our names would be given to INS and we would all be deported." Shahpour hesitated, then said simply, "We can't go back."

I sipped wine and thought hard. Shahpour had said "someone." Was he being coy or didn't he know who his extortionist was? "Who's threatening you?" I asked casually. Most victims know precisely who is extorting them. Blackmail is by nature an intimate affair.

"I don't know," Shahpour said. "That's why I asked about corruption among U.S. immigration officers. My first thought was that the man had some connection to the official bureaucracy. That's the way it would happen in Iran. Someone would notice that a visa had run out. Then he would find the person and make him pay to remain."

The scenario was logical enough, but not particularly compelling. It might have happened that way in Iran or Taiwan or Guatemala. In America the game was played differently. Petty emotions were more important than petty cash.

"It's possible that some bureaucrat is involved," I said finally. "But I doubt it. When INS gets tips on illegals, it's usually a grudge being paid off. A labor union wants to harass a factory that employs nonunion illegals, so somebody whispers in immigration's ear. Bad blood between neighbors in the barrio and La Migra gets a tip. A Mexicano sleeps with one man's sister but marries another. *Adiós cabrón.*"

Shahpour smiled slightly, sending fine lines of humor across his lean face.

"But those are the problems and grudges of poverty," I said, setting aside the wine. "You're a wealthy man. Our immigration system is based on law, even if it is muddled and randomly enforced law. You should qualify for legal status as an investor or under some other special category."

"I've already pursued that," Shahpour said quietly, returning my look with a dark one of his own. "There are quotas from each country. We would have to wait at least five years to qualify for legal entry. And," he added, "we would have to wait in Iran." He hesitated, shrugged and said, "That is impossible."

Shahpour signaled to the waiter, who had been hovering within our peripheral vision. Instantly the man brought our plates. The swordfish was the first of the season, pale and succulent. Sorrel butter had mellowed the pungency of the mesquite wood on the barbecue. The waiter poured wine with a genteel flourish, checked the table for crumbs or missing implements and vanished.

Shahpour and I glanced at the elegantly presented food, but neither of us made a move toward it. Something about extortion sticks in the throat—at least it does in mine. So did the words I was going to say next.

"This might sound callous, but are you sure there's no way you can return to Iran? Khomeini is crazy but somebody is running the country and they need cash just as much as the next guy. More, probably." I talked fast, watching the silent objections tighten Shahpour's lips. I had to know where he stood. "And if it's a question of politics, nothing is impossible. What was a prison sentence yesterday is probably just a shrug and a small fine today."

Shahpour's reaction was immediate and unequivocal.

"I'm an American now," he said, his voice tight and his words precise. "This is the only place I want to be. I will not take my children back to the Dark Ages to listen to some mad imam cursing the kind of men I want my sons to become. And my daughter—shall I condemn her to a shadow life where she must hide her face and her quick mind beneath veils of prejudice?"

He picked up his fork and speared a leaf of spinach. It was a gesture that had more to do with anger than with hunger, for he made no move to eat. "There are other countries that would welcome the Zahedi family. We don't want them. We want the United States. I doubt that you understand that. Americans seem to believe that any country is better than their own."

"We complain a lot," I agreed. "We don't emigrate much, though." Our eyes met and we exchanged sardonic smiles.

"I won't emigrate again," he said quietly. "I will fight to keep what I have here in America."

That was all I needed to know. Shahpour wouldn't fade if the going got rough. When he had fled Iran it wasn't because he was afraid to fight; it was because he knew there was no longer anything worth fighting for. That wasn't the case now. Like most immigrants, Shahpour would defend his acquired heritage with a ferocity that the native-born rarely appreciated and never understood.

Shahpour's fork rang cleanly against the china plate. The spinach leaf quivered, impaled on a silver tine. He took a deep breath, a man about to dive into troubled waters.

"Even if we wanted to, we can't go back," Shahpour said. "We are Jews."

So that was it. The televised image of the religious fervor in Khomeini's eyes flashed through my mind. No, the Zahedi clan couldn't go back. Unlike politics, religion isn't a matter of fiscal negotiation. Not in Iran.

"There were many Jews in Teheran," Shahpour continued. "We did well under the Shah. But the Ayatollah decided that we were all agents of Israel, which was an agent of the Great Satan. For the Zahedis, returning to 'Dar al-Islam,' the land where Muhammad reigns, would be . . ." He paused, searching for the word that would summarize centuries of religious intolerance. And then he found it. "Death," he said simply.

"What else did the blackmailer say?" I asked, ignoring the swordfish cooling on my plate. Nothing had happened to improve my appetite. The way things were shaping up, nothing would.

"He called me an 'agent of Israel' and said it 'would do Jews good' to contribute to the spread of Islam."

"What language did he speak?"

"English, with a heavy Arab accent, perhaps Syrian or Yemeni."

"Take the conversation from the beginning, as much as you can remember."

Shahpour raised his eyes and stared out across the dining room to the razor line separating the competing blues of sky and ocean.

"He asked for me by my full name, as though he were a parent calling a child to attention. I said I was Shahpour Zahedi. He called me 'the son of the enemy of the people.' I said nothing. He said my family and I were now required to make 'restitution' to the one God. Then he launched into a tirade against Jews and Israel."

Shahpour sipped the golden wine several times, as though taking a bad taste from his mouth. "Finally I interrupted him, for I wasn't learning anything. I asked how much he wanted. He told me five thousand American dollars a month wasn't much to pay, not for a Jew who wanted to stay in Dar al-Harb."

"Dar al-Harb? Is that what they call the United States?"

"That's what Muslims call any place that is governed by infidels." Shahpour closed his eyes. "The blackmailer read to me the names of my family in America. All of them."

The idea of such knowledge in the hands of an enemy was the one thing that frightened Shahpour. I didn't blame him a bit. I'd had experience with someone I loved being held hostage. It wasn't something I'd care to repeat.

I looked at the scars on my hands and tried to think. The blackmailer's approach was open to the point of being brazen. No hiding behind an extortion note crudely made from cutout words pasted on blank paper. *The names of my family in America. All of them.* The extortionist either had done his homework very well or knew Shahpour intimately.

"Were there any errors, any gaps, in the blackmailer's knowledge?" I asked.

"One. He mentioned my sister's husband, but Sayyed died of a heart attack."

"After he left Teheran?"

Shahpour nodded.

"Does anyone in Iran know you're here?"

"None of our enemies," he said. "There are a few members

of the family who weren't able to get out. We send them funds
to keep them alive."

"Money orders?"

He nodded again.

"With your return address neatly filled in?"

Shahpour looked at the horizon for a long moment, then
closed his eyes and cursed in a language I'd never heard.

"How stupid we have been," he said finally. "My father's
brother is still under house arrest by the Revolutionary Guards."
Shahpour frowned suddenly. "But wait," he said. "The blackmailer wasn't Iranian. I spoke Farsi to him at one point. He
didn't understand me."

"Are all Muslims Iranians?"

"Would that they were," muttered Shahpour, "for then
they would all choke to death under their blessed Khomeini
and that would be the end of it!" He sighed. "You're asking if
Muslim cooperation cuts across national boundaries. Yes, it
does."

"When did he want the money?"

"Yesterday. I refused. I told him that even a banker couldn't
take that much money from a drawer."

"How are you supposed to pay? Cash? Check? Money
order?" Ordinarily I wouldn't have to ask. Cash and carry is
the blackmailer's motto, but when religion and politics mix,
anything might happen.

"My father was supposed to bring the cash. Alone. The
blackmailer said he would call again this afternoon with the
rest of the details."

I nodded absently. I was juggling facts as though they
were individual notes, seeing if there was a pattern. It was
like trying to forecast the melodic line of a jazz improvisation;
there is an inevitability to it, if it is done brilliantly. And if it
is done only adequately, there is a predictability. The Arab
blackmailer had done his homework but he had made a few
mistakes, too. One was leaving the window of time during
which Shahpour could plan and execute a response.

"Shahpour," I said, focusing on him suddenly. "How good
an actor are you?"

He smiled. "Am I not a banker?"

"And your father?"

"He taught me everything I know about banking—and
acting."

"Good," I said. "What I'm about to suggest has its own

risks, but in the long run it's less dangerous than depending
on the goodwill of an extortionist."

"I know how blackmailers work," Shahpour said.

"Then you know there's no end to greed."

"Only death," said Shahpour, flashing a knifelike smile.

I smiled in return.

Suddenly the swordfish smelled irresistible. As one, Shahpour and I began eating lunch. While we ate, we talked. It
didn't take long—the talk or the lunch—for we didn't have
much time. My plan called for a different persona and a drive
to meet Shahpour's father.

Three hours later I was in L.A., dressed in a three-piece
pinstripe, looking every inch the successful, cutting-edge Gold
Coast lawyer who can fix your divorce, your bookie or your
extortionist with equal ease.

Shahpour's father, Imbrahim Zahedi, had long since retired
from the walnut desks of Teheran or Paris, but the white-haired
man with the olive skin and shrewd eyes hadn't forgotten how
to wear a three-piece suit. Unlike Shahpour, the elder Zahedi
was an utterly civilized man. If he had ever fought or bled or
hated, it didn't show. Nervousness did. With quick, fragile
movements he ushered me into his four-bedroom house on an
Encino cul-de-sac. He shook my hand and made polite in-
quiries as to my family and my body, pretending for all the
world as though I had come to dinner rather than to take him
to a meeting with a blackmailer. It made me feel crude to come
to the point so quickly. But then, I've felt crude before and
survived it.

"Did the Arab call Shahpour?"

Imbrahim hesitated and the social mask slipped, revealing
the fear beneath. "Not yet, Mr. Fiddler."

"Just Fiddler. I'm the informal type."

Imbrahim's smile was small, gone before I could respond.
"Yes, I have heard. I hope it—you—" He made a helpless
gesture. "We have come so far," he whispered, "lost so much,
only to find it was all in vain."

I looked carefully at Shahpour's father. Though old, he
was obviously healthy. He didn't shuffle or need a cane to walk
over the gorgeous rugs of his home. He didn't stoop. But
mentally? "Are you sure you're willing to be the tethered goat?"
I asked bluntly. "Extortionists aren't nice people."

"I trust my son's judgment," Imbrahim said in a low,

cultured voice, "and he believes that you have a gift for"—
Imbrahim stopped, then smiled diplomatically—"for dealing
with people who are unpleasant."

"Gift or curse," I said, shrugging. Like my perfect pitch,
which heard notes far more clearly than my hands had been
able to reproduce them on the violin. "I do what I can."

He stopped me with a firm brown hand on my arm. "Answer two questions for an old man."

"Sure," I said easily. The finesse of the gesture put me
on notice that the questions were not simple ones. For all his
civility, this old man did not touch people casually.

"First, is there physical danger?" he asked.

It was a natural enough question under the circumstances.
I answered him honestly, because I wanted Imbrahim to know
that he was putting himself on the line. "There's always danger
when you deal with criminals," I said.

It was both true and general enough that I didn't feel
constrained to tell Imbrahim that I carried a nine-millimeter
Detonics in a holster at the small of my back. There was no
point in making him more nervous than he already was.

He nodded like a man who has had his opinion confirmed.
"Then why are you doing this for strangers?"

That stopped me. Not because there isn't an answer but
because the answer is nearly impossible for most people to
understand. I looked at the old man. His soft-looking eyes
were deceptive. They were watching me, reading my face like
a ledger sheet. I would have hated to play poker with Imbrahim
Zahedi.

"First of all, you and Shahpour aren't strangers."

He waited, watching me.

I returned his look with the kind of interest a banker would
understand. "When I was young, I was a good violinist. Very
good. I gave it up because I wasn't perfect. The notes I heard
in my mind were more beautiful than my hands could ever
produce. Now I'm not a good violinist because I haven't played
in years."

There was a curious softening to Imbrahim's expression,
as though he were hearing more than I was saying. Perhaps
he, too, had once been young and foolish and had given up
something precious because it wasn't perfect. I hadn't learned
that lesson in time to save my marriage, but I had learned it
eventually. I didn't let go of precious things now, no matter
how imperfectly satisfying the results.

"I'm also good at things like this," I said simply, meeting Imbrahim's careful eyes. "Not perfect. Just good. I always have been. I don't want to lose the touch, like I did with the violin."

The old man weighed me awhile longer. There was more than seven decades of wisdom in his gaze, but no hostility. He smiled and said softly, "Thank God you are not an altruist."

It was a banker's supreme compliment.

Imbrahim lifted his hand from my arm and took my elbow, leading me to the living room. I've been in lots of homes in Southern California, one way or another. I've even been in a few in Encino, which is an enclave of the wealthy and the foreign-born Gold Coasters. But I wasn't prepared for Imbrahim's living room. It was extraordinary—skillfully lit and carefully presented, with a half dozen glass cases and a display cabinet that took up one wall. The cases and the cabinet held breathtaking pottery and tiles, exquisite bottles and pages from ancient manuscripts. The colors were as clear as notes perfectly played, brilliant blue and green, molten gold and scarlet. These were the colors that would be most striking to a desert people, natural but rare in arid lands. They did well in California's unflinching light.

After a few moments I realized my surprise must have been as clear as the colors. Imbrahim was watching me with a combination of pleasure and genuine amusement.

"Do you know Middle Eastern art?" he asked.

"No." I looked around, fascinated by the contents of the cases. "My loss, obviously."

"Come, then. There is always a moment for the pleasures of the mind. That is why man built civilization out of chaos."

He took my elbow again. In the next few minutes he led me past a dozen plates, three extraordinary turquoise vases and six panels comprised of hand-painted, cleanly glazed tile. Even a novice could tell that all of the pieces were of museum quality.

Imbrahim's living room symbolized much of what fascinates me about life along the Gold Coast. Call it unpredictability. You never know which beach cottage in Laguna is owned by an international playboy and which by an avant-garde artist who bought it for five hundred bucks during the Depression. You never know which Central American refugee's house in El Monte will yield a million dollars worth of pre-Columbian art, and which one will yield a million dollars worth of cocaine.

"Is that from the Koran?" I asked, pointing to an illuminated page from a manuscript.

Imbrahim nodded. "Nearly all of my collection is Islamic. I was a Jew, living most of my life in a Muslim world. I studied the civilization that once held all but China in its thrall. I know the Koran better than the Talmud because I needed every edge I could get just to survive. And," he added dryly, "their religion is not entirely foreign. We Jews share the old Testament with Muslims as well as with Christians. Maybe that is why the Muslims hate so well. They are the youngest brother in a very competitive family."

Imbrahim let me look for a few minutes longer before he led me through a small hallway to a sitting room where he poured dark, strong coffee in small cups and we sat waiting for the phone call from Shahpour.

"I sent my wife away to watch over her grandchildren," he said as he poured. "I am accustomed to negotiating with hostile Arabs. She is not."

I nodded and began going over the plan. "When the call comes in, remember that what we want is time and information. The Arab was brazen enough to use the phone, so he's feeling powerful. I suspect he'll want to strut in person rather than just pick up the money at a drop. You tell him you can't drive. He'll agree to having your chauffeur along."

Imbrahim nodded and sipped at the thick, heady coffee.

"You're supposed to be worried about your safety, so the meeting has to be in a public place," I continued. "I gave Shahpour the address of a coffee shop. Once we draw the extortionist out of the woodwork, I'll become your lawyer. We're not going to refuse to pay, but I'm along to conduct the negotiations for you.

"This is the bait," I said, drawing a thick envelope from the breast pocket of my coat. "Extortionists, even Arab extortionists, will have eyes for just one thing—this package. I want you to show it to them right away, to get their attention. But don't give it to them unless and until I say so. All right?"

Imbrahim closed his eyes, nodded and then opened his eyes again. He took the crisp envelope with the Gold Coast Bank logo on it and checked the sheaf of one-hundred-dollar bills inside.

"I recorded the serial numbers in case you decide to involve the police," I said. "An Arab with a pocketful of somebody else's money is the kind of evidence even a suburban cop can understand."

"You were once on a police force, were you not?"

"Long enough to learn the rules of the game, but not long enough to like them."

"Does that mean you consider yourself above the law?"

"Nope," I said. "But the rules and the law are two very different things."

The phone on the small coffee table chimed. The old man jerked, startled. His nerves were strung taut. He answered, speaking Farsi. The conversation was short and crisp and I didn't understand a word of it.

"That was Shahpour," said Imbrahim, hanging up. "The Arab would not agree to your meeting place, but he suggested another, a coffee shop on Encino Boulevard. In thirty minutes."

"Okay," I said. "Shift to plan two. Call a taxi and have him pick up a fare at that coffee shop. Tell him there's an extra twenty dollars if he's there in ten minutes."

Imbrahim was nervous, but game. He took a deep breath and started dialing as I left the room and headed for the Cobra.

3

I hated to leave the Cobra in a shopping center parking lot. There are always a few kids around who love to play a little game that involves running the tip of a metal key along the side of a car. I suppose it has something to do with leaving your mark on the world, and what easier, safer way to do so than on the sleek metal hide of a stranger's car? So I parked the Cobra close to the street, in plain view, where a chicken-shit key artist might hesitate for fear of being spotted.

Car thieves are also a problem. Streetside visibility might panic some booster with a lock puller when he discovers he will have to grapple around under the hood to shut off the Mason alarm I had installed. Not that the alarm really meant a damn. Any self-respecting car thief who knows enough to heist a Cobra will also know enough to overcome a Mason. Given enough time, a good crook can compromise any security system. Locks and alarms merely test the burglar's nerve.

When I first arrived at the shopping center I cruised the parking lot once, quickly. A professional extortionist would have backup somewhere nearby. I didn't spot anything out of the ordinary and began to hope this whole thing might prove to be a local amateur production.

The cabbie I had called was a minute late. I gave him the twenty dollars anyway, in exchange for which he did two more loops around the lot. On the first pass I watched a young man with a thin face and Semitic features drive a flashy green Firebird into a parking space. He parked where he could see the front of the coffee shop.

On my second circuit he was still there, windows rolled down as though he'd settled in. The violin in the back of my head cut into a quick rondo, sharp-edged and piercing. My instincts told me this was either the blackmailer or a friend. Whichever, this wasn't amateur hour.

The cab got me back to Zahedi's house with just enough time for both of us to get into his Mercedes and return to the shopping center. I parked the car as close to the front door of

the coffee shop as I could. Out of the corner of my eye I saw
the sentry still lounging in the Firebird. As we entered the
restaurant, I caught a glimpse of him leaving the car and walking toward a phone booth.

The coffee shop was pure convention. We could have been
at Denny's or Sandy's or Pinky's or Bob's Big Boy—they're all
great if you like moderately good coffee, Argentine hamburger
and processed American cheese, served up with french fries
and a slice of chocolate cream pie. Cholesterol City. Good for
twenty extra pounds between the bottom of the rib cage and
the butt, judging from the look of the two truck drivers and
the Alpha Beta grocery checker sitting at the counter. The rest
of the place was empty. I picked a booth toward the back of
the place, out of earshot of the other customers. Imbrahim
followed without a murmur.

The waitress brought us two cups of coffee and grumbled
about the extra steps. "This section is supposed to be closed."

I showed her a five and she brightened considerably.

The phone call must have been short. The dark-haired
sentry was back in his Firebird by the time we were settled
with our coffee. Three minutes later another Firebird, this one
a deep metallic red, pulled into the parking lot and parked in
front of the coffee shop. I wondered if the Arabs got fleet rates.
Three men got out, all studiously ignoring their colleague in
the green Firebird.

I studied the three as they crossed the parking lot. All
were dark-skinned and dark-eyed, in itself nothing surprising
in modern Southern California. From a distance they could
have been full-blooded Indios from Panama or Chippewas from
Minnesota, rather than the descendants of Bedouins or Alex-
ander the Great. All wore dark glasses. Two of them were
young, dressed in designer jeans and cotton shirts. One of the
shirts was an expensive knit and the other a T-shirt with a
message that I couldn't make out at this distance. They had
the casual Southern California style knocked.

The third man was the King David of this particular
honeypot. If the others were college kids, he was a professor.
He wore a dark European-cut suit, silk by the looks of it, and
a white shirt without a tie.

At first glance none of the three looked the part of sneak
thieves or extortionists. But looks are nearly always deceiving.
Fiora looks like she doesn't have a brain in her pretty little
head, and I look like I'm too big to be fast on my feet.

These clean-cut men came through the front door and headed toward us without hesitation.

"Palestinians," Imbrahim said under his breath, as though it explained everything. His voice broke over the word.

"How do you know?" I said.

He shrugged and spread his hands as though there were too many reasons to enumerate. "The shirt says, 'In today's world, no one is innocent, no one is neutral.' That is a PLO slogan. The rest of the slogan reads 'You are either the oppressed or the oppressor.'"

I glanced at the youth in the T-shirt. The message was in Arabic script, and, though enigmatic to my eyes, it was clear and ominous to Imbrahim. The youth turned to glance around the coffee shop, checking the rest of the customers like a coyote on the prowl—cautious rather than afraid. As he turned I could see PLO in block letters across his back. Nobody in the coffee shop noticed or cared. In Southern California everyone flaunts his political sentiments or personal predilections on T-shirts and car bumpers. To the rest of the people drinking coffee, the letters could have stood for Pasadena Library Outlet or Poor Losers Overseas.

The Arab in the knit shirt took a seat at the counter, paying no attention as the waitress brought him a glass of water. Behind the dark glasses his eyes roamed the shop and the parking lot outside. Without a word the other two men walked to our table and slid into the booth across from us. The man in the suit was clearly in control. The kid in the T-shirt glared at me from behind the safety of sunglasses. The older man removed his glasses. I noticed that his left hand had a scar across the back, a dark furrow that could have come from a knife or a bullet. He stared at me with eyes that were dark and empty.

"This man is no chauffeur," he said to Imbrahim, pointing at me. "Is he police?"

"And if I were?" I asked politely.

"Then I would ask why you gentlemen requested this meeting with me," the Arab replied smoothly, showing me his sharp white teeth.

Imbrahim automatically raised his hand in a conciliatory gesture. He had spent a lifetime trying to pour civilized oils on savage waters. "This man is not a policeman," the old man said. "He is my lawyer and adviser. He is no more a threat to you than I am, Mr.—?" He paused, waiting for the Arab to fill in the blank.

The man with the scarred hand studied me for another long moment, demonstrating his mistrust. Then he turned to Imbrahim. "You may call me Salameh."

He paused as though to let the name sink in. Its significance was lost on me. I sensed Imbrahim taking a quick breath. When he spoke his voice was almost detached, as though the hope that had made him nervous had fled, leaving nothing but the flatness of despair.

"It is a well-known name," said Imbrahim.

"It's a proud *nom de guerre* for a Palestinian," retorted the Arab. "But your lawyer doesn't seem to grasp its implications. Like most Americans, he is ignorant of the rest of the world."

The man who called himself Salameh turned to face me again, as though he felt uneasy when not watching me. Perhaps he saw some of his own predatory nature reflected in my gray eyes. A shrewd man, Salameh. He was handsome beneath that arrogance. The angular planes of his face were oddly complemented by the long black lashes that framed but didn't soften his obsidian eyes. He radiated a feral alertness. Maybe he sensed the pistol under my coat. Some men swear they can smell gun oil; Salameh struck me as someone who might have had the chance to cultivate such a talent.

"Salameh was one of the greatest leaders in Black September," he continued evenly, watching me. "You know the name Black September, don't you?"

"I saw the 1972 Olympics," I said.

"Salameh was the man who planned the incident," the Arab said. "The Zionists killed him with a car bomb in 1979. They were so eager for revenge that they were willing to kill twenty innocent bystanders to take the life of one freedom fighter. I am proud to wear his name."

There was something jarring about sitting in a West San Fernando Valley coffee shop, hearing such rhetoric from a human being who otherwise appeared to be rational. But Salameh's eyes told me that however stilted his words, he wasn't strutting for the peanut gallery. He meant every syllable.

"Tell me, Jew," he said, turning again to Imbrahim, "are you a Zionist?"

"Would it make a difference?" Imbrahim asked, his voice unnaturally calm.

The youth in the PLO T-shirt leaned forward and smiled unpleasantly. He had a broad, flat face with a brow that was creased and knotted in almost simian concentration. He wasn't stupid, however, merely intent.

"We take the same amount from each Jew, but we enjoy taking the money of Zionists more," he said. It was a statement of fact rather than a taunt.

"Since my client's political sentiments make no difference on the bottom line," I said, "there's no point in discussing them." I looked at Salameh as though I'd never seen an Arab before. "You do know that extorting old men is against U.S. law, don't you?" I asked, letting both curiosity and contempt color the tone of my voice.

Salameh shrugged.

So much for guests following the custom of the country. I'll bet he hated kids and small animals, too. I motioned to Imbrahim, who produced the envelope. I opened the flap and revealed the edges of the sheaf of money as coyly as a Victorian maiden showing her ankles to a suitor as she climbed a stair. The younger man came to a visible point. Salameh didn't take his eyes off me. Like I said, a shrewd man.

"Before my client pays any money, I want a signed release stating—"

Salameh began laughing. In his shoes, I would have, too. But I wasn't in his shoes. I was in a pair of handmade calf leather beauties that fit me the way the holster fit the Detonics—perfectly, not a rub or a rough seam anywhere. Even so, I tried to look as though my feet hurt, and my feelings, too. No one likes to be laughed at, especially lawyers.

"I suppose he is collecting a fee for this meeting," said Salameh to Imbrahim, looking at the Jew with an expression somewhere between sympathy and contempt. "American lawyers can think of a thousand ways to complicate and thereby profit from what is otherwise a simple transaction."

At least we both felt the same way about lawyers.

Imbrahim shrugged. "I do not understand American law. He does."

Salameh's smile was like a knife sliding from a sheath. "Old man, you don't need to understand American law, because we're both outside it. Understand this: You will pay what I ask or the authorities will receive the names and addresses of all the Zahedi war criminals who are in America. You will be shipped back to Iran, Jew. Then you will be executed and your women will be stoned to death as whores."

This time it wasn't an effort for me to look pained. "You

can't expect my client simply to turn over the money without assurances, can you?" I said quickly, hoping for a new topic, something to take the sudden gray from Imbrahim's complexion.

"What do you mean, 'assurances'?" demanded Salameh.

"How do we know that you won't take the money and turn in my client anyway?" I said.

"We are Palestinian freedom fighters," he said. "We are men of honor."

"You may be, Jack," I said sarcastically, dropping the courtly act, "but what's to keep Junior here from coming back next week and asking for a little more money on the side?"

"We are the—" began the young man hotly, but a gesture from Salameh stopped the words before I learned anything new.

"We are members of a group that has better discipline than most armies," said Salameh.

"How about the person who betrayed the Zahedi family?" I asked, fanning the money inside the envelope, hoping to tempt and distract Junior into indiscreet words. "Does your control stretch to the Mujahideen in Iran?"

Salameh regarded me closely again, a faint expression of appreciation enlivening his empty eyes. "You're intelligent, for a lawyer," he said. "Perhaps too intelligent." He weighed his instincts against my appearance. Appearance won, although I could tell that the contest was getting closer.

"The Mujahideen in Iran supplied us with the information," he conceded, "and they will share in its fruits. They won't present additional demands."

"There is also the question of—" I began.

"No," said Salameh. He put his palm flat on the table and looked at Imbrahim. "You have two choices, old man. You either pay or you don't pay. It's really quite simple." He glanced at me and added, "If your lawyer needs any extra incentive, perhaps Moussa can provide it."

Salameh nodded at Junior. Moussa glanced about quickly, making sure no one else was watching. Then he smiled contemptuously and lifted his shirt a few inches, revealing the dark metal and white plastic handle of a small automatic. It looked like a .25 caliber assassin's gun and Junior looked eager to use it.

End of negotiations.

Salameh had proceeded to the threat of violent death more

quickly than I would have in his place. Maybe he hated lawyers
more than I did. And maybe his instincts were different from
mine, more direct even than my notoriously retrograde approach. Salameh had caution in him, but it took a back seat to
his belief in American naïveté. Not that I could fault him there,
either. Damn few Angelenos would believe that a bunch of
Palestinians could march into a local restaurant, display a gun
and extort an elderly Jew and his family.

I looked at Imbrahim. He was sweating a bit but still in
control. I tapped the envelope against my palm as though
making up my mind. I wasn't doing anything of the kind. I'd
known the minute I'd seen Salameh's eyes that the five thousand dollars was forfeit. With a shrug, I tossed the envelope
onto the table. Salameh looked at me for a long moment before
he scooped up the envelope in a slender, well-manicured hand.
The white rectangle vanished into his breast pocket.

"We'll speak to you again in a month," Salameh said to
Imbrahim. The Arab looked at me with contempt. "That, my
legalistic friend, is your greatest guarantee of our good faith.
Our freedom fighters need money and guns, so we won't kill
the— What is the American phrase? We won't kill our golden
goose."

His eyes narrowed and his fingers twitched subtly, as
though seeking the familiar shape of a weapon. "That immunity
doesn't extend to a goose's lawyer. Don't presume to stand
between me and a Jew again."

Salameh slid out of the booth and walked away without
looking back. I waited until he and the other two were at the
front door before I passed the Mercedes keys to Imbrahim.

"Are you all right to drive?" I asked quickly, sliding out
of the booth. "I have a man to see about a goose."

"Fiddler," said Imbrahim suddenly, grabbing my arm. "I
believe that boy has killed before. He enjoyed it. Let him go.
What is five thousand dollars compared to life?"

"Will you do one thing for me?" I asked.

He closed his eyes. After a brief struggle with himself he
nodded tiredly, knowing that he had lost the argument before
it had really begun.

"See the green car next to the streetlight in front of the
drugstore?" I asked.

Without turning to look, he said, "The Arab in it watched
us when we arrived."

The old man didn't miss much. "Keep an eye on him.

When he leaves, go and pick up a gray suit you'll find on the floor of the men's rest room."

Imbrahim looked puzzled until I reached for the knot on my sedate Brooks Brothers tie. The fabric hissed against my collar as I jerked the tie free. The lawyer Fiddler began to vanish. Imbrahim smiled slightly and nodded, understanding what I was going to do.

Once I got to the rest room, it took me less than thirty seconds to alter my appearance radically. I had a pair of light running shorts and a tank top underneath the gray worsted suit, and a pair of sunglasses and a soft-brimmed cycling hat rolled up in one suit coat pocket. The Detonics went inside the hat, which I rerolled and carried in my hand. I kicked off my leather shoes and socks and left them beside the suit. Enough people go barefoot in California that I wasn't too noticeable, and I'd stashed a pair of sandals and jeans in the Cobra.

As I slipped out the side door of the coffee shop, I was feeling pretty smug—until I hit the street. Then I hotfooted it for the Cobra. Literally. The blacktop had been brought to a high simmer by the July sun. A Fiji firewalker would have felt right at home. I gritted my teeth and wondered how all those barefoot beach bunnies managed to stroll so slowly across broiling parking lots.

The green Firebird was already pulling out when I got to the Cobra. I let him get a half block ahead before I followed. The afternoon traffic was beginning to back up on the surface streets. I had to rush a signal or two to keep him in sight, but he didn't seem to notice even when I ducked into a diamond lane to avoid a line at the metered signal getting on the Ventura Freeway.

The Cobra is not the greatest surveillance vehicle in the world. One look and you remember it for a long time, if you care anything about cars. The dense rush-hour traffic also tended to defeat the Cobra's natural attributes. Four hundred twenty-five horsepower doesn't mean shit if you can't get above fifteen miles an hour. Unfortunately, the beat-up BMW airport car I kept for just these occasions was getting its solid German steel ass hammered out. Some jerk behind me had been looking at the cruising boys in Laguna rather than at the traffic in front of him.

At least the Firebird wasn't going anywhere fast. Once on the freeway he faced a limited number of options: stay or get off. As the latter choice was only available every few miles, my job was made easier. When the Firebird headed for the number one lane, I knew he wasn't likely to take the San Diego Freeway cutoff, so I let him range a bit ahead. I lounged around in a pack behind him, staying in his blind spot as much as I could and trying to keep the revs high enough that the 427-cubic-inch Ford V-8 didn't burn itself up in the stop-and-slow.

He stayed on the Ventura. If he checked his mirrors a lot, I didn't see it. He gave no sign that he had even considered the possibility of being followed. That's the problem with the kind of countersurveillance assignment he had; while you're watching your comrade's ass to make sure he's not being watched, you also have to watch your own ass. It was a game of double paranoia and he lost. Unless, of course, somebody else was watching me. I checked that a time or five, then remembered the Ice Cream King's advice: *If you fly in circles that get too tight, you sail right up your own keister.*

The Arab in the Firebird stayed on the Ventura to the Hollywood and then joined the looser traffic headed inbound toward the Civic Center. I stayed closer now, because the exit options were coming more quickly. I managed to be no more than one hundred yards behind when he moved over into the far right lane and took the Harbor Freeway south. Again, the rush hour had clogged the lanes and we both fought for every inch we got. It was almost six o'clock when he moved over into the number four lane and signaled off at Exposition Boulevard.

Fifty years ago the neighborhood around the Los Angeles Memorial Coliseum and the University of Southern California was just about the classiest the city had to offer. It has fallen on hard times, now, in more ways than one. In the area called Watts, the stylish Victorians and early modern bungalows east of the Harbor Freeway have been hacked into duplexes or worse. Blacks who moved in during the 1940s are being supplanted by recently immigrated browns, legal and otherwise. This is on the dark side of the Statue of Liberty, where poor immigrants get ground to dust as they always have by the demands of the land of the free and the home of the brave. In these transition neighborhoods the competition and intolerance are thick and harsh, and only the tough survive. It is, however, a yeasty kind of place, particularly if you're into something besides Wonder Bread.

The surface streets were quiet in contrast to the freeway

that passed overhead. There weren't too many commuters in Watts. It was a place you fled if you had a job. The Arab's shiny Firebird stood out against the drab houses. So did my Cobra. It wasn't as out-of-place as it might have been. With USC—a.k.a. the University of Spoiled Children—close by, lots of flashy cars swooped through the ghetto on the way to one of America's most expensive diplomas.

The Arab headed down Exposition and turned into one of the small streets that fringed USC but wasn't part of its walled enclave. I was a block behind. I caught a flash of green as the Firebird went up the spiral ramp of a cement parking structure. Several four-to-six-story office buildings hunkered near the garage.

I pulled in behind an oleander hedge and left the Cobra. I was close enough to see the Arab when he came down the garage stairs and crossed to a five-story smoked-glass tower. There was no way I could follow him immediately without being burned. I went back to the Cobra, pulled on my jeans, tucked the Detonics into the small of my back, and did some thinking. It was dinnertime; foot traffic was getting sparse. I would have worried more about standing out but for the Ferraris and Porsches and Jaguars that cluttered the streets, and the joggers who sweated industriously through their shorts and tank tops. I fit right in.

The parking structure and the nearby lots all had card locks. I could take a chance on getting caught as I jimmied one or I could park on the street. I chose the street a block away from the smoked-glass tower. By adjusting the mirrors I managed to keep an eye on the door the Arab had used as well as the entrance to the parking structure.

Thirty minutes went by. I sat there enjoying the cooling of the July day and fighting to stay awake. That's the problem with the waiting game. If you concentrate on something interesting—like trying to figure out what the hell is going on with Salameh, Junior, the Mujahideen and an old Iranian Jew— you might get so involved with thinking that you overlook something, like an Arab walking by right under your nose. But if you stay away from interesting thoughts, sitting around waiting for something to happen gives you a jawbreaking case of the yawns.

Another thirty minutes crawled by. Summer school must have been in session, because the foot traffic increased at a few minutes before seven. USC still has cachet with upscale and establishment Southern California. As a result, the students on the streets tended to be handsome and bright and rich. It was a preppy fashion show, lots of Izods and designer jeans and Topsiders. The boys were tousled teenaged louts. The girls had smooth faces that were just beginning to accumulate the character lines that come from life's little surprises.

College students make me feel old. Not ancient, mind you, just solidly past childhood. It's the freshness, the innocence, that makes the difference. I watched a young couple walk by, arm in arm, the boy a tall, thin poet with a bulging book bag and the girl looking as enthralled by the sound of his voice as he was. She was slim and blond and had an attractive, earnest face. But in some way, perhaps in the smiling, speculative look that was also in her eyes, she seemed much older than he was. It was as though she was indulging him and he was blissfully unaware.

It struck me that he had better grow up quick. Or maybe she was part of his growing up in a more important way than he was of hers. I wanted to tell him that when it comes to young women, wisdom is rarely found in a book bag. I didn't, though. If the young could learn from the errors of the previous generation, the world would be a different place, and I probably wouldn't be sitting in the silky California evening waiting for an extortionist to walk by.

A few minutes after seven, the night-school students vanished into their protected classrooms. Foot traffic was sparse again. The people walking by were older, probably graduate students heading back to their teaching-assistant cells to grade midterms or wrestle with the chimera of original scholarship in a world that really didn't value maverick thought. The graduates were of all races, but quite a few reminded me of Salameh. Not in looks, particularly. It was something undefined, an intensity about their expressions, as though more than grades or jobs depended on their classroom careers.

The women who passed by tended to be serious-looking with straight hair and black Samsonite briefcases. Except for one. She was strikingly beautiful in an unusual way. This wasn't Bunny or starlet material. Much of her appeal was in the intelligence animating her face. I watched her closely for the simple reason that intelligence and beauty in one person is rare in a world where most people have to be content with one or the other. Or neither.

Where the woman's short dark hair caught the evening

sunlight there were mahogany highlights that married exotically with her clean, almond-eyed Mediterranean features. She wore dark blue slacks and a dark blue blouse. Her clothes were businesslike but couldn't hide the elegantly feminine curves. She walked well, like a woman alive to the possibilities of her own body. In all, she certainly was too attractive to be buried in a library carrel somewhere.

As she walked past she threw a quick glance my way. It wasn't a come-on. It wasn't even a once-over. I admit that I was piqued that she seemed more interested in the Cobra than in its driver. The price of driving a memorable automobile. Maybe I should take up Rabbit diesels after all.

Then, like a thousand other beautiful women, she was gone from my life. Her passage left me with plenty of material for idle male speculation. I damn near missed the Arab from the green Firebird as he walked by me on the other side of the street. He carried a graduate student's briefcase and was headed for the campus. If he saw me, he didn't let on. I let him go for a long sixty count and then followed.

It was a brisk five-minute walk across the campus to the Physical Sciences Building. I leaned against the sun-warmed trunk of a sycamore as if waiting for a date and watched through the building's glass doors as the Arab took an elevator to the fourth floor and stopped. I gave him a couple more minutes before I checked the building directory. The only thing I could find under a fourth-floor listing was the Sub-Atomic Physics Laboratory. The hallways were so deserted that I was guaranteed a burn if the Arab reappeared suddenly. I withdrew to my warm-barked sycamore.

Fifteen minutes later the Arab still hadn't come out. I waited a few more minutes, then turned and went back toward the car. I knew where the Arab had gone but I still didn't know where he had come from. I checked the Cobra to make sure nobody had swiped the hubcaps and steering wheel, then crossed over to the smoked-glass office building.

USC is noted for networking, not scholarship, but the campus appeared to have its share of think tanks, judging from the directory in the lobby. The Institute on Aging in America; Transcontinental Business Studies; International Association of Band Directors. Really scintillating stuff. All except the fifth-floor listing: Muslim Student League.

Why not? Everybody's got to belong to Something.

Building security was good but not great. Although the

doors were duly locked to the outside world, a credit card laid the latch bolt back in two seconds. In two more I was inside the well of the fire stairs. Five flights up I had a clear view of the Muslim Student League offices through a safety-glass panel in the stair door. To the naked eye there was nothing sinister or even interesting about the place. There was a suite of two offices served by a small receptionist's desk and waiting area on one side, and a pair of double doors in the opposite wall that probably opened into a meeting room. The lights were on but nobody was home.

I stood in the shadows for a few minutes, watching through the glass panel and listening to sounds penetrating the descending night. Somewhere below my feet a phone rang faintly. I jumped when the third-floor door opened, its sound magnified by the echo chamber of the stairwell. I held my breath and prayed that no one was coming my way. Some people use stairs for the sake of their cardiovascular systems. I hoped I looked like one of those dedicated urban climbers. I let out a long breath as the sound of footsteps headed down the stairs. I counted the scuffing steps and enjoyed the clear, pure notes of someone's innocent whistling. When I heard the ground-floor door slam shut, I relaxed again.

Access from the stairwell to the building proper was controlled by a card lock. It was less impressive than it looked. The slotted screws that held the faceplate were exposed. They came off with a few twists of the Proto screwdriver on my keychain. The circuit was simple enough. When I ripped off the two wires on the card reader and crossed them, the door buzzed happily and popped open.

I went inside and did a quick turn around the floor, just to make sure I was alone. The two offices were empty. They were also one hell of a lot more secure than the rest of the building. The desks in each were clean and locked, and the file cabinets were the special kind with hardened-steel hasps and thick locking bars sunk into a crossbeam in the floor. Each office had its own safe.

I wondered which one held Imbrahim's five thousand dollars. Double doors opened into what had once been a conference room. Now it was just different enough to confuse me for a moment. It was empty of furniture. The tiles on the floor and partway up the walls had the same brilliant colors that I had seen in Imbrahim's museum cases, but the execution of the design was not even in the same league with his. Just

inside the door was a small basin of water in a stand that
reminded me of a Christian baptismal font. There were no
pews around, and certainly no crosses. The floor was bare
except for what looked like small rugs rolled and stacked neatly
along one wall. There was no altar, only two small alcoves
against the eastern wall of the room. A dome between the
alcoves was supported by wooden posts.

Thick, slanting sunlight was coming through the smoked
glass behind me. It fell on the dome naturally, a radiant reminder of the path to Mecca. There was an inscription in both
Arabic and cursive English on its cornice:

> Guide us on the straight path,
> the path of those whom You have Favored,
> not of those who have incurred your wrath,
> nor of those who have gone astray.

Religious folks, these, and hard-edged. The sentiments
reminded me of a fire-breathing, Bible-thumping Baptist I had
listened to a long, long time ago. The folks who worshiped
here weren't evangelical Baptists, but they would do until the
millennium came along, when God got a chance to sort things
out. I wondered idly whether the Muslim Student League had
heard of liberation theology in the religious academies of the
Middle East. I doubted it. Muslim fundamentalism. That's as
redundant as rice paddy. You've never heard of Reform Muslims, have you?

I know next to nothing about Islamic religious practice,
except that it requires prayer five times daily. One of those
times was probably in the evening. *If I should die before I
wake* . . . That's always been one of my favorites. I doubted
that it was on the Muslims' ten best list. In fact, if my memory
serves me, their favorite prayer runs along the lines of "There
is no god but Allah and Muhammad is His prophet." If Muslims
did indeed have their own version of vespers, I'd better find
another place for myself and do it now. I was probably standing
in the only mosque for miles around.

I made one more pass through the suite on my way out,
wanting to check on the bulletin board by the elevators. Routine stuff mostly, announcements and phone numbers and a
reminder about a fund raiser for the Muslim Student League.
Daylight was just bleeding into twilight as I headed back

to the Cobra. The streets were being reclaimed by the natives. There were black kids and brown kids cutting through the campus enclave, headed for the ice cream stores and Seven-Elevens on Vermont. The Cobra was still in one piece. So was a loose-limbed young black who was leaning against a tree studying my car as though he were trying to figure out where I kept the stereo. He spotted me as I crossed the street. I expected him to split. He didn't. As I got closer I saw that he was younger than his big body looked. He had probably been in training as a power forward since he was nine. He had the shoulders and thick, muscular arms of somebody who worked out seriously, yet his face had the transparent, wary innocence of a twelve-year-old who had spent too much time on the street.

"How's it going?" I said as I passed by and started to get into the Cobra.

"That your car, man?"

I turned. "Something wrong?"

"Don't know," he said, approaching me. He was only an inch or two shorter than I was. He had the lithe, light-footed grace of a natural athlete. "I'm just supposed to tell you something, if that's your car."

"Shoot," I said, more curious than wary.

"You're supposed to look in your trunk, 'cause somebody been messing with your car."

If I had been raised in a different part of the world— Beirut, for instance—I would have known enough to start running like hell. But I was born in America, so I walked around to the back of the Cobra. I ran my fingers lightly around the square trunk door. No wires showing, nothing unusual to the touch. I eased open the trunk.

It took a few seconds for my eyes and my mind to accept the reality of the three sticks of dynamite taped together and wired to a timer in the Cobra's clean, small trunk.

As Uncle Jake used to say, Oh shit oh dear.

4

The bomb was nothing spectacular to an expert, I suppose, but it looked both ridiculous and dangerous to me. It had wires and a very prosaic device I took to be a timer, complete with an archaic-looking Timex wristwatch, the kind with hands instead of an LCD readout.

"John Cameron Swayze, where are you when we need you?" I said out loud. Then I laughed, a combination of adrenaline and disbelief.

"Who?" the power forward asked.

He had wandered around until he could see the bomb. His jaw dropped and for a second he didn't say anything. I looked at the three sticks again, hoping irrationally that they were just highway flares. Somebody's idea of a joke.

No such luck. Highway flares have strikers on one end. These deep-red, paper-wrapped sticks had plain, folded ends, like dynamite. Worse, I could also see a glint of copper-colored metal in the end of one of the sticks. The primer cap was in place.

That's when I got pissed off. Mostly at myself. I had been suckered but good. The Arab who had walked me across the campus to the physics lab had been a nice piece of bait. Probably the girl in the dark blue slacks and blouse had been part of the game, as well. She had eyeballed me closely enough to confirm that I might once upon a time have been a Brooks Brothers lawyer. Salameh and his people had been onto me for at least an hour, probably more.

Well, Fiddler. You can't say they didn't warn you.

Okay. Okay. I've been warned. Now what the hell do I do?

Gently I braced the trunk lid open with its notched bar. Shock was being replaced by old-fashioned, irrational anger.

"Hey, bro," I said quietly to the power forward, without taking my eyes off the ticking watch, "I think you'd better haul ass out of here. I really appreciate you sticking around to give me that message, though." Mechanically, I reached into my pocket and handed him a five.

"S'all right, man," he said quickly. "The dude gimme ten dollahs."

"What dude?"

"Big one. Walked kinda like John Wayne."

My mind was already occupied but that stopped me for just a second. John Wayne? I pushed the five into his shirt pocket.

"Go down the street and around the corner," I said as I studied the homemade bomb. "If you hear a big bang in the next five minutes, call the police and tell them what you saw. If there's no bang, I'll be along shortly and I'll give you another five. Okay?"

"Gonna mess with that?" he asked doubtfully as I moved to the front of the Cobra.

I bent over and rummaged in the glove box for a flashlight. "It's a dirty job, but . . ."

Light dawned. The kid backed up in high gear, hands held in front of him as though to ward off the blast he expected.

"Shee-iitt!" he said, retreating hurriedly. "That's a nice car, man, but not that nice!"

I gave the bomb a long look. My first impulse was to grab it and chuck it into the nearest trash bin. You can die of first impulses. Rule #1 for dealing with a bomb is don't touch until you're sure it isn't booby trapped.

So I looked. Hard. I had no intention of dying, but then, I suppose you never do. There's nothing like anger and adrenaline to make you feel bulletproof. Even so, I wished that the Ice Cream King of Saigon were at my elbow. This was right up his spooky black alley. Unfortunately, Benny Speidel, a.k.a. the King, was too far away to do me any good.

Judging from the timer, everybody else in the world was, too. Except me.

The little old bomb maker, whoever he was, could have made things a lot tougher on me by camouflaging everything. Even a paper bag over the watch and wires would have slowed me down fatally. But he was probably more interested in shock effect than in design awards. Or maybe he just liked to show off his handiwork.

The Timex watch was brand-new, the stainless-steel case unscratched. Someone had popped the crystal to expose the hands and the face, and then had drilled a hole in the number three spot on the watch face. The hole had been filled with solder. There was a wire embedded in the solder. With a beam of light, I followed that wire from the timer to the copper top of the primer embedded in a stick of dynamite.

That was one half of the circuit.

The other half included a wire that came from a small square nine-volt battery. The wire was joined by a liberal glob of grayish metal solder to the minute hand of the watch. Right now the minute hand read seven minutes past the hour, and all was well with the world, the Cobra and me. It took no genius to figure out that the situation would change radically at quarter after the hour. The two halves of the circuit would become a whole charging unit and a nine-volt spark would pop the cap and the cap would whap the dynamite and turn its solids into gases that would spread through the air and the aluminum skin of the Cobra and the more delicate skin of yours truly at a rate of about 2,500 feet a second.

Elementary physics, my dear Watson. Pretty basic, too.

The sweat that was running down my arm into my palm made the barrel of the flashlight slippery. I shifted my grip and wiped first one hand and then the other on my jeans. It didn't help much. I realized that I hadn't been breathing enough in the last few minutes. I backed off a bit, gulped a few deep breaths and tried to slow down. This was one time when adrenaline wasn't going to get the job done.

When I looked back into the trunk, the minute hand had jumped ahead three notches. I also saw that the workmanship on the improvised timer was not as precise as I'd thought. The wire had been lapped on the minute hand so that contact might come anytime after thirteen minutes past the hour. That didn't give me much time for thinking. Reflexes took over, and anger. In that instant I knew there were a bunch of things I was *not* going to do, and one of them was to stand by like a ninny and watch a beautiful, irreplaceable Cobra blown to trash. That I would be trashed with it if I didn't move fast made no impression on the chemical storm that had overwhelmed rational thought.

I shifted the light and leaned in as close to the bomb as I could without touching it. I heard my own shallow breathing and the faint metallic lisp of the mainspring, and I smelled an acrid tang that might have been the dynamite or my own fear. I couldn't see anything fancy, no extra wires or loops in the circuit, nothing that might go boom if I jostled the dynamite. No surprises. Just your basic-model bargain-basement bomb. Okay. Somebody put it together, so it can be taken apart.

Even if you've never done it before.

The worst part was simply touching the bomb. Reason told me that nothing would happen, but if I'd been listening to reason I'd have been a block away and gaining speed with every stride. Gingerly I touched the battery, turning it over very carefully. In a configuration like this, the last connection ought to be the battery. So the battery connection probably would be the easiest to remove from the circuit. No battery. No spark. No bang. All I had to do was disconnect one wire from one little terminal.

The circuit wire had been soldered securely to the negative post of the battery. The wire on the positive post had been stripped for a few inches and then passed through the center of the wire coil that formed the post. The stiff copper whiskers of the stripped wire had been tied once in an overhand knot and the knot had been pulled tight. I wasn't going to be able to pull it loose without ripping the wires themselves apart. I suspected doing that might lead to a rash of very bad luck.

That was when the Swiss Army came to the rescue. I pulled out my little red knife and went to work.

Whoever thinks the neutral Swiss are pushovers doesn't know that every Swiss male is a reserve soldier armed with a full assortment of Swiss Army knives. You can get them in many sizes, but all you really need is the Pathfinder model: blade, tweezer, toothpick, file and scissors—best damn scissors in the free world. Cuts right through copper wire. I know, because that's what I was using to cut the nine-volt battery out of the circuit, snipping first one wire and then the other.

The copper didn't do the edge on the scissors any good, and I dropped the knife three times before the job was done. I was glad Benny couldn't see my fingers shaking as I picked up the battery and put it in my pocket. Then I went and sat on the curb by the front end of the Cobra for a few minutes, sweating and shaking and trying to figure out how many years of normal stress had just been subtracted from my life's allotment. Somebody owed me, and I was going to collect.

After a few minutes my pulse rate had dropped from frantic to the normal rate for someone who has just finished a hundred-yard dash in full combat gear. Feeling like an old man, I got up and went to deal with the dynamite. I pulled the blasting cap out, wrapped the bright copper in a dust-cloth and put the package in the tool case. Even if the cap went off there, it wasn't powerful enough to do any real damage. That left the dynamite, by now the most stable element in the equation. I tossed it on the front seat and covered it with a windbreaker I always carry in the Cobra.

Then I went off to dismantle the power forward and discover who had just tried to kill me.

It took me only a few minutes to find out that the kid was a pretty decent, largely innocent child named Esau Biggs. He was thirteen, just over six feet tall, and the shortest forward in his Peewee basketball league. But he told me he figured he would be able to crash the boards with the rest of them in a few years, once he got his full growth.

Esau wasn't able to tell me much except that the big dude had been hanging around the neighborhood for a couple of days. All the kids figured he was some kind of cop because he acted like he was watching somebody. He had a strange accent that Esau had never heard before. And yes, he had been with a woman today, a woman whose hair was both dark and "kinda" red. All Esau said he could remember was that she had a fine ass and was dressed in something blue. She was driving a car that had a funny kind of license plate on it, but even for a twenty Esau couldn't remember the license number.

I let him keep the twenty anyway and gave him a ride in the Cobra to a convenience market on Vermont where he had been headed when the big dude had buttonholed him. I even let Esau hold the dynamite in his lap. By the time I pulled into the market parking lot, he was pretty comfortable with the sticks, tossing them from hand to hand to impress the gang of kids who were eating Moonpies and drinking Cokes on the curb. Before he got out, I gave Esau a personal card with the phone number of the answering machine on it. He promised earnestly to call me if he saw either the big man or the woman again or if he remembered the number on the license plate. I didn't have much hope of that happening. Esau was willing, but unless it was basketball, his heart wasn't in it.

I gave the gang a thrill by scratching out of the parking lot in the Cobra, all 425 horses howling and smoking the Pirellis. I know you aren't supposed to play drag racer with a sports car, but I had a little excess adrenaline to burn off. Esau and the boys got a hell of a kick out of it, too. Good kids, as long as your car doesn't have an in-dash stereo.

After the initial hard rush, I headed back down the Gold Coast as decorously as an old maid on the way to get her hair dyed blue. The drive, unlike the minutes that had preceded it, was uneventful. I found the Ice Cream King sitting on the balcony of his West Newport house, drinking cold beer and watching the breakers turn white in the city lights. The King remains a New Zealander in many regards, but drinking warm stout is not one of them. He favors cold lager, an American habit he picked up in Vietnam, along with the severed spinal cord that put him on permanent wheels.

Fifteen years before, Benny had been the quality-control engineer for a U.S. food conglomerate that manufactured dairy products for the half million Americans serving in Vietnam. His day gig was making ice cream in three flavors, plus the all-important flavor of the month—nunc mam sherbet. At night he had another job, one that involved planning and operating a superspook microwave communications system that nobody ever acknowledged we had there. It was an unusual kind of moonlighting that paid in gold to a numbered Hong Kong account, but by the King's standards it was honest work. Except for the silly accident when some punchy American M.P. mashed down on the trigger of his M-16 in a moment of boredom and severed Benny's spine, he rather enjoyed Vietnam.

He still makes his living in applied electronics. Mostly he builds bugs and debugs and listening devices and other state-of-the-art gimcracks for cops and spooks and spies. He won't work for just anybody, even if they carry business cards proclaiming that they're on the right side of the law. His talents are special enough that he makes a hell of a good chunk of dough without catering to crooks and crackpots. He owns one of the nicest houses in West Newport and one of the best-equipped workshops anywhere. I hang around with him because he keeps me humble and because about once a week he teaches me something that I didn't know before. He hangs around me, he says, because nobody else would have me.

I tossed him the three sticks of dynamite when I walked onto the patio. He caught them one-handed and fired them back at me.

"I don't need it," he said. "C-4 is more powerful and you can use it to start your barbecue, too."

"How about this?" I asked, giving him the timer. I kept the blasting cap, still wrapped in the dustcloth, in my hand.

The Ice Cream King inspected the watch closely and then gave me a speculative look. "You make a habit of going to garage sales, mate?"

So I gave him chapter and verse, beginning to end, from

the Zahedis to Esau. He picked it apart, as I knew he would. That's why I put up with him. He has a mind like nobody else's.

"In the first place, this isn't really a bomb," he began.

"Why?" I objected. "Because it doesn't have a primer?"

I tossed the dustcloth gently into his lap. He unwrapped the blasting cap with blunt, deft fingers.

"No," he said, nonchalantly inspecting the cap and testing its weight in his palm. "It isn't a bomb because it's an improvised explosive device."

"That strikes me as a difference without a distinction."

"There is a hell of a difference if you're standing nearby," he retorted. "An improvised explosive device goes bang. A bomb goes *BOOOOM!*"

He took a hit on his beer bottle. "Actually," he said, eyeing the collection in his lap, "this is a pretty hack effort. See, the timer is diagnostic, like red spots with measles. This style of bomb—"

"Improvised explosive device," I said blandly.

"Screw you," he said without interest. "This was invented by some wise-ass Palestinian about twenty years ago. He probably stole the design from the Haganah or Palmach and then refined it. Years ago the Israelis were pretty good at this sort of thing, before they became the establishment and the other guys became the terrorists.

"Anyway," Benny continued, nibbling at his beer, "these Timex things have shown up all over the world since the 1960s—the Red Brigades, Irish Republican Army, Venceremos, everybody who got any PLO or PFLP training, uses this timer." He smiled the kind of smile you associate with knives and dark alleys. "Pretty soon those buggers will have to think up a new trick. The Timex folks are phasing out this particular model. Ah, the march of progress. How I love it."

"It looked a lot more impressive fully assembled and ticking in the Cobra's trunk."

The King tossed the timer back to me. "You done good, boyo. No doubt about it. But before you get too puffed up with pride and stupidity, you better know that the PLO probably wasn't all that interested in blowing you to hell."

"Looked like a fair effort to me," I said, remembering the adrenaline and the shakes.

Benny shrugged, then gave me a look from dark eyes that had seen more of hell than any man should. "Listen up, Fiddler. If the PLO really wanted you, Arleigh McCree would be spending the next week in Watts, retrieving pieces of you from black folks' lawns and rain gutters."

"Who's Arleigh McCree?" I asked, changing the subject because Benny's description had been a little too vivid for my peace of mind.

"He's the head of the LAPD bomb squad. He's also about the best bomb tech this country has ever produced. But even he wouldn't have been able to disarm this if those buggers had wired a good shaker switch into the circuit."

Benny finished draining his beer bottle before I asked, "What's a shaker switch?" Then, because the King has been known to get carried away answering technical questions, I added real fast, "Not the specs, just enough so that I'll recognize the damn thing and run like hell if I ever see one."

Benny reached into the battery-driven, wheeled ice chest that follows him around like a stainless-steel hound. He fished through the glittering ice, pulled out a bottle of beer, opened it and handed it to me. He repeated the process for himself. Then he sat and watched foam rise in the long amber neck of the bottle. As he watched, he talked.

"The best shaker switches around today are the flat little mercury switches in the expensive burglar alarms on cars like your Cobra," he said. "One good shake of the car, like if somebody sits down in the seat without turning off the alarm, and an airhorn goes off like a bleeding banshee. Only in this case, a bomb tech moves the device about two inches, the mercury rolls down the chute and everybody is blown to bloody rags.

"The Puerto Ricans use shakers as the primary switch on some of their bombs," he continued. "Leave the bomb in a car in a tow-away zone, and when the police truck comes along and puts on the hook, up comes the front of the car, and blam goes the bomb. Hateful little shits, them. Ought to be outlawed."

As though to underline his feelings, Benny flipped the blasting cap he had been toying with over the lip of the balcony. The cap hit the concrete at the edge of the kitchen patio below and exploded with the flash and report of a cherry bomb. The King listened as though assessing a musical performance, nodded, then looked at his beer without drinking any.

"In other words, boyo," he said, pointing a stubby index finger at me, "you're cocking around with people who have been killing each other for a long time and will go on killing for a lot longer. You did fine today, but this was just a scrimmage. It wasn't the big game."

The Ice Cream King likes to call himself "half a Jew." This may have given him a little deeper feeling about the matter. Even so, there was an unusual edge to his words.

"I appreciate your concern, Benny," I said, watching him watch his beer, "even though I know it's selfishly motivated. You know if anything happens to that Cobra, you're going to be nominated to put it all back together. But if it's any comfort to you, remember this: I have one important advantage in this little game."

He waited, watching me now rather than his beer.

"The game is being played in my ballpark," I said succinctly.

Benny waited for a three count, then tilted the longnecked beer bottle in my direction. "Guard your spine, Fiddler. It's the home team that buggers you every time."

It was coming up on midnight when I finally pulled off the Pacific Coast Highway onto the dusty little road that leads into Crystal Cove. The cottage I call home is one of about fifty that have accumulated over the past seventy-five years in the little crease called Las Trancas Canyon. The open land on either side of the cove is part of a billion-dollar parcel of property, the last major undeveloped portion of the Gold Coast except for the Marine Corps enclave called Camp Pendleton.

The Crystal Cove cottages will be bulldozed someday soon. One of two things will happen then—either it will become another public beach pocked by smashed beer bottles and carpeted with trash or the Irvine Company will sprawl some fancy, earth-toned $250-a-night resort hotel down the bluffs to the sea.

Either way, I'm going to lose. I've reconciled myself to it, most of the time. I'm not even sure that I resent it anymore. Until Armageddon comes on the back of a D-9 Cat, I'll enjoy the hell out of that old cottage, with the glass picture window so old it has bubbles in it and the koi pond where fish turn like autumn leaves in a dark wind and the sunsets are so beautiful they are music written in tones of light.

I found some cheese and sausage in the refrigerator and opened a bottle of Napa Pinot Noir. I took the meal out to the pond. My palate was really looking forward to the wine. I was just settling down to eat and feed the fish when the phone rang. It was too late on the East Coast for Fiora to be calling, and I'd just tucked a rather grim Ice Cream King into bed. More curious than alarmed, I picked up the receiver.

"Congratulations, Mr. Fiddler. You're a very lucky man."

Not even so much as "hello," but then Salameh didn't seem to be aware of courtesy as an alternative approach to human relations.

"Tell your intrepid bombardier that he'll have to learn to construct a new timer," I said, chewing noisily. "Timex is phasing out that model."

"You're a fool," the Palestinian said.

No sense of irony, that one.

"All Americans are Jews or fools," continued Salameh.

"If you called me to trade ethnic slurs, Sally, I'll do my best. Let's see, what was the phrase—towel head? Rug jockey? No, that's not— Camel jacker! That's it. I've been waiting to use that one since I opened the Cobra's trunk."

Salameh laughed, but it wasn't a friendly sound.

"We have your address," he said. "Think about it. Then tell your Jew friends the Zahedis that you cost them an extra five thousand dollars. I doubt that the friendship will survive the loss of money. For the last time, Mr. Fool, goodbye."

He hung up with emphasis.

I stood there with the phone in my hand, studying it as though it would give me a clue to the way Salameh had traced me. I didn't think I'd left that many tracks. But the longer I thought, the less magic it seemed. If the Palestinians had spotted me tailing the green Firebird—as they obviously had— they would have gotten my license number. With the license number, you can get a home address from the Department of Motor Vehicles. I'd figured that out a long time ago and had made a mental note to change the address on my vehicle registration to a post office box.

First thing tomorrow I'd do it.

There was another part of that equation, some other pertinent little fact that was eluding me. I was pursuing it, maybe even gaining on it, when the telephone rang again. This time I was smart. I went and got my plate and glass of wine before I answered it. If I was going to trade insults, I'd need strength.

The woman's voice threw me for a moment. Husky, intimate, yet definitely not a come-on. Just her normal speech.

"Mr. Fiddler?" she asked, but there was no real question in her voice.

"Fiddler," I corrected her.

"Very well . . . Fiddler," she said. "My name is Sharai Landau."

A beautiful name. As beautiful as the woman who had walked by the Cobra this afternoon, perhaps?

I kept my speculations to myself and enjoyed her voice as though it were a good wine: smooth, complex, infinitely intriguing, a voice to hold any man's attention. The tones were cultured, the delivery well modulated and the whole package wrapped in just enough of an accent to be exotic.

"We have a friend in common. Esau Biggs."

That answered the question of how she had gotten my number. I took a sip of the wine and tasted the tarry richness of the Pinot Noir. "Do you have dark hair that turns sunlight into fire?" I asked.

There was just enough hesitation that I could almost see her smile. Then her voice changed. "I'm calling to suggest that you really don't want to be associated with the Muslim Student League. You were"—she hesitated again, but this time not for a smile—"breathtakingly foolish this evening."

"I should have let my car blow up, I suppose?"

"Cars can be replaced."

"Not that one." I took a bracing sip of wine. "Just out of curiosity, which side are you on?"

"We warned you about the bomb, didn't we?"

"I don't know about 'we'," I said, swallowing another bit of wine, savoring its arid finish. "Esau said he was hired by a man, some big guy who walked like John Wayne."

"John Wayne?" she said. She laughed softly. "Let me reassure you that neither John Wayne nor I are on the side of the Arabs." Her voice changed, almost impersonal again. "What attracted you to the Muslim Student League offices?"

"I was sight-seeing for a friend," I said unhelpfully. Then I decided to try a little bait of my own. "To be precise, they're not just Muslims. They're Palestinians in league with the Iranian Mujahideen."

That caught her attention.

"Iranians," she said quickly. "Are you sure?"

"Look," I said, smoothing a bit more wine across my beer tarnished tongue. "I know that you're the well-dressed lady I saw on the street this afternoon just before somebody tried to kill me. I'm always glad to talk to beautiful women who walk like dancers. But this conversation is pretty one-sided. Unless you plan on holding up your end of Twenty Questions, I don't have any more time to play."

There was a three-count pause at the other end of the line, but the bait I had dangled must have been tempting enough.

"All right," she said. "I work for the Israeli consul general in Los Angeles. Does that make any difference in what you're willing to tell me?"

I chewed on a morsel of sausage while I examined the terrain for land mines.

"Consulate staff, huh? That could be anything from a file clerk to Mossad, and I can guess which one would be more interested in Palestinians and Iranians. Tell me, Sharai, does the American government know Israel is conducting a surveillance operation against Palestinian students at USC? Would you be embarrassed if the FBI found out?"

She didn't flinch. "Tell me, Fiddler," she said in a musical tone, "did you report the fact that someone tried to bomb your car? Would you be embarrassed if the police found out about that?"

"In other words, if I don't show them mine, you won't show them yours," I said, taking a sip of the wine and wishing I could chew a Stoned Wheat Thin without making any noise.

"Let me put it this way," she said. "I think our situations are quite similar. I don't know anything about your friend or client or whomever you represent, but the Israeli government tries to look out for the interests of all Jews, not just those who have chosen to live in Israel. Perhaps we could strike some sort of rapprochement on that basis."

The bait was nicely presented, neither too shy nor too bold. I sipped at the Pinot Noir again, ticking through the possibilities. I probably could fence with her long enough to get another tiny fact or two, but would it be worth the time and effort? Assuming she had told the truth about her job, she undoubtedly had bosses to answer to, men who had a smallish and embattled country to worry about and who were used to holding their cards flat against their hairy chests.

"Sharai, it's been a long day for me. I can't say any more until I talk with my principal, and you can't say any more until you talk with your people. Why don't we get together for lunch tomorrow and discuss this whole thing more candidly."

I could hear her put her hand over the receiver and speak with someone else in the room. The sound changed again, allowing me to hear her gentle breathing.

"All right," she said, after a moment. "Where?"

"I'll pick you up at the consulate about noon."

"No. I'll meet you."

Mentally I sighed, knowing that now I'd have to shake down my list of contacts for someone who could tell me if a Sharai Landau really worked at the Israeli consulate, and, if so, was her job a cover for something else. Maybe Benny could help. And maybe not. Consulates are like Chinese boxes when it comes to getting useful information: the more you unwrap, the less you get.

"Fine," I said. "Do you know Spago?"

"You have very expensive tastes. Twelve-thirty."

She hung up. I finished the rest of the Pinot Noir as I fed the fish. Lord Toranaga, shogun of the pond, was unusually friendly, nibbling at my fingertips as though he hadn't eaten for weeks. He must have been missing Fiora, who usually drops by to feed him from her hand at least once a week. Despite Toranaga's muscular demands, I found myself paying a great deal of attention to a new koi, a rather small, beautifully formed fish named Sky for the clear cerulean spot on its back. Blue is an intriguing, disturbing color, evoking everything from memories of Fourth of July picnics at the lake to a depression as deep as the Mariana Trench.

Sharai had worn blue when other women with her coloring might have chosen green or black or red.

I watched Sky turn gracefully in the pond's subtle currents. Blue. The color of water, pacific and unruffled. But there is the blue of the ocean depths, too, the supple blue that conceals the turbulence of a thousand currents and undercurrents. When I finally went to bed I dreamed of blues and of sliding beneath the surface, slipping toward the depths. It wasn't an unpleasant experience, but then it was a fairly short dream.

I got a chance to experience the rest of it later.

5

The sun was still struggling to shine through a thick layer of marine clouds when I was awakened by the damnedest metallic skreeling sound. King David's ever-blooming flower was running low on nectar, and three of the noisy little bastards were hovering outside my window, cursing me roundly for dereliction of duty. Whoever dreamed up the term "a charm of hummingbirds" had never seen more than one at a time. A "shrill of hummingbirds" would be more accurate.

Once I brewed up the sugar elixir and got the hummers out of my hair, I was free to take up my life again. For openers I managed to turn in a fairly respectable time on the three miles up the canyon and back. The thought of Salameh squeezing an extra five thousand out of the Zahedis in my name helped my speed considerably. By the time I cooled out, showered and dressed, Shahpour was in his office at the bank, shuffling currency around the short-term money markets of New York.

I told him what had happened, including the surcharge. "You'll probably be getting another call from Salameh demanding more money," I said. "Take five grand out of my account, since I'm the cause of the second assessment. If there are any more surcharges, use my money. No sense in your paying for my mistakes."

"No," said Shahpour calmly. "Not a cent. My father told me he would pay far more than five thousand dollars to watch you handle Salameh again."

"I'd rather never see the bastard, if it's all the same to you."

Shahpour made a sound halfway between a laugh and a sigh. We both knew that Salameh wasn't going to dry up and blow away on a desert wind.

I dressed for lunch a bit more carefully than usual, and even called Spago ahead of time to make sure they would have a decent table for two at twelve-thirty. I also took a moment and called the Israeli consulate. Sometimes an ordinary question results in a useful answer.

"Israeli consulate, *shalom*," said the bright and faintly

accented voice of the switchboard girl. The familiarity of the accent was a reminder of exactly how extensive the Işraeli population had become in Los Angeles.

"Sharai Landau, please," I said.

"Moment . . ." I heard the only sound I needed to as the girl plugged me in to some extension. I could have stayed on the line to hear what section answered, just to satisfy my own curiosity about Sharai's cover job, but it didn't really matter. Chief assistant to the assistant chief, maid, switchboard, secretary, liaison to the East Sinai Quilting Society—they all amounted to the same thing, a legitimate title in an often illegitimate world. I hung up before learning which plausible lie Sharai worked under.

One of the few useful legacies of my time in the newspaper business is relatively free access to the Los Angeles *Times* research library. It's an involved, gritty story, but I once did a favor for somebody who since has become part of the *Times* hierarchy. Quite a substantial part, as a matter of fact. That's what too many lunches in the Picasso Room will do for you.

The paper granted research privileges to a few local freelance writers and I'm on that list. When I called the library clerk at the *Times*, he checked my name against the list, then ran the clips on the Muslim Student League for me.

"The envelope's pretty thin," said the clerk, returning to the phone after a short run through the files. "Three stories. A brief about a demonstration they held at the Federal Building in 1979 against the Shah of Iran. A mention in a society-page feature last year. And"—pause while papers were rustled—"a story from last week's business section."

An odd mix, I thought. The society pages are usually reserved for those with clout, and the business pages for major representatives of capitalism. The news sections are different. Any asshole can make the front page.

"What's the society thing about?" I asked.

"It's a profile of F. Robert Jarvis, the chief executive officer of International Constructors. He's also the last of the red-hot donors. This says he runs a bunch of charities, stuff like the Hospital Guild, the Children's Home Foundation and the Muslim Student League."

"That's the only mention?" I asked.

"Yup," he said. "You want me to read the last story?"

"Sure, why not?"

"It's from the Business Briefs column just last week. It says that the Gold Coast Industrial Council is sponsoring a horse show at Dry Canyon Ranch this week."

"What's the connection to the league?" I asked.

"It's an Arabian horse show. Get it? Arabian?"

I got it, but I wasn't going to brag about it.

"It's true," said the clerk. "The student league gets all the proceeds of the show. And the show is Arabian horses. You want Xeroxes of the clips?"

I was in string-gathering mode at this point, and what the hell, you can never have too much string, right?

"Yeah. Leave them with the Spring Street guard. I'll pick them up in an hour."

I snagged a fat Yellow Pages telephone book from the table near the phone, looked up the number for the Gold Coast Industrial League, punched it in and waited until a secretary answered.

"Who's the president of the league this year?" I asked.

"F. Robert Jarvis, sir. Did you wish to speak with him?"

"No, thank you. Not right now," I said, hanging up gently. Another piece of string.

I called the *Times* library again and identified myself.

"While you're at it, could you run off a copy of everything you have on this guy Jarvis?" I asked.

"Sure thing," said the clerk. "It's about a ton of clips. You want me to go to the data bases?"

"Sure thing," I echoed dryly and hung up.

One of the anomalies of modern life is that the press, that faithful champion of civil liberties and individual rights, has the best and most accessible dossiers that have been gathered this side of Orwell's Oceania. Makes you wonder who is watching the watchers. But I try to be adult about my speculations. In other words, I use what I can get my hands on and let the op-ed pundits worry about journalistic morality. Not that the subject ever comes up; we all know that the Fourth Estate contains the only genuine saints remaining in a lamentably fallen world. Right?

Sure thing.

I looked at my favorite clock, the one that told time around the world. People were knocking off for the day in England. Publishers in New York were more than halfway through the prandial marathon they call a business lunch. Hollywood types were tying their stomachs in knots worrying about their upcoming meetings at Spago. Would it be a nice table this time, discreetly removed but not banished to the fringes? Would the right people glide by for a round of kissy-kissy? Would Wolfgang anoint me with his presence?

Or, in my case: Had Spago hired any Palestinians since my last visit?

It hadn't. The valets were all Muscle Beach types. One was named Bruce and the other was named Keith and they had nice white teeth and big hard pectorals and soft little smiles. I let Keith park the Cobra. He slid it into the place of honor right beside the parking lot shack. The slot on the other side was occupied by a Rolls-Royce Silver Cloud.

Yes, Spago is pretentious. No doubt about it. But a chef like Wolfgang Puck has to be pretentious to make his clientele feel at home. He's very good at it. Human psychology is his second calling. Selling quality food is his first. He lets just a whiff of the kitchen drift into the dining room. The tantalizing scents swirl around the white cane chairs and linen tablecloths. Spago is, without question, the toniest pizza parlor in the world, complete with the smells of extra virgin olive oil and vine-ripened, sun-dried tomatoes and basil so fresh you can damn near eat the aroma.

As good as it is, Spago isn't a usual lunch for me. There is a very good French deli much closer to home, and nothing can equal the decor of my patio, where hummingbirds dog-fight against the gigantic blue backdrop of the sea and the wine list is tailor-made for my palate. Nonetheless, here I was.

I decided I must have been trying to impress the graceful lady with fire in her hair and secrets in her voice. And why shouldn't I try? A woman like Sharai didn't come along every day or even every decade. Even if she was an Israeli spook.

Traffic had been lighter than usual. I had time to kill before Sharai arrived. I ordered a bottle of crisp, cucumbery Sauvignon Blanc for company as I leafed through the Xeroxed newspaper clippings. It didn't take much time to add some strings to the growing snarl I had already collected.

The Muslim Student League stories were just as the kid had described over the phone. Inconsequential. The connection between an international entrepreneur and a group of Middle Eastern students was the only intriguing bit, but the reporter who wrote the articles didn't seem to think so. He ignored the connection entirely, as though every corporate president routinely adopted a batch of Third Worlders. Maybe it was a new variation on the sixties take-a-minority-to-lunch cliché.

The files dealing with Jarvis and International Constructors were more thoroughly researched, but not by a hell of a lot. The clips extended back over thirty years and chronicled the growth of IC from a medium-sized civil engineering outfit doing subdivisions and municipal sewers into one of the top five construction firms in the world.

F. (for Franklin, a name he publicly loathed) Robert Jarvis was singlehandedly responsible for IC's unnerving growth, according to the folklore of the industry. A half century ago he had been born in the California boondocks, in a place called Indio, where the Great Sonoran Desert spills over onto the west side of the Colorado River. From distinctly humble beginnings, Jarvis had worked himself into a full scholarship at USC, an engineering degree and ultimately a job with a little local engineering firm. Within five years he had bought out the firm's founders and had begun to work his fiscal magic.

Today, judging from the pictures that accompanied the most recent stories, Jarvis was a shrewd old man with a smoker's wrinkled and parched skin. He was also the chairman and CEO of a firm that did five billion a year in business all over the world, from Stockholm to Seoul to Stockton.

Much of the business was in countries where the power was in the hands of guys with names like Muhammad and Abdullah. Jarvis and his firm seemed to do everything for these folks from drilling the wells and capping the wellheads to welding together the pipelines and erecting the pumping stations and the catalytic cracking towers on their refineries. He left the supertanker business to the Greeks, but F. Robert and his IC surrogates had a hand in everything else from crude to carburetor.

I found one perceptive little profile which claimed that Jarvis was himself part Bedouin—spiritually, if not genetically —because his upbringing in the California desert gave him an easy compatibility with the princes of the House of Saud and with the other Muslim leaders who controlled the wastelands of the Middle East. The piece even quoted Jarvis:

"One must admire and respect the men who rule the Middle East," he said, "for they are direct, forceful and steadfast in their politics, their friendships and their religion."

He didn't say where the Arab terrorists and their supporters fell within that hagiography.

I was more than a bit put off by this apologia, but what can you expect from a guy who makes a zillion dollars a year off the Arabs? I'm just a romantic, I guess. I still have this view of captains of industry as steely-eyed visionaries, but Jarvis apparently couldn't see any farther than the bottom line when it came to judging his associates' morality.

I read through the rest of the clips quickly. The most recent ones suggested that the bloom was off the rose for International Constructors. With the decline in oil prices, the instability of Iran and the general Muslim bloodletting of the past couple of years, the building boom in the Arab world wasn't. Profits were down at International Constructors. No one predicted an immediate upswing.

The most recent business analysis piece in the clipping file suggested that Jarvis was scrambling for building projects that had nothing to do with the Arabs or petroleum. He had promised the stockholders that his first priority in the new fiscal year would be to wean IC from its dependence on oil-based construction. Recently, the firm had won a big contract from the People's Republic of China for a phosphate plant not far from Beijing.

I closed the small manila envelope, stuffed it into the breast pocket of my sport coat and allowed the waiter to pour me a second glass of wine. In my mind I was trying to fit a few of these new strings to the fiddle inside my head—or at least into a mental game of cat's cradle—when a stir in the room distracted me.

Spago is a very sophisticated, male-dominated lunch spot. Hotshot producers schmooze with the studio chiefs who control their destinies and both defer to the three or four stars whose faces are thought to control the P and L statements of the industry. These men see more beautiful women in a day than most guys do in a year. Washington lures attractive, intelligent women but L.A. draws stunning ones.

So when half the guys in a room like Spago come to point for a woman, she has to be striking. Sharai was. Striking. Yet she seemed oblivious to the attention the room was paying to her as she walked toward me.

She was taller than I recalled, but every bit as beautifully shaped. She was wearing an indigo silk shirtdress, simple and belted to catch a small waist between fullness above and below. The intense blue color darkened her café-au-lait skin and black eyes. Even here, in the subdued light of the restaurant, her short hair shone with the lustrous richness of Moroccan leather. She walked with the healthy, natural grace that comes of physical strength.

"Runner, dancer or swimmer?" I asked as she approached the table.

Sharai looked surprised that someone should notice. "Swimmer," she said. "I'm an oddity. Israelis are supposed to be desert people, but I was raised partly in Haifa."

"I don't know which part Haifa was responsible for," I said, "but the rest of the country didn't do too badly by you, either."

Sexual innuendo isn't really my style, but there was something about Sharai that both intrigued and almost irritated me. I had an irrational urge to pry beneath that rich feminine surface and uncover the woman hidden beneath shades of blue. I watched closely for her reaction to my smart-ass remark.

For an instant she almost smiled. Then it passed and she shot me a look that had NO TRESPASSING posted all over it. "I was also raised here in L.A.," she said coolly. "But we didn't come here to talk about parts of me. Or of you."

Ouch.

Well, she was intelligent beneath that silky indigo shell. A quick, sharp tongue. Despite the flare of feminine response, I sensed she wasn't interested in anything from me but conversation. Too bad. If it isn't mutual, it just isn't—period. So I stood, held out her chair and gently tucked her under the table.

The waiter moved in quickly, pouring Sharai a glass of wine. She took it in both of her hands and sipped. As she did, I caught sight of another gleam of the deep blue that seemed to be her signature: a ring with a large, beautifully shaped oval stone mounted simply. Lapis lazuli, clean and rich and perfect, bezel-set within yellow gold. The stone was like a deep, serene eye staring unflinchingly at the world.

Lapis is a soft stone. Most of it, even the best, is shot through with flecks of iron pyrite, fool's gold. Sharai's stone had no such distractions. It was pure blue, like a Mediterranean cove a hundred feet deep. The grain of the stone itself was as fine and smooth as the skin of the woman who wore the ring.

"Afghan?" I asked.

"Yes," she said, following my eye to the ring on her hand.

"The setting looks more Navajo than Middle Eastern. Fine without being effete."

I sensed the surprise that rippled through her. She looked at me again, as though she hadn't really seen me the first few times. And maybe she hadn't. On the outside I don't look like the type of man who would appreciate fine wine or intelligent women. I definitely look the beer, busty barmaid and brawl type.

"You're unusually knowledgeable," said Sharai. "The stone was given to me by someone who had traveled in Afghanistan. I had the lapis set by a jewelry maker here in Los Angeles. A Navajo, or at least he was until the tribal elders disowned him. He was forever transcending the strictures of his culture by creating not-quite-traditional designs using nonnative materials."

"There's strength in hybrids," I pointed out, savoring the subtly changing flavors as the Sauvignon Blanc warmed slightly. "The best grapes began that way."

This time Sharai definitely smiled, enjoying my pleasure in the wine. The smile faded into the silent blue depths of whatever haunted her. For she was haunted. It was as clear to me as the husky music of her voice.

"To be hybrid is dangerous," she said softly. "The ones that survive are strong, yes, but the rest die trying to combine attributes that would rather be at war. And even the ones who seem to survive . . ." Her voice faded, then returned, stronger, almost harsh. "Shortly after my friend made this ring, he went on a drinking spree. He crashed his car at high speed and died."

"Maybe that was what he wanted. It's faster than alcohol, and a damn sight cleaner in the end."

Surprise flickered behind her expressionless face. "And I used to think Israelis were cruel," she murmured.

"Sorry, I didn't mean to be. It's been my experience that people who drink hard and drive fast have a death wish. Sometimes it's granted."

Sharai moved her head slightly, making light run like tiny flames through her hair. "You're right. He meant to die. It's just that Americans usually refuse to understand that death can be welcome." She closed her eyes. When they opened again they were very dark and she looked older than she was. "How did you get involved with the Muslim Student League?"

Before I could answer, the waiter appeared like an expectant hummingbird. And like a hummer, he was also quite demanding in his own wordless way. Sharai invited me to order one of Spago's pizzas and salads for both of us. When the waiter hummed off to the kitchen, I answered Sharai's question.

"Three Palestinians have been trying to extort five thousand dollars a month from a family I know," I said. "I followed one of the blackmailers back to the league offices. Someone spotted me and put a bomb in the Cobra. At least"—I shrugged —"I assume it was an Arab. I haven't pissed off anyone else lately."

She nodded. "An Iraqi named Saied put the bomb in your trunk a few minutes after you left your car and followed the other Arab onto campus. Why are your friends vulnerable to extortion?"

I smiled and shot her a look that said: *Honey, you really don't expect me to answer that one, do you?*

"They're Jews," she said in that husky, fascinating voice, "and they're in America illegally."

I nodded, confirming what she already knew.

"Your friends aren't alone," she said earnestly, "although I'm sure they feel that way. We've recently become aware of several Jewish families who are having the same problem. It appears that the Palestinian terrorists have somehow discovered a way of identifying and exploiting Iranian Jews who have come illegally to America."

"Revolutionary Guards," I said.

"Iran's?" she said, quickly following my elliptical response.

"Yeah. Apparently some of those bastards can read more than the Koran. They vet the mail, write down return addresses in America, and the PLO types here check them out."

There was a moment of silence. I could almost see her assessing the possibilities, discarding some and keeping others, thinking quickly, cleanly. To me that was as sexy as her very female body.

"Very neat," she said, referring to my information rather than to the process of blackmail it described. "The PLO has tight connections in Teheran, and other Middle Eastern capitals as well. I'm sure they could use the apparatus of almost any Muslim state to gather information for them."

I freshened her wine just a bit and asked, "Why are you interested in USC's Muslim Student League?"

"Israel is always interested in Muslim terrorists. It has to be."

"Somehow, the University of Spoiled Children doesn't seem like a natural hotbed of terrorism," I retorted.

"The University of—?" she began questioningly. Then she made the connection. "Oh," she said smiling. "USC. Appropriate, yes? Especially for the sons of petrodollars. You see, most of the Arab states are educationally in the Dark Ages. If it isn't in the Koran, it simply doesn't exist. But you can't build a twentieth-century technology using the sayings of a seventh-century holy man."

Sharai sipped her wine as gracefully as she did everything else. When the tip of her tongue licked her lips in unconscious appreciation of the wine's flavor, it brought every male sense in me to full alert. Her unconscious gestures were sensual, and yet her conscious gestures denied that sensuality. The tension between the two made me want to take up arms on behalf of her unconscious.

"Arab governments send students all over the world on scholarships," she continued, touching her tongue to her lips again. "The PLO claims that it is an Arab government without a country, so it must do the same. But the PLO doesn't waste scholarships on moderates. It sends only those students who are"—she smiled sadly—"fanatics."

She kept talking softly, speaking in a voice that was meant to describe intimacies rather than atrocities. "Many of these 'students' have killed long before they get to the U.S. They are terrorists, born and raised—in all their parts," she added ironically. "There are several hundred such men here in California alone. They mingle with other Middle Eastern students—Iranians, Iraqis, Syrians, Kuwaitis, Turks—in places like the league."

"Those league meetings must be kind of interesting, what with the war between Iran and Iraq, plus Shiite versus Sunni hostilities in other countries," I said.

"Muslims fight one another, yes, but they are bound together by two things," she said. "Their love of Allah and their hatred of Israel."

"I got the impression yesterday that the extortionists were less moved by love than by hate."

Sharai shrugged slightly, a motion that emphasized every curve of her breasts. It was unconscious. For all she seemed to care about her impact on men, she might as well have been veiled in yards of black and hidden behind seraglio walls. Her indifference wasn't an act, either. She simply did not acknowledge the world, men or herself in sexual terms. Perhaps that was part of the tension that lived in her, haunting her eyes, for she was a sensual woman. Even as she spoke, her fingers stroked the smooth, crisp finish of the linen napkin lying across her lap.

"Hate is a religious experience to a Muslim. To love Allah you must first hate infidels." Sharai's full mouth turned down slightly as she read my expression. "To you that's an unfair summary of Islam, I suppose. But Islam is a relatively new religion, and their day of glory is already past. Like the Irish, hatred and holy war are all they have left. They like it that way. It's the Manichaean dichotomy of light and dark, good and evil, life and death. There are only two kinds of people in the world—Muslims and all the rest. There are only two places in the world—those ruled by Muslims and those ruled by the Great Satans. The destiny of every good Muslim is to spread Islam by the sword."

Her unpolished fingernail snapped against the wineglass, sending a crystal sound through the silence like a cry through twilight. "Muhammad was a desert man not given to subtle distinctions or philosophical intricacies. Power, death and hatred were all that he understood. Islam reflects that."

"You feel very strongly, don't you?" I asked.

"Even if I weren't a Jew, I'd feel this way. Any culture that systematically degrades its women in the name of holiness is contemptible."

"Don't Jewish men ritually thank God every day that they weren't born a woman?" I asked.

"Orthodox Jews still do, I believe. The rest of us have grown up."

Whew. I was glad Sharai wasn't directing that controlled rage at me. The anger just beneath the surface of her words crackled like the fiery light hidden within her hair. Fiora would have approved of every slashing sentiment. Like Sharai, Fiora had to bear the indignity of being born into a world of less intelligent men, men who treated her as a cross between a pet and a pincushion.

Sharai took another sip of wine as though to put out a concealed fire. Except for the echoes of her words expanding through my mind, I might have imagined her flare of emotion. Her façade was firmly back in place. She was a very controlled person, despite her passion. Or perhaps because of it. Was that what haunted her? Had she taken her passionate nature and hammered it into the cold shape of hatred? I'd done that myself in the past. Thinking about the man who had tried to murder Fiora could still make me hum with an icy eagerness to kill. But that was a hell of a way to live. It eats you the way napalm eats flesh. Slowly. Irrevocably.

So I had opted to live and not to hate. At least not very much. Had Sharai chosen? Did she know that she had a choice?

On the other hand, did she have a choice?

The Israeli secret service is spread more thinly than any spook stable in the world. Sometimes it has to rely on pickup talent for noncombatant help. This woman conducted herself professionally, but she was just too damn beautiful and therefore too memorable to be much use in the field except as a Mata Hari. Despite Sharai's obvious commitment to Israel, I didn't see her turning tricks in the name of national security. Whores are basically cold people. Sharai was not.

Which left me with the question of what she was. Had she been recruited against her will, or at least her basic inclinations? If so, who was her target? I doubted that I was. She had been watching the Arabs before I'd arrived in the Cobra. If anything, I was a complication added to her original assignment.

The sense of being watched called me out of my thoughts. I realized that Sharai was looking at my hands. As usual when I was thinking hard, I was rubbing the pads of my fingers over the smooth globe of the wineglass, then nestling its curve into my palm for a moment, then running my fingertips over the glass again. My hands are large and hard and scarred by the vagaries of the life I have chosen. The wineglass looked very fragile against my palm.

I looked up suddenly, catching an entirely different expression on Sharai's face. I knew then that she was wondering how my hands would feel on her body, and whether I would be half as careful of her as I was of the wineglass I was holding.

"Look, Sharai—" I began, but she spoke quickly, as though she knew what I was going to say.

"The four Palestinians—what did they look like?" she asked.

I waited for a long five count. She watched me calmly, nothing speculative at all in her expression. She was as deep and serene as the lapis ring on her hand. So I gave her the only thing that she seemed willing to accept from me: a description of the four men. She listened carefully and said nothing until I described the leader.

"Did you notice anything unusual about him physically?" she said.

"He had a scar across the back of his left hand, either a deep cut, a burn or a bullet crease," I said.

Sharai's irises were too dark for me to see if her pupils expanded, but I could see her eyes narrow quickly, briefly, in a reflexive indication of intense interest. "Recent?" she asked.

I shook my head. "Old," I said, looking at the shiny pink of the new scars on my hands. "Whatever marked him happened years ago." I took a sip of wine, gauging her sudden tension. For an instant something very like hate looked out of her eyes, but not at me. It was the Palestinian who had stirred Sharai's depths. "He used a *nom de guerre*," I added matter-of-factly, watching her wrestle with whatever dark emotion had claimed her. "Salameh."

Sharai's reaction to the name was complete and visceral. Hatred. She looked away, into the mirror on the wall beside our booth. At first I thought the gesture was an effort to conceal her emotions from me. By reflex I followed her glance and caught the reflection of a man who was seated at the bar across the dining room from us. He had been largely concealed from me by a pillar, but when I shifted to look in the mirror I could see him clearly.

The man was in his fifties, big and raw-boned, with weathered skin that was different from the beach tans that inhabited the rest of the room. He sat alone at the bar, smoking and toying with a glass of beer in front of him, dressed in a blue blazer and white shirt without a tie. His eyes seemed to be fixed on Sharai. Then he shifted and our gazes locked for an instant in the mirror. He had a faint squint, like a man used to looking across long distances against intense sunlight. He radiated both intelligence and hardness. He had the eyes of a watcher, a hunter, a man who has seen enough death to know that it isn't mysterious or special or ennobling. It's simply final.

Something about the man's eyes, his parchment skin, his animal alertness, reminded me of another man: Aaron Sharp, a shooter whose deadly skill had saved my life, and Fiora's.

As the man looked away I remembered what Esau had said about the guy who had paid ten bucks to give me a warning. Yeah, this man had something of John Wayne about him. But this wasn't John Wayne at his most popular, fighting for Old Glory. This wasn't even Rooster Cogburn pulling a gritty little girl out of a nest of rattlesnakes. This was John Wayne playing Ethan Edwards, the Indian killer of the Malapai, half savage himself.

Sharai was looking at me again, but it was too late.

"Invite him over," I said. "I'll buy him lunch."

She pretended she didn't understand.

"No problem," I said gently, needling her and knowing it. "I'd have seen him sooner or later."

She shot me a look that said she didn't know what the hell I was running on about, but would I please switch subjects so she could participate in the small talk.

"Don't be embarrassed if you don't know his name," I said, oozing sympathy and understanding. "There are so many Israeli spooks around Los Angeles, maybe you weren't even introduced." I held her steady gaze, and added helpfully, "He's the one in the blue blazer behind the pillar."

I looked in the mirror again. Our eyes met and the man realized he was burned. He went very still for a moment. Then he picked up the beer in front of him and walked across the room toward our table. As he approached, I saw why Esau had been reminded of John Wayne. The man was big, broad-chested, solid, and walked with the rolling gait of a cowboy or a sailor or a man with a bad knee. In this case, I voted for the knee. The gait might have been the source of Esau's impression of John Wayne, but the closer the man got, and the more clearly I could see his eyes, the more he reminded me of Ethan Edwards.

He and our lunch arrived at the table simultaneously. The waiter was discreetly puzzled. Table-hopping is de rigueur at Spago, but the three of us weren't exuding the usual kissy-kissy vibes. The waiter didn't know whether to bring another plate or signal the bouncer.

"Another plate, more salad and perhaps some pasta primavera," I said, rising, watching the big man's hands. "Oh, and bring another draft beer for Mr.—?" I waited politely.

"Rafi Yermiya," said the big man. "I'm Sharai's father."

6

I didn't know whether to laugh or to apologize to Sharai for giving her a rough time. Whether she was an experienced operative or a total tenderfoot, she was playing the game with an almost unbelievable handicap: a case agent who was her father. I wondered which conspiratorial genius in Tel Aviv had authorized this little tap dance.

But then I suppose it made no more or less sense than the man who sat across the table from them: an independently indolent gringo doing a favor for a friend. The game of spies and spooks is stranger than the average civilian might expect. Today the pros and the amateurs are thrown together more frequently than used to be the case. That's probably because the game reaches deeper into society than it used to in the fifties and sixties, back during the cold war. Then there were only two sides, and both fielded professional armies of full-time spooks, men and a few women who fought for ideology because they loved to fight.

Today, there aren't two sides. There are a dozen or a hundred, as many as there are nations and interest groups and ideologies. Jews and Druze, Muslims and Gentiles, Hindus and Holy Rollers, Communists and Libertarians all get dumped into the same boiling pot in places like Los Angeles and Washington and Paris, Ulster and Teheran and Beirut.

The game has changed from the days of the cold warriors. Today, the targets of espionage are factories, not military bases; the targets of military attack are embassies and consulates, not armies or armed fortresses. The most damaging spy in recent history was a $150-a-week clerk at TRW who had a cocaine habit and an antisocial itch. The most telling combatants in the struggle for international domination are likely to be aerospace draftsmen with middle-age panic and Xerox privileges or students with scholarships and green Firebirds.

Modern wars and skirmishes are fought once removed, by proxy, as though they were mere battles for corporate control. This is the era of the low-tech truck bomb and terrorism by telephone. There are professionals around, to be sure, but they conscript their cannon fodder in rather unexpected places. What I was trying to prevent was the use of unsuitable conscripts. I had bought in as a Zahedi replacement, and that's the way I wanted it to stay.

I wondered if Rafi Yermiya would agree that the Zahedis didn't belong in the front line of his little war. I doubted it. He had already recruited his daughter, who, in her own way, was as unsuited to well-planned death as gentle old Imbrahim Zahedi. Rafi was fully suited. He was as tough a man as I've ever traded stares with.

I watched him across the table as he studied me with those hard eyes of his. I wondered if he was trying to intimidate me or was simply being himself. The latter, probably. Men like Rafi don't have to work to be intimidating. They simply are.

Rafi produced a package of Dunhills from his inside pocket, politely offered me one that I declined and took one himself. He lit it with a Zippo lighter that had some kind of military insignia on it. I could smell first the thin sharpness of the lighter fluid and then the rich scent of burning tobacco. He smoked deeply, with the air of a man who didn't have to worry about the long-term medical prognosis, because in the long term he didn't expect to be alive.

I looked from Rafi to Sharai. No doubt she was his daughter. There was a clear impression, refined but unmistakable, of him in her features. I realized that in his own dark way Rafi was as handsome as his daughter was beautiful, and as enigmatic.

There was something about the way that Sharai watched her father that was hard to decipher. This was a grown woman, an intelligent and independent person, yet when she looked at Rafi there was something else as well. Not quite childlike, not quite obedient . . . and not quite loving. Perhaps it was the way she held her hand beside her face as she looked at him; the blue inner eye of the ring watched him steadily, unblinkingly. I wondered what it saw that I didn't. There were some very complex currents between father and daughter. I felt a stirring of sympathy for both of them. I suppose none of us ever completely overcomes the bonds forced on us by the accident of birth.

"Fiddler met a man who calls himself Salameh," said Sharai, her voice so tightly held that it was almost harsh.

There was no external change in Rafi, but a few years of

learning the hard way how to judge men told me that Rafi had risen to the bait with even greater violence than Sharai.

"When," said Rafi, looking at me.

It was a command, not a question. I took a bite of the fragrant pizza in front of me and chewed for a while. Rafi took a hit on his cigarette but had the grace not to exhale all over my lunch. For that bit of courtesy, I answered his question.

"Yesterday."

"Any distinguishing characteristics?" asked Rafi. His voice was under control again, the tone politely curious rather than demanding.

I had another mouthful of pizza by then, so Sharai ran her finger across the back of her hand, a silent retracing of the scar I had seen on Salameh. The gesture was more confirmation than I needed of her familiarity with the Palestinian. Rafi's only response was the sudden red-hot glow at the end of his shrinking cigarette. Sharai began to tell him about the extortion when Rafi made a tiny, almost invisible motion with his hand. She shut up instantly. Despite the familial relationship—or because of it—she worked well with him.

"Perhaps Fiddler would tell me himself," offered Rafi quietly. "He might remember something new."

I swallowed another bite of pizza, thought about switching to beer, but decided that the wine wasn't as bad a match for the lunch as it sounded.

"Salameh is running an extortion racket, using men who can pass for college kids or graduate students. He could almost pass himself, until you get in close. I'd peg him as thirty-three, give or take a few years."

"Coloring? Height?" asked Rafi very quietly.

He didn't look at me while he spoke, as though he were wary of alienating me by leaning too hard. Like Salameh, Rafi was a shrewd man accustomed to command. Unlike Salameh, Rafi wasn't restricted to it. Like all good commandos or terrorists, both men were quick, intelligent and deadly.

"A bit lighter than you, but nothing that a trip to the beach couldn't cure," I said. "Smaller than you by a good five inches, leaner, probably quicker." I looked up and caught the intensity with which Rafi was listening to each word. "Funny thing, Rafi. He reminded me of you in another way."

"Yes?" asked Rafi, his tone polite and his mouth set in a hard line.

"His eyes were a lot older than he was."

Sharai moved slightly, as though her chair or my words were uncomfortable. Rafi simply smiled. I decided that my first impression was right: he'd make a better ally than an enemy. I also decided that I'd rather not get between him and something that he really wanted. Like Salameh. On the other hand, it wouldn't be the first time that I'd found myself on the slip face of violence between two opposing forces. So I smiled in return.

I guess my smile wasn't reassuring, because Rafi suddenly exuded the feral alertness of a predator sniffing the twilight wind. Sharai stirred again, watching me with a combination of interest and wariness that was essentially feminine rather than combative. Until that moment she'd thought of me as rather big, rather foolish and on the whole rather harmless. She was revising that opinion. Surprisingly, she wasn't put off. Or perhaps it wasn't so surprising. If she'd spent her life measuring men against her father, a lot of them must have come up short.

"What's your interest in Salameh?" asked Rafi almost gently. Almost. He had more respect for me than he had had a moment ago, but he didn't like me any better. That's okay. There are parts of myself I don't like very well, either.

"Salameh collected five thousand dollars, a 'war tax,' from a friend of mine."

"A Jew," said Rafi.

It wasn't a question. I shrugged. Apparently Salameh's extortion racket was old news to Israel.

"In this country illegally," continued Rafi almost absently, as though he were thinking aloud.

I declined the deft offer to think aloud with him and took a bite of pizza instead.

Rafi sipped his beer and watched me over the rim of his glass. His eyes were as black and unyielding as marbles.

"Why didn't your friend contact the Israeli consulate?" he asked.

"Do they hire you out as a bodyguard?" I asked.

Smiling faintly, Rafi shook his head.

"In that case the consulate can't do much about my friend's dilemma, can it?"

"Then you're a bodyguard," said Rafi.

"Actually, I'm a retired violinist."

"Who fiddles around in his spare time," Rafi suggested dryly.

I couldn't help it. I laughed. Unlike Salameh, Rafi still had a sense of humor behind his too-old eyes.

"And nearly got yourself blown up in the process," continued Rafi. "Actually, it wasn't a bad job for an amateur."

"The bomb or the dismantling?"

Rafi almost smiled at me. "The dismantling. You had enough imagination to know the consequences of a mistake, enough control not to panic and enough courage to get the job done even though your hands were shaking. You would have been wasted as a violinist."

Sharai looked at her father for a long moment, plainly surprised at his implicit praise. I would have been flattered, except that I knew there were real thorns amid those verbal roses, and it was just a matter of time before he drew blood. Rafi wanted something from me, something a lot more costly than a few words about a man called Salameh.

"Did you trace Salameh to the student league?" asked Rafi, stubbing out his cigarette.

"No," I said. "He and the two men with him disappeared. The fourth guy was outside in a parking lot as backup. He's the one I followed to USC."

"As I thought," Rafi said to Sharai. "Salameh won't come anywhere close to those crazy students. He will pick up the money, but nothing else. He is very careful." Then, to me, "Do you have any way of contacting Salameh?"

"I could pin a note to the bulletin board in the league offices."

Rafi's lips thinned into a cold smile. "Something a little less . . . obvious."

"My friend will hear from him," I said. "Salameh was so disappointed when his bomb didn't go off that he's charging my friend an extra five thousand dollars."

"Is that all?" asked Rafi ironically. "He must have been in a good mood."

"He also offered to kill me if he saw me again."

Rafi's smile was thin and dark. "The thought doesn't seem to bother you. Don't you believe him?"

"I wish he'd try. Might solve a whole lot of problems at once," I said, shrugging. "But he's not likely to. He tends to pick on illegal aliens. That's the trademark of a very cautious man."

"He is that," murmured Rafi. "Next time he'll send one

of his tame Arabs to collect the money. Salameh never does the same thing twice. That's why he's still alive."

"You sound like you've been hunting him a long time," I said, initiating a little gentle fishing of my own.

Sharai gave me a sidelong glance that was half amused, half disbelieving. Apparently she was accustomed to people walking on eggs around her father, especially when he was in Ethan Edwards mode.

Rafi's laughter had surprising warmth. "Don't bother, Fiddler. My interest in this man doesn't overlap yours. You have your concerns and I—we—have ours."

Professionals can be insufferable. Their idea of cooperation is you reciting chapter and verse while they take notes.

"Well then, I don't think we can do business," I said, showing my teeth in what only a blind man would have taken for a polite smile. I turned toward Sharai and felt my smile softening. Something about her appealed to me in a way that transcended her obvious beauty. Later I realized that it was because she was a strong person balanced on the breakpoint of irrevocable choices; the future was rushing toward her like the jaws of a trap snapping shut. I wanted to smooth away the lines of strain from her mouth, to help her if I could and to comfort both of us if I could not. But I didn't know that yet, so I said brightly, "Do you think Spago's pizza lives up to its press releases?"

Before Sharai could answer, Rafi interrupted. He was more than astute enough to know that I meant exactly what I'd said: business was over unless he wanted to tell me something I didn't already know.

"I suppose," he said in a voice that was darker than his eyes and even less reassuring, "we do have some obligation to help Jews who are in trouble. If you would just answer one more question, I may be able to help your friend. Did you report the bomb to anyone of authority?"

I didn't figure that the Ice Cream King qualified as an "authority" in that sense, so I shook my head.

"How do you plan on helping your friend?" asked Rafi.

"That's two questions," I said, draining the wineglass. "You only get one at a time. Then it's my turn."

Rafi looked angry for an instant before he reined it in with the kind of control that only comes from practice. "I will confirm that the Israeli government has been hunting Salameh for many years, but if you call up the consulate they will deny they've ever heard of me and will tell you that Sharai is simply a cultural attaché."

Two bits of information and I'd only asked for one. Rafi was indeed a shrewd man. I'd be much more inclined to be generous if I thought he also was being generous.

"The Muslim Student League is a charity, of sorts," I said. "Did you know that?"

Rafi shook his head and glanced at Sharai. She said nothing.

"It gets a lot of corporate attention and contributions," I continued generously. "My guess is the corporations do a lot of business in the Middle East."

Rafi nodded slowly. His eyes were oddly alive now, as though he were thinking or living very hard. He might not know where I was going, but he was beginning to believe that I might lead him somewhere useful.

"American corporations are quite shy about controversy," I said. "I doubt very much that any of the benefactors of the league have the faintest idea that their tame Arab students might be out strong-arming local Jews." I smiled. "If the sponsors knew what was going on, they would probably wash their hands all the way up to their collective armpits. The last thing corporate angels want is something ugly growing out of their generous, humane and highly publicized philanthropies."

Rafi pondered the idea for a moment, and then nodded. "It might be a useful lever."

At the time I thought he was referring to getting my friend off Salameh's hook. I was partly right but mostly wrong.

"I'll get the names of the league students who were involved yesterday," said Rafi. "That will give credibility to the case you present to these corporate angels." He lit another cigarette, watched me through its haze for a moment, and asked quietly, "Who will you approach with your information?"

I reached into my breast pocket and flipped him the brown envelope full of clippings. The first one he saw was the society-page feature.

"Jarvis." Rafi said the name like a prayer. Or the answer to a prayer.

For an instant his mask slipped and something very old and eager and frankly ugly surfaced in his eyes. It came and went so quickly that I wasn't sure if I'd seen anything more than a reflection of my own buried rage at Salameh's casual attempt to kill me. That's why I was surprised when Rafi looked straight at me and told me to take my little plastic pail and play in somebody else's sandpile.

"Not Jarvis, Fiddler," said Rafi, leaning over and stuffing the clippings back into my breast pocket. "It won't work. Find another way to help your friend. If you can. And when you finally admit that you can't, give your friend's name to me, if he's still alive by then. If not"—Rafi shrugged and smiled coldly—"he won't be the first Jew who died trying to avoid a fight."

Rafi stood and looked at Sharai. At the time I thought he was signalling her to leave. Later I wondered if it hadn't been a signal for the second skirmish to begin, the one for my heart and mind. That is a question that still bothers me late at night, when my old mistakes sometimes come back to visit me. Eventually I decided that it didn't matter whether Sharai was acting alone or according to some previous plan when she refused to leave with Rafi. Either way, nothing would have changed my response to her.

"You'll have to forgive my father for his rudeness," Sharai said when Rafi made an imperious gesture with his hand, silently commanding that she get up and leave with him. "He's spent so much of his life with Arabs that he's forgotten women aren't lapdogs."

Rafi frowned and hesitated, suddenly more of a father than a commander. "Remember," he said quietly, "what is at stake here."

"I have better reason to remember than you do," she said, her voice husky with something close to pain. "You've asked Fiddler your questions. Now I will ask mine."

"Sharai—" began Rafi, then he shrugged. "So ask your *questions*," he said sardonically. Then, almost gently, "I hope the answers please you. Then, perhaps, you will stop looking back at what can't be changed or forward to what you're incapable of handling."

He took his own advice. He turned and left without looking back. He looked everywhere else, though, like a man accustomed to being followed by professionals. Sharai watched him go with a trace of irritation in her eyes but with no real animus. Their elliptical conversation had contained as many undercurrents of affection as it had of anger.

I had a choice between asking Sharai questions she wouldn't answer—such as what the hell her father had been talking about—or I could try being subtle just for the novelty of it.

"What exactly does a cultural attaché do?" I asked as I served both of us from the platter-sized pizza.

Sharai examined the question as though it were a fully loaded gun. "Right now I'm arranging musical tours for the Israeli Philharmonic Orchestra and overseeing a lecture series by a group of poets and writers," she said. "Both are part of a Bonds for Israel drive. The idea is to make Jews here in West L.A. feel as though they're part of the cultural life of Israel. It's important work. Last year we raised eight million dollars."

"What kind of preparation does it take to be a fund raiser in the arts?" I asked, pouring more wine into her glass.

Again the hesitation, the examination, the decision and the marvelous voice making English into music.

"I was educated in art and history, but I've had to learn to adjust to the realities of the world. I use all of it in my work—the art and the history and the adjusting."

"A realist," I said, smiling and wondering just what came under the category of adjusting. In my case it had been the realization that my hands would never be as good as my ears when it came to music. A simple thing, but then watersheds usually are. "Like your father. A hard case."

She smiled sadly. "Yes, he's a hard man. But he's had a hard life, too. He was in the Haganah in 1948 and since then—" The music stopped. She was looking at me and seeing only the past. Whatever her memories were, they weren't happy.

"Since then he's been with the Central Institute for Intelligence and Special Missions," I said blandly as I bit into the succulent pizza.

Sharai's dark eyes watched me for a long moment, entirely focused in the present once more. She made a sound that could have been a sigh or a single word. *Mossad.*

"He was in Arab territory, working under the deepest cover, when I was born," she said, looking at me, waiting for a reaction. When it didn't come, she relaxed. "I'm the product of his last weekend at home. I was walking and talking before he ever saw me."

"Your mother must have had some choice thoughts about that situation," I said.

Sharai's laugh was painful. "She tried, but in the end she couldn't take the pressure of being Rafi Yermiya's wife. And he—he wouldn't give up that kind of work, even after—even though some terrible things happened along the way. They separated when I was ten. Mama came to America. I shuttled back and forth between them, half Jewish-American Princess, half sabra, until Mama died."

"And now you're a full-time sabra. Did he recruit you?"

It was as though I'd thrown a shadow over Sharai, darkening her. She toyed with the stem of her wineglass, studying it, hiding her eyes. Then she looked up and gave me that dazzling, dark-eyed smile. There was no laughter in it, simply irony and intelligence.

"I'm no more what you think I am," she said huskily, "than you are what I first thought you were. Let's just leave it at that. We know all we really have to know. We're on the same side." She shifted in her chair, a subtle movement that reminded me how much of a woman she was. "Tell me," she murmured, "have you always been an independent fiddler?"

She was offering to begin again with a clean slate, or as clean a slate as life hands out in a situation like this. I could take it or leave it—and her.

"If it were just me," I said conversationally, "I'd accept your gentle offer of truce. But it's not just me. I've already cost my friend five grand and whatever goodwill may have existed between extortionist and extorted." I paused. "Other than that, I'm just your average goy with a penchant for trouble."

Her soft laughter was even more intriguing than her voice. "You don't expect me to believe that?" she asked. Instead of rancor, there was a very feminine amusement in her voice. "You're more complex than that," she continued. "If I had any doubts, my father took care of them. He doesn't praise people often, or easily."

"Only when he wants to use them, right?"

Something like pain crossed her beautiful features. "You're very quick. It took me years to figure that out about Rafi. And then it took much heartache before I found out I was wrong."

She chewed a bite of pizza, half closing her eyes in sensual appreciation as the flavors curled across her tongue. It was the first time in my life that I'd been jealous of a damned pizza.

"Were you born with money?" she asked after a moment.

"No. I was born with an uncle six years older than I was and not nearly as quick. He died young and foolish and left me a steamer trunk full of untraceable money. My wife took it and turned it into real wealth."

"Your wife?" asked Sharai carefully.

"Ex-wife," I said. "We're one of those dreary statistics

newspapers cite in stories about the breakdown of the modern family."

"I'm sorry," Sharai said, sensing the emotion beneath the casual words.

"So are we," I said, "but we survived. We're still—close. She's back East right now, learning how to make more money. It's her way of fiddling, and she's damn good at it. How about you?"

"What do you mean?"

"Married? Divorced? Living in? Living without?"

Emotion flashed in her dark eyes like the beam from a lighthouse, stark and intense and passing quickly. I wished that I hadn't asked.

"I was married," Sharai said. "He died."

"Now I'm sorry," I said.

She managed a pale smile. "It happens to many Israeli women. Men, too, sometimes. But it was more than ten years ago. Time passes. The wound scars over."

I looked at the scars on my hands and wondered. Scars weren't a true healing. They were simply an end to bleeding. But in this life you take what you can get in the way of comfort. Time is the surest relief this side of death. Sharai had had more than a decade of time's indifferent medicine, yet pain still transfixed her as though days rather than years had passed. I wondered which war had widowed her, then decided it wasn't worth asking. There were so many to choose from. They all run together there in the Middle East, the boundaries between wars blurred by police actions and retaliatory raids and intelligence missions, any of which could kill. I've known more violent death than most Americans, I suppose; but I doubt very much that I know violence with the intimacy of the average Israeli.

As though Sharai had followed my thoughts, pain flashed through her eyes again, bleaching the colors of her life. I reached for her instinctively in an effort to lure her out of cold thoughts of death and back to the warm day. Her response was also instinctive. Her fingers curled around mine. Her skin was smooth and soft and warm. For a moment there was only that, and then electricity passed between us like a rolling power surge, startling both of us. We looked at one another and then at our hands. The first touch always tells a lot.

Not everything, but a lot.

Sharai studied my face for a moment, her fingers still

curled around mine. She looked extraordinarily vivid, as though thinking of her dead husband brought life back to her. "It was a long time ago," she said softly, "but it was good, very good, so it still hurts. It always will. That's why there won't be another."

Slowly she slid her fingers beyond my touch and wrapped them around the neutral territory of her wineglass. She sipped carefully, fastening all of her attention on the pale liquid. When she lowered the glass, her face was composed and calm again, as though we had never touched one another. I watched her dark eyes, seeking . . . something. The pain was gone, but so was the incredible vitality she had shown. The intensity in her had vanished as though it had never existed. But it had existed. I had seen it. I wanted to see it again, to share it, to increase it until she hummed with pleasure and life.

Outwardly calm, Sharai leaned forward and sank her neat little teeth into Spago's best crust. We ate in silence. When we were done, she stood gracefully, gestured for me to stay in my chair and then hesitated, poised on the brink of leaving.

"What will you do about the Palestinians?" she asked.

"Exactly what I told Rafi I was going to do," I said. "You didn't have to hang around to find that out."

"That isn't why I stayed."

I gave her the arched-eyebrow of civilized skepticism.

"I stayed because I was hungry," she said, her voice unusually husky.

For what, she didn't say. I wish it had been something as simple as lunch or sex, because then things would have turned out differently. Feeding a woman's body I can manage. Feeding a woman's soul is a trick that I've apparently never gotten the hang of. Ask Fiora.

"Look," I said gently. "Life isn't a circle. It doesn't always take you back to the same place."

"You're wrong," she whispered. "It always comes back to the same thing. Death."

I've never forgotten Sharai's answer. Nor have I forgiven myself for being unable to keep her words from coming true.

7

I settled up with the waiter, the maître d', the cashier and the Muscle Beach boys in the parking lot. I ignored their exhortations that I have a nice day, knowing that by now the words were as automatic with them as flexing their pectorals at each other. Bruce watched me rather oddly as I gave the Cobra the kind of once-over that a minesweeper gives a suspect shipping lane. I didn't find anything.

Driving in your rearview mirror becomes a habit after a while. Looking for tails commanded no more real attention from me than shifting or braking. While part of my mind took care of mundane traffic matters, the rest of me tried to figure out what I could expect from Sharai and Rafi.

There was no easy answer to Sharai. Outwardly, Rafi was much the less complex of the two. He was a hunter and Salameh was his prey. In an odd, very basic way, there is no closer relationship than that which exists between hunter and prey, unless it's the one between a man and a woman. For better or worse, men seem to find the hunting relationship to be the easier one. There's no problem with changing roles. No problem with feeding souls. Nothing but cunning and adrenaline, the chase and the kill.

Rafi had been a hunter since World War II. Maybe he had been a hunter long before, chasing dream prey through his mother's womb. And Salameh? There was some of the hunter in him, but not much. There is no cunning, no silent stalking, no instinct in a truck bomb. Letter bombs and packages that go boom also don't rate high on the skill-and-finesse scale. For Salameh, the world was a shooting gallery where everything was a target. *You are either the oppressor or the oppressed.* In the former case, blow it up. In the latter case, recruit it to blow up the former. Not that Salameh was stupid. He wasn't. No stupid man could have eluded Rafi for years. It just takes a different kind of mind to run than it does to chase.

The automatic pilot in my brain began blinking, telling

me that something wasn't quite kosher. A few moments of full attention told me what was wrong: the Ford Grenada that had picked me up a block west of the restaurant had been hanging on for the last few miles. He wasn't close enough for me to see anything more than the large male form on the driver's side.

I had a cast-iron hunch that the tail was Rafi. His heart really wasn't in this chase, though. When I found an open block and goosed the Cobra lightly, he lost a few hundred yards without trying very hard to make them up. I finished losing him on the esses where Sunset winds through the foothills toward Sepulveda Pass. Just because the Cobra is memorable doesn't mean it's easy to follow. There's a big difference between a Ford Grenada and a Ford Cobra. I exploited that difference without a quiver of conscience. By the time the Grenada got to the San Diego Freeway and had to make a choice of directions, I was out of sight. He must have guessed south, because I went north and didn't see him in my mirrors again.

I stopped by a branch bank on Ventura Boulevard to cash a five-thousand-dollar check. After twenty minutes of calling and checking and verifying and conferring with assistant branch managers and then with branch managers, I was beginning to understand the appeal of C-4. It would have been quicker to blow the doors off the vault and rob the damn place. Not that my account didn't have five thousand dollars; not that there was any question about my identity; it's just that ever since Southern California got hit by a rash of Pyramid games a few years back, the paternalistic bastards that run the bank put a two-hundred-dollar-per-transaction limit on cash withdrawals. *For your convenience*, as the sign reminded me.

Bullshit.

I was tempted to take off my belt, open the hidden compartment, and pull out five of the thousand-dollar bills I always carry. But getting big bills to replace them would be even more of a pain in the ass than cashing the check. Besides, this didn't qualify as an emergency. The banks were still open. Reluctant, recalcitrant and irritating—but open.

My impatience must have shown.

"It really is for your own protection, sir," the assistant manager assured me for the third time, smiling dutifully.

The guy had lots of polished teeth and a wide green tie. He was sitting at his formica-topped desk, drumming his fingers on a VDT keyboard and trying to make the current balance of my checking account come up on his screen. I could tell when he succeeded, because he went very still, then peered at the screen, counting zeroes.

"Are you sure that five thousand is all you need, sir?" he asked. Then, as though he couldn't help himself, "You know, don't you, that you're missing out on a good deal of interest by keeping that much money in a no-interest checking account?"

"No-interest checking account" came off his tongue like a line from a litany.

"I know," I said.

He opened his mouth to pursue the subject. I looked at him as though I'd found him swimming in my soup. He jumped up, went into the vault and came back counting my money.

Imbrahim was at home when I arrived. His wife, a white-haired woman with a full face and limited English, met me at the door and ushered me back to her husband's sitting room. The banker hadn't been expecting me. He was dressed casually in an open-collared shirt and an old man's cardigan. He seemed smaller, both restless and resigned at the same time. Suddenly I knew that he had been sitting there with nothing to do but think. Sometimes that's good. And sometimes it's nothing more than time spent naming and numbering old regrets.

The small television set on one of the bookshelves was tuned to a UHF station whose programming consisted of a Dow-Jones ticker printout that filled the screen. The audio commentary was turned off; Imbrahim didn't need somebody else's market analysis. All he needed was raw data.

We shook hands and made small talk until Imbrahim's wife left to prepare coffee. As soon as her slow footsteps faded, he said in a low voice, "They want more money."

The stepped-up demands had shaken him. It showed in his voice and in the shadows beneath his eyes. He was willing to play by the rules, but they kept changing the rules. If you want to drive someone crazy there's no better way. Ask the sadists who electrify laboratory rat cages.

"Here, this will cover it." I handed Imbrahim the envelope. He took it before he realized that there was money inside.

"No," he said. "The Zahedis do not need that."

"My fault, my money. Besides, it's in the nature of a loan to Salameh, although he doesn't know it yet. I'll get it back. With interest."

"Whether from Salameh or the Zahedis," said Imbrahim, "you will indeed get your money back. With interest."

I changed the subject, knowing how fragile Imbrahim's pride was when it came to dealing with Arabs. He was neither a hunter nor a warrior, but life seemed to demand either one or the other from him. Nor was he a coward. He was a diplomat and a philosopher in an age when those were just two more words for target.

When I mentioned F. Robert Jarvis, International Constructors and the Muslim Student League, Imbrahim smiled almost sadly, as though he were enjoying a joke at his own expense. As he quickly made clear, he was.

"When I was in the Shah's government, I negotiated with International Constructors on several major projects. I met Jarvis twice, once in Teheran and once at his offices here."

"Would he remember you?" I asked.

"He might," said the old man. "The projects we negotiated were worth a bit more than four billion dollars."

I had read enough about Jarvis to doubt that he would be moved by the problems of an old man with whom he had once done business. Jarvis's magnanimity seemed to be limited to those who were in power, or who, like the Muslim students, might someday attain power in the Byzantine world of Middle Eastern politics.

On the other hand, a four-billion-dollar deal might have left Jarvis with some goodwill toward Imbrahim and his clan. If so, Jarvis might prove to be a more likely prospect than appealing to the immigration service for special dispensation in behalf of the Zahedis. Immigration cops are bureaucrats; it is both their nature and their role in the big scheme of things. Their job isn't to interpret or evade the law, it's to enforce it. Jarvis, at least, might want to hedge his bets in case the Shah's circle ever came back to power.

Imbrahim's wife brought coffee and a plate of thick, honey-rich baclava. When she had served us and left, I told him the rest of it—Rafi and the Israeli from the consulate.

"If you like," I continued, discreetly licking honey from my fingertips, "I could do as Rafi hinted and dump the whole mess in his lap."

Imbrahim thought for a moment. "You say that the Israelis already knew about the extortions?"

"They didn't know about you personally, but they knew that the Palestinians were strong-arming Jews in Los Angeles."

Imbrahim hesitated as though he were reluctant to think, much less to speak, what was on his mind. "The Israelis are —passionate? Is that the word? I think so. They are very passionate about the correct way to deal with Arabs. Israelis see the world as a war zone where they must fight ceaselessly to survive." He shrugged and sighed. "Perhaps that is true, for Israel. I do not believe it is true for all Jews. The Israelis"— again, Imbrahim hesitated—"the Israelis see all Jews as soldiers in a war with no end. Yet I am not a soldier," he said softly. "I have spent my life avoiding that war."

I watched the old man search for words.

In the end he spread his hands and said simply, "I do not know whether what I have done is correct. I have supported my people's dream according to my talents. For this, men like Rafi look at me with contempt. Did God assign them to be my judges?" Imbrahim smiled sadly. "I think not. I think no one can be sure what is right and what is wrong. 'For who knoweth what is good for man in this life . . . who can tell a man what shall be after him under the sun?' "

Having spent my youth on some hardwood Lutheran pews, I recognized a quote from Ecclesiastes, the King James version at that. I was startled for a moment, until I reminded myself that the Christians lifted the Old Testament from the Jews. So did the Muslims. They lifted some of the New Testament from the Christians, too, but not much of it. Jesus was a bit too soft for Bedouin tastes. In Islam, the Golden Rule seems to be *Do unto infidels*.

"Whatever God decides about me," continued Imbrahim, lifting a delicate cup to his lips, "I do not think that Rafi would be a wise choice for the Zahedi family. If the Israelis were interested in ending the extortions, they would have ended." He sipped lightly at the cup of black coffee. "They have not ended. This probably means that Israel has some other interest in the league, one that is not necessarily congruent with that of the Zahedi family."

I was beginning to have the same suspicion, although I was still in the dark about the true nature of the Israeli interest.

"Will the Israelis object if we pursue our own interests?" asked Imbrahim.

"I doubt it. I had the feeling that to Rafi we were merely a complication, not an obstruction. Complications he brushes aside or gives to his daughter to handle. Obstructions are like tank traps. He blows them up."

Imbrahim nodded. "The Israelis are like that, even to the rest of us Jews. I suppose we should not be bitter. They are trying to make our ancient dream come true. We give money. Some of them give blood. So much money, so much blood." He sighed. "The Israelis' virtue is in their willingness to fight. Their vice is in their eagerness for battle." He looked at me with haunted eyes. "I will trust my family to your gentler American instincts."

I looked at my scarred hands. Gentle? Well, maybe. I usually try being nice first. If that doesn't get it done, there's always the Israeli method.

"I can't promise to keep the lid on," I said. "The PLO isn't a humanitarian organization. I'll see if I can cut some kind of deal with Jarvis. If that fails, the choices get less gentle."

"If I can help . . . ?"

"How long since you've taken on the kind of female dragons that guard Jarvis's lair?"

Imbrahim smiled. I wouldn't have called it a gentle smile, either. Philosophers can be real pragmatic about some things.

It took him less than ten minutes on the telephone to penetrate the sanctum. The sanctum sanctorum, old F. Robert Jarvis himself, would take more than a telephone call. Even so, Imbrahim had saved me two days of soft-soap and glad-handing. The rest was up to me. I changed into the shoes and the Brooks Brothers pinstripe that Imbrahim had cared for after retrieving them from the coffee shop's bathroom floor. Then I headed for the steel-and-glass towers of International Constructors.

Malibu is not my kind of Gold Coast. It's a little too crowded, mostly with insecure types who made a couple million in films or records or commodities. Those are essentially irrational processes, controlled more by luck than skill. The money spends fine, but the problem is that the guys spending it don't know what they did to get lucky, so they're terrified of getting *un*lucky. The salt air along Coast Highway in Malibu is rank with the smell of nervous sweat.

A bit farther north you get back into my country again. Up here, it's one of two ways: people know what they did to earn big bucks and can do it again, or else they know they did nothing to attract good financial fortune and aren't worried about it. F. Robert Jarvis falls into the former category and I fall into the latter, but we both seem drawn to the kind of rolling seacoast landscape you find between Ventura and Santa Barbara.

The headquarters of International Constructors is strung in perfect harmony along the last coastal ridgeline before the land tumbles down to the ocean's edge. In spring these hills are as green as lake moss, but by midsummer the grasses and brush have turned to Mediterranean browns and yellows. The green of the sea and the blue of the sky offer primary contrast to the subtle earth tones of the land.

And the air—the air is incomparable.

There is a style of California painting called Plein Air. The artists of that school were fascinated by Impressionism and the dazzling effects of sunlight refracted through crystalline air, much as some French Impressionists were drawn to the Mediterranean. Many of the Plein Air painters ended up along this stretch of the Gold Coast seventy or eighty years ago. Six out of seven days the coast is quite pretty. The seventh day, along about evening, the view is so perfect it breaks your heart.

It was the seventh day when I pulled up to the discreet security gate at the top of the hill overlooking the Santa Barbara Channel. As I looked back down the slope to the restless sea, I saw why F. Robert had chosen this spot for his smoked-glass and stainless-steel castle. It probably cost him a fat bundle each year to truck the majority of his work staff up here from the flatlands every day, but when you're F. Robert, you can afford to pay for a view.

The guard who checked my name against the visitors' log looked less than enthusiastic about his surroundings. Summers were sweet and clean, but the other nine months must have been righteous bastards for someone who had to stand out on the slope and check cars in the teeth of a wind that hadn't seen land since Japan.

"Yessir," he said. "Mr. Calvin called down a while ago. Said you'd be coming."

The guard smiled reflexively, put a check in the box beside my name and noted the time on his watch. Finally he raised the long steel arm of the gate and signaled me through. As I drove in, I saw in the side mirror that he was writing down my license plate number. Polite but thorough. I'd seen less efficient industrial security at missile installations.

The lobby was worth the drive. Corporate decor is fascinating; it tells you almost as much as a balance sheet. Judging by the lobby, International Constructors had been in big, big chips when the place was built. The lobby understated that fact very nicely, while underlining IC's global reach. Part of the effect was created by a wall of highly stylized clocks that displayed the time in parts of the world even *National Geographic* hadn't visited lately. But the magnitude of IC's influence was emphasized by the centerpiece of the lobby: a massive, three-story world globe. The framework of the hollow globe, as well as the continents, were outlined in burnished copper wire and the entire piece revolved at a stately pace that made you dizzy if you stood too close.

It was masterfully executed, massive without being ugly. The crowning touch was a spray of lights—cobalt blue, malachite green, incandescent gold, hot ruby. They made the globe glitter like a sultan's treasure chest. Assuming that each light marked an IC project, the geographical sweep was impressive. There were dozens of lights in North America, including a string that designated a transcanadian pipeline. There was a scattering of several colors through the Pacific Basin. Then the globe turned silently to reveal a burst of blue and green braided thickly through the Middle East—too many lights to count. In contrast, the two ruby lights glowing along the coastline of Europe looked quite lonely.

I waited until the Middle East rolled around again. Pinpricks of light showed on every side, but the small stretch of Mediterranean coastline between Egypt and Lebanon was dark. No IC projects in Israel, undoubtedly the cost of doing so much business in the Arab world.

The uniformed security guard at the kiosk in the lobby was every bit as polite and efficient as the one at the outside gate. He asked for identification, filled in a bunch of blanks in his log and keyed up something I couldn't see on the video display terminal in front of him. Then he picked up one of the color-coded telephones, confirmed my authorization and issued me a plastic badge that said "Visitor. Escort Required."

"If you'll just wait here, sir, someone will take you up to see Mr. Calvin."

The guard picked up a white phone, quietly said a few words into it and hung up. A moment later an attractive, tastefully sun-streaked blond wearing a fake-suede blazer appeared from across the lobby.

"My name is Barbara, Mr. Fiddler. Please come with me,"

she said, giving me a smile that revealed rows of perfectly straight teeth.

It would have taken more effort than it was worth to tell her to forget the Mister. She had been well and truly programmed for courteous behavior. Calling people Mister was courteous, and therefore it was probably company policy.

Barbara led me across the lobby to the biggest open escalator I had ever seen. As we rode up the three flights, she chatted politely, pointing out the architectural marvels of the building and reciting little facts about the corporation. She reminded me of the pleasant, relentlessly nice young people who run the rides at Disneyland. So I did what any polite visitor would have done. I asked questions.

"What do the colors of the lights mean?" I asked as we moved past the middle latitudes of the slowly revolving globe.

"They indicate all of our current or completed projects," she said. "Blue is for civil engineering, such as waterworks; green is for petroleum-related projects like pipelines or refineries, and so forth."

"What are the red lights in Europe?"

"Those are nuclear power-generating plants in France and Belgium. We were just awarded those contracts. It's part of International Constructors' continuing effort to diversify its engineering product."

I wondered if she ate company reports for breakfast. I would have asked, but politeness seemed to be infectious. "Isn't IC a bit too dependent on petroleum projects, particularly with the decline of OPEC and the Middle East?" I asked. Well, maybe politeness wasn't all that infectious.

"Oh, I wouldn't know about anything like that," Barbara said, blinking soulfully at me, giving me the kind of look that sets women's rights back a generation. She didn't even realize what she was doing. It was automatic with her, like flexed pectorals at Muscle Beach. She started chattering about multistage flash desalination plants in Abu Dhabi, just like she knew what they were. Imagine that.

When we reached the fourth level of the building, things suddenly changed. The austere modern plastics and stainless steel of the first three levels were replaced by rich dark wood paneling that looked like it had been stolen from a nineteenth-century London men's club. The long hallway was beautifully lighted and hung with paintings. I slowed down. Nearly every painting repaid the study.

In a hundred feet I recognized a Winslow Homer, a Bierstadt and a Moran. The rest were often ravishing pieces by lesser-known American artists, the type of paintings that a critic refers to as "important" because history has yet to confer on them the mantle of immortality. I've seen worse collections in museums that considered themselves "significant." Somebody around here had very good taste and an even better bankroll.

"Nice, aren't they," said Barbara, her tone unchanged from her earlier canned chatter about municipal sewers.

Nice? There was more life in any one of those paintings than there was in the two of us together. The paintings reminded me of Sharai—intensity tightly leashed, sensuality seen as much in shadows as in light.

Politely, inexorably, my Barbara smiled her way through the extraordinary hall of paintings, dragging me behind. The area opened up into a chamber the size of a small church. Half the room was filled with secretarial desks; the other half was a waiting area arranged so that there was virtually no way to avoid looking at a mammoth oil portrait of old J. Robert himself. I was left to worship at this altar while my guide announced me to one of the secretaries.

The portrait was a real work of the sycophant's art. It captured and amplified everything that I had seen in the newspaper photos of Jarvis, all the shrewd analytical power of the eyes, all the plain, even homely strength of the features, all the unflinching acceptance of fiscal reality that separates the great capitalists from the merely greedy. There was dedication rather than humor in his mouth, firm leadership in the way the aging hands rested on the gold-headed cane. At least that's what the artist—and presumably F. Robert himself—had wanted to convey.

In short, Jarvis was a man who believed his own bullshit.

I had no doubt that the living flesh would be much less impressive than the picture before me; but then, it's the talent of the portrait artist to capture what exists in the patron's self-image rather than the mundane exterior reality. Whoever had painted Jarvis had earned every nickel of his fee.

It presumably was a mark of respect for Imbrahim Zahedi that the executive vice-president of International Constructors came out of his office to greet me. The old Iranian might be a refugee out of power, but what goes around comes around, as the Khomeini well knows. There was always a chance that Iran's populace would get fed up with being taken back to the

Dark Ages, chuck their oh-so-holy man and invite back the Shah's offspring. Or at the very least their business managers. Thomas Wilton Calvin was well aware of those possibilities as he walked through the ranks of secretaries and secretarial assistants, hand extended in greeting.

His suit was a custom job, cut from dark gray Saville Row wool. The shoes were black Italian calf leather, nicely buffed. The shirt was white cotton, unwrinkled at the end of the day, which meant he changed it at least twice. The tie was a deep wine color. Silk. Conservative and nicely understated.

"Tom Calvin, Mr. Fiddler," he said, extending a big hand, perfectly manicured. "Nice of you to come all the way out here to talk with us."

I smiled my corporate smile. "Mr. Calvin. It's nice of you to take the time to talk with me."

I took Calvin's hand, giving exactly as much of a squeeze as I got. He did the same with the once-over he gave me. As the bill for my clothes came in well over a grand but was still less than his, I passed inspection. He led me toward the big oak door of his office, which was immediately adjacent to the even bigger oak double doors that presumably led to the office of F. Robert Jarvis. Calvin's room offered 150 degrees of what California realtors call a "forever view" down the rolling hills, over the coastal plain and across the glittering ocean to the Channel Islands. I knew that Jarvis's office had to have a better view, but I was damned if I could figure out how.

"Sit down, please," Calvin said, gesturing to a leather couch off to one side of the office.

He drew up a high-backed red leather chair and sat across the low walnut table from me. He was a handsome man in his late forties, with a tennis tan and gold-rimmed glasses. He produced a pipe from his pocket. As we talked he tinkered with the pipe, loading it and firing it off at random intervals, each of his movements precise, practiced and efficient. We exchanged a few pleasantries on the view, government regulations and the prime rate before Calvin opened the bidding.

"Minister Zahedi said something about your interest in the Muslim Student League."

It wasn't quite a demand, which would have been crass. It wasn't even really a question. I had to answer it just the same, or else get bounced higher than the view. One look at Calvin had told me I wasn't going to get past him to Jarvis on the first try. The real utility of power and wealth is in buying insulation. Tom Calvin was very expensive insulation. At the first sign that I was trouble, he was going to throw me out on my ass and deny that we had ever met. So I discarded all but one of the plans I'd made and began lying like an accountant at an audit.

"I hope we may speak candidly," I said. I waited, making him nod his agreement. "Good," I continued, flexing my big hands as though I were nervous or angry or both. "I'm trying to wrap up a deal in the Middle East. Arabs. The deal is a solid eight figures. Not much for IC, maybe, but respectable."

Calvin sucked on his pipe and nodded. "I'm still enough of a country boy to be impressed by eight-figure deals."

"Then we're both from the same part of the country," I said. I ran my fingers through my hair, adding to the image of an earnest, harassed opportunist. "I've been dealing with several VIPs in the Middle East, and with a couple of their underlings here in Los Angeles. The men here aren't what I'd call sophisticated, even by country boy standards. To be blunt, they came on pretty crude. They said that if I wanted to do this deal, I had to pay into the Muslim Student League fund."

I gave Calvin a moment to be shocked. He took the time to clean his pipe.

"I don't mind the money, particularly," I said. "That sort of thing is just part of the cost of doing business. The method, though, put me off."

I paused for outraged reaction. Calvin used a specially designed pipe lighter to set fire to the carefully tamped weed.

"I was a little worried about who to pay," I continued. "I mean, these boys were *crude*. So I did some research and found out that Mr. Jarvis sponsors the league. That made me feel a bit better. But I wanted to check things more carefully before I committed."

Calvin shook his head sadly and balanced his pipe in the crystal ashtray in front of him. "Different cultures," he murmured. Then he sighed. "In behalf of Mr. Jarvis, let me offer an apology for the unfortunate way you were treated. If you give me the names of the people who were involved, I assure you that it won't happen again. We're very well connected in the Southern California Arab community."

I looked harassed and apologetic. "No names. Sorry. My deal is at a very delicate stage," I said, then added hastily,

"Don't get me wrong. I can afford the squeeze. I just want to know if the league is the right place to drop the payoff."

Calvin suddenly looked as if he had sucked something sour through his pipe.

"Sorry," I said again. I made an obvious effort to gather up my M.B.A. party manners. "That was badly put."

Calvin didn't disagree, but he saved the moment with the grace of a good insulator. "Contributing to the welfare of Arab students is a gesture of goodwill that might be appreciated by the people you're doing business with. Hands across the ocean and all of that. Also, you would be in good company. In addition to Mr. Jarvis, the House of Saud sponsors the Muslim Student League, as do the Seven Sisters."

All of them? I wondered silently. Then I remembered that all seven of the major oil companies had interests to protect in the Arab Middle East.

"Each of us," continued Calvin, "needs to shoulder part of the responsibility for educating the youth of the Middle East."

I heard an echo of Kipling there, the White Man's Burden. The more things change, the more they stay the same. Extortion gets my nomination for the second oldest profession, just edging out government by a nose.

"Is the league involved in politics?" I asked.

A warning light must have gone on somewhere in Calvin's mental DEW line. "Why do you ask?"

I shifted on the leather couch as though it were a picket fence that I was straddling. "I do some business in Israel, too. I don't want to get too close to one side or the other."

Calvin picked up his pipe and sucked on it thoughtfully, choosing his words with the same care I imagined he used to choose his ties. He was a cautious man but he was also a salesman, and right now he was selling the Muslim Student League. I wondered how he felt about ringing the bell for the Arabs like a Salvation Army street crier. If the job bothered him, he didn't let it show.

On the other hand, there probably were a lot of things that Calvin didn't allow to show.

"My experience," said Calvin slowly, "has been that Israel is confident of its position in American affections. The Arabs, on the contrary, need . . . reassurance. It has also been my experience that petrodollars spend more easily than shekels."

Well, there it was. As close to the bone as you were ever going to get with Thomas Calvin.

"Yesss . . . ," I said, stringing out the word, sounding doubtful without actually saying it, begging to be convinced.

Calvin picked up the beat instantly. There are two kinds of salesmen on any used-car lot, liners and closers. The liners are the nice guys who show you the car and let you kick the tires and drive the demo around the block. Closers are the guys who get your signature on the sales contract, and on the finance contract, and on the extended warranty contract, and —if they're really good—on the credit insurance contract. Thomas Calvin was a closer.

"Look," he said, leaning forward earnestly. "The way the league approached you was regrettable, but it points out just how very much the students need a Western education. F. Robert is both a shrewd and a generous man. He knows that someday the league's students will be the leaders of their countries. It's good business to be involved with them. As for politics," Calvin smiled coolly, "F. Robert believes that good business is good politics. Don't you agree?"

How could I decline such a shrewd and generous offer?

"I can't think of a better way to invest my twenty-five grand," I said. "Whose name goes on the check?"

A light began blinking on the phone console beside Calvin's huge desk. We both saw the summons from the corner of our eye. We both ignored it.

Calvin smiled and waved aside my question about check writing with the stem of his five-hundred-dollar pipe. "I'm sure F. Robert will want to thank you personally for your generosity. He's having a league fund raiser tomorrow night at his ranch down in San Diego County. Your contribution will be a wonderful icebreaker."

I looked puzzled. The phone console began to chime discreetly. Calvin ignored it, more intent on landing the fish than on answering the phone.

"Fund raising is a special skill, one that F. Robert has refined to an art," said Calvin. "There's nothing quite like a solid opening donation to loosen purse strings."

"I'll look forward to meeting Mr. Jarvis," I said honestly.

"Good," said Calvin, rising and going toward the door.

I took the hint and followed. The phone console began to ring a good deal less discreetly.

"Are you a horse fancier?" asked Calvin.

"Not yet," I said. I had a feeling I was about to become one.

"F. Robert has some of the finest Arabian bloodstock in Southern California," Calvin said. "He has a little show planned after dinner. I think you'll enjoy meeting F. Robert's friends, and you'll get a marvelous meal in the bargain."

Gee, what more could anyone ask for a mere twenty-five grand?

"Feel free to bring a companion," continued Calvin, smiling man-to-man. "Be sure she brings a wrap. Evenings are chilly in the desert."

Just as Calvin reached for the door, one of the secretarial assistants stuck her head inside.

"Sorry to interrupt," she said breathlessly, words tumbling out like she was on a piece rate, "but Mr. Jarvis urgently needs the file marked 'Yellow Cake–Al-Makr' and he says that you—"

"In a moment, Miss Adams," interrupted Calvin, his voice like a whip. He shot me a look out of the corner of his eye, measuring my reaction to the mention of the file.

"Thank you for your advice, Mr. Calvin," I said earnestly, shaking his hand.

"My pleasure," he answered, his smile as firm as his handshake. "Leave your address with my secretary. The tickets will come by messenger, and someone will contact you about the mechanics of your contribution." He looked at the chastened assistant. "I would take care of the tickets myself, but—"

"I understand. You have more urgent matters."

Like firing a loose-lipped secretarial assistant, maybe.

I walked away wondering what the hell Yellow Cake–Al-Makr might be, and whether knowing about it would give me any leverage with the Muslim Student League.

8

First chance I had, I pulled over and ran some silver through a telephone. I needed confirmation from an expert, and I only knew one. The Ice Cream King answered on the twelfth ring, about par for him.

"Does the name 'yellow cake' strike a familiar note?" I asked.

"Happy birthday to me, happy birthday to me, happy birthday to— Like that, mate?" he asked cheerfully.

"Not music, Benny," I said. "I was thinking more along the lines of science and engineering."

"You gotta spell out that kind of distinction for me, boyo," he said. "Yellow cake is uranium concentrate, refined ore, so to speak, but not terribly radioactive unless—"

He stopped in midsentence. Then I thought I heard *Bloody hell, sod all illiterates* and a few more of Benny's favorites. Then he took a deep breath and reverted to mostly American English.

"Mate," he said carefully, "you can piss about with plain old high explosives and Timex watches all you want, but if you're into nuclear proliferation, there's bugger all I can do to keep you from going BOOM."

"Relax. Nothing's ticking at the moment, as near as I can tell."

"Then what are you doing fiddling with yellow cake?" he demanded.

I traced the trail from the league to Jarvis, IC and yellow cake, then got down to specifics. "IC is a big company, projects all over the world," I said. "But that fancy globe is a lie. It shows only two nuclear plants, both in Europe. 'Al-Makr' doesn't sound European. It looks like Jarvis and his minions are helping somebody in the Middle East go nuclear."

There was silence followed by the sound of Benny's wheels humming up and down the aisles of his workshop. Once he told me he thought better on his feet. Now he thinks on his wheels. I heard the hollow sounds of computer keys responding to his touch.

"Not a bloody thing on the standard data bases, mate," he said finally. "The word is Arabic, of course. It has the sound of a place-name."

"Any possibility it might refer to uranium deposits someplace?"

"Doubt it. God gave the Arabs petroleum, not pitchblende, which shows that the old bastard isn't entirely crazy. Nigeria has some, and Chad. Matter of fact, word is that Colonel Khadaffi Duck started that little war in Chad just to get his hands on a steady supply of fissionables."

"Benny, do me a favor," I said. "Run that name by some of your old friends in McLean and see what happens."

"It isn't a one-way street, Fiddler," he said. "They're going to want to know all about a new reactor in the Middle East."

"If I find one, you'll be the first to know."

I hung up and got back on the road. Even with the Cobra's help and a road nearly empty of California Highway Patrol units, it was past dinnertime when I turned off the highway to Crystal Cove. Thoughts of dinner triggered a rather complex chain of sensory memories. It was cleaning day, the day that Luz Amarillo Pico comes to reimpose order on the chaos of my house. Luz is a descendant of the last Mexican governor in Alta California, but she bears no malice toward the gringos who displaced her Spanish ancestors. After all, the Mexicanos had displaced the California Indians, who had displaced Diggers, who had displaced. . . .

You get the idea.

Luz makes a very decent living managing the households of the incompetent or the lazy. Don't ever call her a "maid," or even a "cleaning service." She's more like a majordomo. She arrives with five nieces from Guadalajara, picks up and cleans, does the laundry, restocks the pantry and takes care of the household plants. She does it all in about two hours flat. I always try to be out of the way because I get the uncomfortable feeling that if I don't move fast enough, I'll end up in the washing machine with the rest of the dirty laundry.

None of this explains why my mouth waters on cleaning day, though. Luz also leaves me enough Mexican food and beer for a small army. I decided that wine with pizza is one thing, but wine with chiles rellenos doesn't even bear thinking about. Sometimes there's just no substitute for a good, cold *cerveza*.

The sun was still two fingers above the horizon when I

pulled onto the lane that leads to the garage and watched my
dreams of a quiet evening dissipate like the fine salt mist rising
from the surf. There was a Ford Grenada parked beside the
garage—a tan sedan just like the one that had followed me out
of Spago.

I could have lived without Rafi, but at least he wasn't
trying to hide. A visitor who leaves his car in your driveway
isn't planning an ambush.

Muttering under my breath about solitude, peace and
perfect sunsets, I put the Cobra in the garage and yanked a
case of beer out of the extra refrigerator. Beer under right arm,
I stepped out of the garage, half-expecting to be bowled over
by the canine monster called Kwame Nkrumah, the Rhodesian
ridgeback who lives next door and keeps an eye on things for
me when I'm gone. I wondered whether my uninvited Israeli
guest had gotten a chunk taken out of his leg when he climbed
out of his car.

Nkrumah's impressive *woof* came from the back of the
house, but the lazy son of a bitch didn't come out to say hello.
Feeling vaguely overlooked, I strolled across the lawn and onto
the back deck. Nkrumah was there. So was Rafi. He was lying
on his back on a chaise lounge, watching the late-afternoon
light show with one hand behind his head and the other stroking slowly down the huge, indolent body of the rusty-black
dog. Nkrumah thumped his short rope of a tail on the redwood
decking but didn't stir otherwise.

I rattled the case of beer. The sweet clinking of the clear
glass bottles pulled Rafi out of his thoughts. He lifted his arm
and glanced over at me for all the world like someone interrupted while daydreaming in his own bed.

"Go ahead," I said. "Make yourself at home."

"Yes, I believe I have, haven't I?"

He laughed softly and looked about twenty years younger
than he had at Spago. A Southern California sunset is like that.
Relaxing. That's why I'm going to miss this stretch of coastline
when they turn it into one more ersatz Mediterranean resort.

Rafi's right hand smoothed over Nkrumah's stiffly feath-
ered ruff. The dog's eyes were blissfully closed. Rafi appeared
to be watching a spot on the clear horizon. He was looking
way out over the water, away from the setting sun, to the south
where the Pacific turned blue and serene. He began speaking
quietly, as though he were reading aloud.

" 'All the rivers run into the sea, yet the sea is not full; unto the place from whence the rivers come, thither they return again.' "

It seemed to be my day for Ecclesiastes. That didn't surprise me. Rafi was an Old Testament sort of man.

"This is a wonderful place you have," he continued quietly, the harshness gone from his voice as it was from his face. "I've rarely been more at peace than I have in the last hour, seeing the sky change and discussing the state of the world with your Rhodesian. The aerial circus," he added, nodding toward the hummingbird feeder, "is enough to bring pleasure to even the most jaded man."

Just beyond us, but nearly within reach of Rafi's powerful arm, a pair of ruby-throated hummers were suspended in the late sunlight. They swam in the air like tropical fish in a golden ocean, eyeing one another evilly. There was a sudden, startling hum, a flash of incandescent scarlet, and the two birds fled. An instant later a third hummer teleported into position by the ever-blooming flower. He chirred and skreed and cursed at Rafi, who watched with an indulgent half smile.

"King David," I said, belatedly introducing the hummer.

"Does he think I'm Goliath?" asked Rafi, amused.

"You don't look like Bathsheba," I pointed out. "Or would you rather be the baby that got divided up?"

"That was Solomon, not David."

"Don't suppose it mattered to the baby."

Rafi chuckled and shook his head. "Do you take anything seriously, Fiddler?"

I looked out over the languid transformations of the sea and the brilliant, slowly darkening colors of the sky. "This," I said. The air was crisp, almost succulent, a feast for the senses. The moment was so still and deep that I could hear my heartbeat echoing the slower, more massive beating of the sea. Like the sea, I felt both relaxed and powerful, at rest and endlessly questing. *Alive.*

I realized that Rafi was watching me. He nodded slowly, his eyes focused on a point about two inches behind my eyes, as though he could see into me as clearly as I saw into the sky.

"That is what she saw in you," mused Rafi. "Life."

"Sharai?"

Rafi looked startled, as though I had read his mind. I realized that he had come unraveled in the sun and calm, his guard lowered to the point that he had spoken his innermost thoughts aloud without realizing it. He looked away from me, out over the ocean, and said nothing more.

I pulled two long-necked bottles of Corona from the case. They began to bead with moisture the instant the warmer afternoon air wrapped around them. Beer glowed through the colorless bottles. Corona is a Mexican beer; its brewers don't believe in effete gringo nonsense like twist-off caps. I embedded the metal teeth in the soft redwood edge of the table and rapped the neck of the bottle with the edge of my hand. The cap popped off. I handed the bottle to Rafi and opened one for myself.

When the first bottlecap hit the deck, Nkrumah heaved himself onto his haunches and began to beg. He loved beer almost as much as he loved the green pellets I fed the koi. Rafi smoothed the dog's massive head absently, a surprisingly patient and gentle gesture. He looked at the foreign label on the Corona, sipped cautiously and smiled. He saluted me with the slender bottle before taking a long, appreciative draft of the beer.

"Who do you talk to, Fiddler?" Rafi asked, settling back into the chaise lounge.

I didn't have to ask what he meant. It's hard to find people who don't withdraw from you at the first hint that you might not be civilized all the way to the soft centers of your bones. Finding someone who accepts the good, the bad and the boring—all of it—isn't easy.

"A man who made ice cream in hell," I said. "And my ex-wife, when we're speaking to each other."

"Does that happen often?"

"Too often for divorce. Not often enough for marriage."

Rafi's mouth turned down in a sad, knowing smile. "You too? Let me tell you, my friend, it's no easier after she dies."

There was no answer to that. Rafi sipped appreciatively at his Corona, as comfortable with the silence as he had been with speech.

"Who do you talk to?" I asked, letting the words sift into a pause between the massive heartbeats of the sea.

"My ex-wife when she was alive. My daughter after she grew up. Men like myself. You." He poured a mouthful of beer into his palm and let Nkrumah's broad tongue wash over his skin. "You don't need a lecture and a fistful of photographs to understand the life of an Israeli agent. You know what this life costs—family, home, the freedom to wake up slowly in the morning with a woman in your arms. I can't remember when I last felt at peace with the world, when I was not at war or planning war or hoping for war."

King David dove at Nkrumah, wings humming at full throttle. The dog ignored the noisy foray, having learned already that the bird wouldn't hold still long enough to be eaten and was too fast to catch on the fly. While David's attention was divided, another hummer zoomed over the house, shot between the open slots in the patio cover and thrust its sharp little beak deep into the forbidden nectar.

Instantly David switched his attention. He attacked in a blur of wings and outraged shrilling. The second hummer shot back up through the wooden lattice with the king in hot pursuit. No more than a second later, a new hummer with a royal purple head and throat appeared an inch from the feeder. Hovering in a blur of wings, he turned one way and then the other, making his iridescent feathers flash on and off like a beacon. In the right light he was a blinding, seething purple. Then he would turn and his feathers would look as black as the bottom of night.

Blackbeard got two good licks in at the nectar before another hummer appeared. This one was new, smaller, maybe a female. He chased her off with a thunder of wings, only to be routed in turn by King David.

Rafi laughed, but it wasn't a pleasant sound. "So brave. So vicious. So *stupid*. If they would just stop fighting one another, they could drive the king into the sea. At the very least, they could take turns leading him on a chase while the others drank the well dry. But do they?" He laughed again. "No. They fight each other more viciously than they fight the king; and they lose every time." He drank once, hard, as though he were washing away a bad taste. "The king is grateful for their stupidity. It's all that keeps him alive."

We both knew he was talking as much about the Middle East as he was about hungry hummingbirds. Neither one of us saw the need to point out the obvious. Israel has always been a small, fierce but beleaguered country. It owed much of its survival to its own strength, but it also owed a vast debt to the divisions in the camps of its enemies.

Nkrumah rested his head on Rafi's knee and gazed worshipfully at the golden beer. Rafi poured more liquid into his palm and waited while Nkrumah sloppily lapped up every drop. When the dog was finished, Rafi wiped his palm absently on his thigh and said, "I could have saved you the trip to International Constructors, but it was a nice day for a drive. How did you get along with the shrewd Mr. Calvin?"

I sighed and wondered who the Israelis had bought inside IC. Several people, probably, including the grinning gate guard. I looked at the level of beer in my bottle. It was going to be a long evening. I didn't want to face it on an empty stomach. "Have you ever eaten chiles rellenos?" I asked.

He shook his head.

"If you like Mexican beer, you'll love chiles rellenos."

I went inside, put the case of beer in the refrigerator and checked the dinner prospects. Luz had left refried beans in one Crock-Pot, tamales in another and rellenos in a pan in the oven. As usual, the red and green sauces were sitting quietly, deceptively, in clay bowls on the kitchen counter. Material like that ought to bubble or boil or smoke, something sinister to warn the unwary. But it never does. It just sits there and looks like food. Once, as an experiment, I let a bowl of Luz's verde sauce sit out for three months. Nothing happened. Didn't even dry up. No mold, no degeneration, bloody nothing. No known bacterium could survive in the stuff, much less reproduce.

I got rid of the Brooks Brothers persona, threw together a couple of plates of food and put them on the redwood table outside. By the time I returned with a basket of flour tortillas and another round of beers, Rafi was seated at the table. Nkrumah had his head plastered on the Israeli's thigh, drooling and making a fool of himself.

We both ate in silence for a while. Rafi watched how I used the tortilla as an edible spoon and quickly applied the principle himself. What is called "Mexican food" in Southern California is workingman's fare with lots of starch, grease and spices. Rafi seemed at home with the general idea, if not the specific execution.

After my second relleno, I asked, "Who, where or what is Al-Makr?"

Rafi's face was in the last of the full light, which was the only reason I saw his eyes narrow very briefly.

"It's a place," he said matter-of-factly. "A little nothing of a place in the desert."

"There's a hell of a lot of desert in the Middle East," I pointed out, scooping beans with the tortilla and adding a spoonful of verde sauce.

Rafi followed suit, then hurriedly reached for his beer. The spices had finally burned through his smoker's palate. He let the beer effervesce on his tongue for a moment, then swallowed and said, "I know of a place called Al-Makr in Libya."

I chewed on that, got a chile seed caught between my teeth and put out the fire with half a Corona. Rafi chased a dab of beans around the plate with his fork, cornered it in a puddle of hot sauce, rounded the mess up on a chunk of tortilla and dropped it in his mouth. He finished his beer in a long swallow. A fine mist of sweat gleamed on his suddenly flushed face. I could feel the same thing happening to me as my body adjusted to the sudden influx of Mexican fire. In another minute we'd both be aglow and tingling like freshly washed babes.

"What does Daffy Duck need with yellow cake?" I asked.

Rafi's fork hesitated fractionally in its pursuit of relleno. "Sharai is right," said Rafi, looking up with eyes just slightly darker than the circles below them. "You're very clever. How did you pry that bit of information out of IC?"

I shrugged. "I got lucky."

Rafi shot me a hard look.

I smiled. "You've heard the old saying 'I'd rather be lucky than good'?" It wasn't as elegant as Ecclesiastes but it said volumes.

Rafi stood up, went to the kitchen and returned with four beers. He opened his own this time on the edge of the table. He caught on quick.

"The Libyans want to have a nuclear facility at Al-Makr," he said, sitting down again. Nkrumah took up his former station, muzzle nailed to Rafi's leg. "We believe it's another step toward the Islamic bomb."

I rounded up some more green sauce for my beans.

Rafi looked at me, laughed and shook his head. "That does not terrify you? Most Americans seem to think if it's radioactive, it's Armageddon."

"You seem pretty sanguine yourself," I shot back. "You can't tell me Israel is exactly thrilled by the idea of Colonel Daffy Duck dropping hot ones on Tel Aviv."

"It won't ever get to that point," said Rafi coolly. "We'll do what we did at Osirak. While the West wrings its hands, our F-16s will go in at Mach 2 and blow the installation to hell."

"Then you knew that International Constructors was involved in the project?"

Rafi nodded and followed my example by helping himself to a tamale. He watched me, then unfolded the corn husk to reveal the cornmeal and meat that had been steamed inside. Just as he lifted a forkful toward his mouth, a belated thought came to me.

"I hope you're not Orthodox," I said quickly. "Luz makes her tamales with *carnitas*. That's pork."

Rafi's lips cleaned the fork of every morsel. He chewed, made sounds of appreciation and swallowed. "In 1948, the Palmach sent me into Arab Lebanon to keep track of the Palestinians who operated there. I passed myself off as a Maronite Christian, and in doing so learned to enjoy two things. One of them was pork."

"What was the other?"

"Christmas," he said, smiling slyly.

I laughed and wished that Rafi and I had nothing more between us than the enjoyment of the food, the beer, and the unusual chance to talk with another civilized barbarian. It would have been so easy to trust him. He was sharing more with me than he did with most human beings, even if it was far from full trust. That's the hell of living in the world he lived in. The decision to trust is never yours to make, because if you trust the wrong person, others pay the price.

It was the same for me. I wanted to trust Rafi, but not at the cost of the Zahedi family. Rafi had his own imperatives, his own devils, and I had mine. Until they were the same, we could only trust tentatively and fill the silences with understanding smiles.

Rafi threw a ladle of salsa verde across his tamale and ate silently for a while. The first wave of heat had passed, leaving us in a gustatory afterglow that we were reluctant to disturb with half truths and outright lies. Frankly, I didn't expect many of the latter from Rafi. He was a pro at the game of truth and falsehood. He knew that half the truth went farther and struck harder than the best lie.

"Tell me," Rafi said, beginning a new tack. "Did you see Salameh in IC's corridors?" He smiled a bit coldly when I reacted. "Oh yes," he said softly. "The Palestinian is on IC's payroll, although he's seldom seen there. It's all very legitimate, just part of IC's cost of doing business in South Yemen, which is one of the PLO's staunchest patrons.

"There's even an outward logic to it. Salameh is a civil engineer. When he's not extorting Jews, he's a liaison man on a project to construct the first sewage plant ever built in the People's Democratic Republic of Yemen. The Libyans are financing it in behalf of their Yemeni brethren, who are among the most backward people on the face of the earth."

"Is Salameh working as well on the Al-Makr project?" I asked.

Rafi studied me for a moment. "What Al-Makr project?" he asked indifferently. "It doesn't exist. Remember?"

"Jarvis is playing a very dangerous game," I mused aloud. "How is he covering his tracks?"

Rafi shook his head. "On paper, Al-Makr is being built by a consortium of European firms. They are all respectable companies whose connections to IC are as carefully guarded as the vault in a Swiss bank."

"Why should Jarvis take the risk?" I asked.

Rafi smiled. "As a businessman, Jarvis made a very significant international gamble a decade ago. He backed the play of Sheik Yamani, betting that OPEC would ruin the West by running the cost of oil out of sight. It worked for a while and IC prospered. But now OPEC is falling apart. So is IC.

"The firm has enormous capabilities. There are only a few contractors in the world who can put together a project like Al-Makr. But our information is that unless Jarvis cashes the two-billion-dollar contract on Al-Makr, he and his company go under."

"That would certainly explain why Jarvis is so willing to do little favors for the Libyans, like hiring Salameh and supporting the Muslim Student League," I muttered.

Rafi said nothing. After a moment Nkrumah whined indelicately and then looked away as though startled by his own bad manners. Rafi glanced questioningly at me. I shrugged.

"He's beyond the age of consent," I pointed out, busily adding Rafi's information to my mental snarl of string.

Rafi fed Nkrumah half a tamale. The dog swallowed, drooled copiously and silently begged for more. Shaking his head, Rafi fed Nkrumah the rest of the tamale.

"Do not regard the situation as a simple quid pro quo," Rafi said finally. "Jarvis is too sophisticated to accept orders directly from Khadaffi. And for that matter, the league is very much what it appears to be, a collection of students who are taking postgraduate degrees at universities all over Southern California."

Rafi shrugged and tested the curve of the beer bottle with his hard palm. "Some of the students, unfortunately, are more than they appear," he continued. "They are available to do odd jobs for Colonel Khadaffi's Libya or any other state that rejects the idea that Israel has a right to exist. For instance, your FBI has a large dossier on a young Palestinian who is studying organic chemistry at the California State University at Fullerton. I know about the dossier because I helped two FBI agents put it together six months ago."

"Extortion?"

"Assassination."

The word took more than a little of the glow off the meal.

"The student is the prime suspect in the murder last year of an anti-Khadaffi Libyan living in exile in Loveland, Colorado."

"Charming," I said. "I've heard of working your way through college, but that's ridiculous."

Rafi's laugh made Nkrumah look at him in wary reassessment. Rafi took out a Dunhill, set fire to it and blew out a stream of darkness into the golden light. The dog sniffed, sneezed and retreated with a hurt look.

"Did you tell the FBI about the connection between IC and the league?" I asked.

Rafi shrugged, lined up a beer bottle with the edge of the table and whacked off the cap with a single hard chop of his hand. The same well-placed blow could have killed a man.

"They have been informed," said Rafi.

"And?"

"They filed it in a thick file with dozens of other intelligence reports." He smiled sardonically.

"That's all?"

"That's all."

"Hold it—" I began.

"Hold what?" he interrupted harshly. "Jarvis is a big contributor to the present administration. The FBI is not likely to move against him or his company on one unsupported piece of intelligence from Israel. For all I know, the administration is blackmailing Jarvis into sabotaging Al-Makr as they build it."

He paused, studying that possibility. "That idea has a nice symmetry. I wonder if anyone else has thought of it."

"Christ, I thought Fiora had an intricate mind," I said.

Rafi chuckled. "Fiddler, you're a good man, but you're too direct," he said. "Directness is a virtue in many places, but not in international politics. Someone once called politics a 'wilderness of mirrors.'" He nodded his approval of the phrase.

"I've heard that," I said. "My reaction usually is to kick over a few mirrors and see what's behind them."

"But broken glass can be very sharp," he said.

It sounded enough like a threat that I couldn't afford to let it pass. I looked him straight in the eye and smiled. "Sharp things cut two ways, Rafi." I took a drink of beer. "Does Israel have its own bombs?" I asked, holding the bottle up against the sun, admiring the flush of carmine light through the golden beer.

"The last estimate I saw, which was in a reliable British newspaper," said Rafi ironically, "indicated that we have about a dozen small nuclear warheads."

He smiled. His smile was so much like Salameh's that I felt a chill.

"Don't look so worried, Fiddler," Rafi said softly. "Many other experts say those warheads are just an illusion. Israel has used such illusions in the past. Do you remember the platoons of fantastically skilled sky marshals who materialized instantly after the Arabs started their highjacking campaign in 1968?"

I nodded.

Rafi put his arm across his waist and bowed ironically. "More mirrors, along with some blue smoke," he said. "I was the master in charge of illusions at that point and all I did was put out a press release. The idea, true or false, proved irresistible to the press. It was pumped all over the world and deterred who knows how many fanatic Palestinians. It worked, for a while. Long enough for us to train some men and get them in place."

"Are Israel's bombs an illusion, too?"

Rafi simply smiled again. "Believe what comforts you."

"What do the Arabs believe?"

"What comforts them: that we have the bomb and that soon they will have their own bomb and then they can finally go to war with us again."

"That's insane," I said flatly.

"Was sanity an issue?" he asked.

Rafi took a deep drag on his cigarette, letting the smoke

wreathe and soften the hard lines of his face. Even that wasn't
enough to hide the bleakness of his eyes. He was looking old
again, as though he had never relaxed on a chaise lounge and
watched the day extinguish itself in a shimmer of gold.

"Have you ever heard the tale of the Frog and the Scorpion?" he asked me after a long silence.

"No." And if the look on his face was any indicator, I
wasn't sure I wanted to hear.

Rafi smiled at me as though he knew exactly what I was
thinking. His smile also said that he had no intention of sparing
me.

"The Frog was swimming near the bank of the Nile when
he heard the Scorpion call to him," said Rafi, staring out over
the ocean to the point where the sun burned down to the
water. " 'Please, dear brother, beloved countryman,' said the
Scorpion, 'give me a ride to the other side of the river.'

"The Frog stared at him in disbelief. 'You must be joking,'
he said to the Scorpion. 'I know you, evil creature. If I let you
onto my back you will sting me and I will die.' "

Rafi took another hard pull on his cigarette and exhaled.

"The Scorpion was indignant," murmured Rafi. " 'How
can you misjudge me so?' he asked mournfully. 'Besides, brother
Frog, my own life would be in your keeping. I cannot swim,
so I cannot kill you without killing myself.' "

Rafi's smile gleamed briefly, brutally, in the dying light.
"The Frog thought it over and decided he was safe. He swam
close enough to the bank so that the Scorpion could leap onto
his back. Together, they set off for the far side of the Nile.
When they reached the middle, the Scorpion sank his poison-
ous tail deep into the Frog's neck.

" 'Scorpion,' cried the Frog as he sank. 'You have killed
me. But you have killed yourself, too. *Why?*'

"And the Scorpion answered, 'Because, my friend, this is
the Middle East!' "

Rafi laughed, low and sad, as he watched the horizon lose
its definition to the condensing night.

"Which are you?" I finally asked.

"I am both," he said. "We are all both."

At that moment Imbrahim's picture flashed through my
mind. And Sharai's.

"Are you sure, Rafi?" I asked.

"For myself, I am sure." He drained the beer bottle and
held it up to the thin light. "I'm not complaining, Fiddler,"

he said. "Like you, I chose my life—and would choose it again. My decision has allowed me to take part in the growth of my country, the failures and the successes. It *matters* that I have lived. I've made a difference in our history."

I said nothing. Rafi's intensity, which I had first seen this afternoon, was back in full force, plainly evident in his savage hunter's eyes. He was Ethan Edwards reborn.

"Perhaps that's it," Rafi said slowly. "I've fought and lied and killed to serve my country and myself. It has cost me much of what is human. Those I've loved, and those I love now, have paid the same price, but they don't get to feel the satisfaction of knowing that their sacrifice made a difference."

For a moment he was very still. Then he crushed the cigarette under his heel and flipped the butt off the bluff with a snap of his powerful fingers.

"What about Sharai?" I asked quietly. "Is she both Frog and Scorpion, or is she simply a daughter caught between two parents and two countries, not able to please anyone, especially herself?"

Rafi looked at me a long time, as though he were deciding whether to speak. In the end he said only, "There's much you don't know about Sharai. Perhaps she will tell you. I can only say this. My wife and my daughter bore much of the cost of my life, and my wife is dead now, but my daughter is still very much alive. You interest her, for whatever reason."

Then he shook his head and gave me an amused once-over with his dark eyes. "That was a father speaking," he amended. "You interest Sharai for perfectly obvious reasons, just as she interests you. I approve of that. If it is only that."

A flurry of blurred wings descended on the ever-blooming flower in the last of the light. Four hummers fed and two more hovered, waiting for their turn during the time of the twilight truce. Rafi stared in a combination of disbelief and fascination. King David chirred and skreed from his perch in the lemon tree but made no real move to drive away the other hummers. Night is a difficult time for the little warriors who must eat their own weight in nectar several times a day. If they don't feed properly at twilight they could starve to death before dawn.

I watched Rafi and wondered if he had ever known anything like the twilight truce.

There was a burst of yellow and the pungent smell of tobacco spread through the soft night air. The flare of the cigarette lighter outlined the harsh lines around Rafi's mouth and eyes.

"I have need of Sharai right now," said Rafi roughly. "I don't want to need her. I wish it hadn't happened. But—" He made a chopping gesture with his hand, sending a fine scattering of bright ashes into the darkness. "It is done and there is no going back. I thought she was pleased with her decision to join me. She demanded it, in fact, worked very hard for it, very long. And I had no other choice. Then I saw her watching you. You are *alive* and she—"

Abruptly Rafi stopped speaking, as though he had said more than he had intended. He stood up and moved stiffly away from the table. The jerkiness of his motions startled the feeding birds but did not put them to flight. The necessity for food was too urgent. Rafi limped to the edge of the deck and stood looking out at the pewter sea. It was obvious that his left knee was reacting badly to the increasing chill and dampness of the salt air. He saw me watching him and smiled grimly.

"Yes, I've paid for my life. But before I accept retirement, I will do what must be done. I will kill Salameh, and Sharai will help me."

"Why is it so important that he die? Simply because he's PLO?"

Rafi studied me for a moment, as though deciding something. Then he shook his head. "He is a condemned terrorist. He has committed crimes against the nation of Israel, against all Jews. That is why I want you to give me the names of the Jews he is trying to extort. They owe it to their people."

I could see how Israel would prefer to send a man like Rafi after Salameh. An assassin's bullet had deniability, and it was a great deal more efficient than a formal request for extradition. Rafi was a good solution, one I probably would have chosen, faced with Israel's choices.

But I had my own problems, principally the Zahedis. They had entrusted themselves to me and they deserved better than being staked out as tiger bait, which is what Rafi intended. He would lie in ambush and would put a bullet through Salameh's head the instant he appeared, no matter who was in the line of fire.

The thought of Sharai being involved in that kind of cool, preprogrammed murder made me want to scream and kick and smash mirrors. Some people can kill without paying a price. She wasn't one of them.

"Leave your daughter out of this thing and I might be able to help," I said. "Maybe we could rig a trap without endangering the Iranians."

"Salameh would smell the danger. He always uses the innocent as a shield," added Rafi with deadly contempt.

"You must know him very well."

"Yes," Rafi said. "Now give me the names of the Iranians. They will be heroes of Israel if we kill Salameh."

"If they get lucky and survive? No way, Rafi. It isn't going to happen. Besides, it's not my choice to make."

"As Sharai's choice is not mine to make," he murmured.

Suddenly he looked sad, as though his next words were painful. But he said them anyway.

"Give me the Iranian's name, Fiddler, or give it to the Los Angeles police." He paused for a moment, letting the ramifications sink in. "Extortion is a crime, and policemen don't like competition from free-lance handymen like you. They'd break you eventually. Then they'd bring in the immigration officers, and your Iranian friends would be deported."

He was right. The immigration service was the most heartless bureaucracy in the world. It had to be. It heard a thousand heartrending stories before the morning coffee break. The Zahedis could fight and wriggle and beg and plead but eventually they'd be on a plane for Teheran.

"Understand, Fiddler," Rafi said. "I will do it. I have no choice. I must have Salameh." His eyes were black confirmation of his words.

Anger uncurled hotly in my gut. "All right, Rafi," I said. "Dealer's choice, and you chose hardball. One word, just one hint to the local cops and I'll stampede Salameh all the way back to Yemen."

I watched the realization sink into Rafi. "That's right, Rafi. No winners, only losers. It's called a 'zero-sum game.'"

Rafi didn't give up easily. He rotated the idea a quarter-turn and took another run at it.

"At least take me with you to the league show. There's a chance that Salameh will be there."

"Jesus Christ! How did you know about that?" I demanded.

Rafi made an impatient gesture and said nothing.

"Do Salameh and his comrades know your face as well as you know theirs?" I asked. Rafi didn't have to answer. For once, his expression didn't keep all of his secrets. "Great," I said sarcastically. "I take you, you're recognized, and the Iranians are blown to bloody bits in retribution. No thanks."

"Take Sharai. She isn't known to them."

I hesitated.

"Her or me. Take your choice, Fiddler. Otherwise I'll send the word to IC and you won't get in the door. I'll also tell them that you're a lot more than you appear to be."

"You're a righteous prick, aren't you?"

Rafi just waited.

"Tell Sharai to bring a wrap," I said curtly. "It gets cold in the desert at night."

I should have told him to make sure she left her small black pistol at home.

9

I dreamed of Sharai. The dream was blue on blue, tints and tones of blue like a silent cataract pouring over me. Only it wasn't silent. My dreams rarely are. Sometimes I suspect that I think in music the way other people think in English or French or Arabic. But there were no symphonies in my head this time, not even chamber music. This was a chorus of Zahedis singing about the old-time religion. I tried to sing along but I'd forgotten the words and the notes themselves kept sliding away from me like water drops dancing across a hot skillet. Sharai was the soloist. She sang better than I did, but she kept getting lost in the transitions. The chorus would start another verse of "Battle Hymn of the Republic" and she would keep trying to wedge in a round of "Amazing Grace." Every so often Rafi would kick in with "Swing Low, Sweet Chariot" and really screw things up.

I woke up edgy as hell, in the kind of nasty morning temper that reminded me of why I was no longer married. The best tactic for dealing with myself in that state of mind is a couple of miles in the loose sand. Hard on the hamstrings but good for the sullen spirit. As I ran, I tried to make sense out of the chaos that was passing for thought in my mind. At the end of three miles I was out of breath and in sync with myself. Chaos had settled into some good news and some bad.

The bad news was that this little morality play was acquiring a cast of thousands. In addition to the Zahedis, I found myself worrying about Sharai. She was an extraordinary woman, strong but vulnerable in ways that I could only guess. I did not want to see her pay the price of Rafi's fanaticism.

The good news was that Rafi had given me a new weapon, whether he had intended to or not. He had confirmed that International Constructors was involved in a business deal that was questionable, if not outright illegal. I knew without checking the State Department Munitions list that any high-tech gear more sophisticated than paper clips was on the Libyan embargo list. Even if the IC connection to Al-Makr was carefully hidden, F. Robert Jarvis might be willing to help the

Zahedis rather than test the thickness of his corporate cover. And I knew from Rafi that Jarvis exerted a great deal of influence over Salameh.

I decided that approach was certainly worth a try as I jogged up from the beach in a burst of self-congratulation. King David rasped his metallic little song. It was a note of discord that should have warned me. But I was too busy admiring my own cleverness at saving Sharai and the Zahedis and the whole frigging world to listen to a bad-tempered hummer.

I called Sharai and formally invited her to be my companion for the evening.

"My father told me his plan," she said.

I caught the cool blue tones of my dream in her voice. "To hell with your father," I said. "Either you want to spend the evening with me or you don't."

She hesitated. "I'm sorry," she said. "I didn't mean to be . . . ungracious. It's kind of you to try to make this sound like a date."

"That's what it is. A date. If you're coming along for any other reason, don't bother. I mean it, Sharai. I plan on taking care of my business very quickly. After that, the evening is ours."

Again she hesitated. "What time should I be at your house?" she asked finally.

"I'll pick you up."

"Thank you, but no," she said in a firm voice. "It makes more sense for me to come to your house than for you to make an unnecessary trip to L.A."

It also gave her greater freedom if she decided to opt out of anything more than a business relationship with me. I knew it and so did she.

"Come around three," I said.

"What should I wear?"

"I almost said, 'Something sexy.' But with you that isn't necessary. You'd look sexy in drag."

My flirting was rewarded with a pleasant little laugh, one as pretty as the woman herself.

"It's for charity, so it's formal," I added. "You know the type. Men whose wives put more money on their backs than in the fund bucket."

The laugh this time was fuller, even more musical. "I'm a diplomat, Fiddler, albeit a junior one. I know exactly the type of function you're describing. See you at three."

That prospect kept my day a lot brighter than I would have expected from the way I woke up. Just to keep the mood from getting too mellow, I got a call around noon from a dry-voiced woman who turned out to be "*the* personal secretary to Mr. Jarvis."

Her tone was arch but I could tell that she had checked my credentials with Fiora's firm. Jason, Fiora's secretary, must have done his usual proficient job of legitimizing me or the woman would never have called.

"Mr. Jarvis is wondering if you would be so kind as to arrive a bit early this evening to discuss some of the mechanics of your contribution," she said.

It was more a command than an inquiry, but that's the way it's done in corporate America.

I had decided to chip away at the façade of corporate noblesse oblige, so I decided to start with her. "Sure," I said cheerfully. "I'll be happy to be tutored by a pro on the fine points of shilling."

She ignored my impertinence. "Shall we say seven-thirty?"

"I'll be there with Salvation Army bells on."

"A courier will deliver your invitation within the hour. Just show it to the guard at the gate and he'll direct you to the main house," she said. "And do remember, Mr. Fiddler, that this is a formal event."

I hung up before I got frostbite.

Sharai arrived on time, and there wasn't anything frosty about her. She was wearing a dress guaranteed to raise the blood pressure of a corpse. I'm not talking Hollywood sleaze, either. The dress simply was silk, lapis blue, glowing, designed by someone who knew that the mind is definitely the most erotic zone on the human body. When Sharai breathed, light moved over the deep blue silk in a way that was both mysterious and tantalizing. Her small diamond stud earrings and a bracelet of woven gold chains were nearly as fine as her skin.

"I'd compliment your dress," I said, helping her out of the car, "but I'm afraid if you knew what I was thinking you'd get back in the car and drive like hell."

Sharai's smile was very swift and very female, telling me that it would take more than a few sexy thoughts to put her to flight. The smile also revealed that she had dressed for me rather than for the charitymongers. As she stood up, the wind brought me a hint of the fragrance she wore. It was as elusive as the light curving over her breasts every time she breathed.

"Just a minute, lady," I said lightly.

I was moving before she had a chance to object. She was a tall woman wearing high heels, so I didn't have to bend far. I could tell by the way she froze that she was expecting a kiss or something heavier in the way of a pass. Instead, I put my hands on her shoulders and tugged her gently to me. The softness of her hair caressed my cheek, the warmth of her neck brushed against my lips and I breathed in deeply. She smelled like a garden at midnight, secret and sensual.

"That perfume has to be illegal," I muttered.

Sharai looked at me for a long moment. "This isn't easy for me," she whispered.

"Why not? My God, woman, a thousand men must have told you you're beautiful."

"But I didn't care what they thought."

That stopped me.

She stood on tiptoe, brushed her lips across my cheek and smiled up at me. "If you could see the look on your face—"

I laughed. She tucked her arm through mine and stood close enough to share her warmth and her maddening perfume.

I gave her the full tour, from the old picture window and the new wine cellar, to Nkrumah, the hummingbirds and the koi. Since I had no idea when I would be home again, I covered the small koi pond and explained to Sharai that the steel netting kept the raccoons from having a sushi appetizer on the way to their nightly meal of dog kibble stolen from Nkrumah. Sharai sat on a rock at the edge of the pool for a moment and watched the fish making colorful arcs in the clear water. She immediately noticed the new koi, the white one with the blue patch on its head.

"It looks like a Blue Willow bowl," she said, smiling and holding very still as the skittish newcomer nibbled on her finger. When the koi vanished in a swirl of water, she turned back to me. "Father was right. He said your home held as many surprises as you did."

"I think he'd find any home surprising. It's been about forty years since he's had one."

She studied me with thoughtful eyes. "You really aren't as harsh as you look, are you? And you're right. When Father came to see me last night, he was as lonely as I've ever seen him. He's finally beginning to acknowledge what he has missed. But it's too late. His wife is dead and his daughter is too much like him to settle down and give him grandchildren."

"He didn't complain to me. As for the grandchildren—who knows? That's hardly out of the question for you, is it?"

Sharai looked away from me, studying the fish. They seethed in colorful, graceful patterns, stirred by the prospect of manna dropping from the delicate feminine hand which teased the water. She stood in a ripple of graceful, deep blue light. "We'd better go. Father said it was a long drive."

We took her car, a Mazda RX-7, which was both less breezy and less conspicuous than the Cobra. Without a word Sharai flipped me her keys. I drove, letting her watch the coastline as we headed toward San Diego County. I had the feeling that she was thinking rather than sight-seeing.

Interstate 5 dips close to the water at San Clemente and then follows the coastal shelf all the way from the twin concrete bubbles of the San Onofre nuclear power plant to south of Oceanside. At every available beach, surfers, swimmers and sun worshippers carpet the sand and dot the undulating sea.

"I love the water," said Sharai quietly, not turning toward me. "When I was a girl in Haifa, I swam every day in the sea. Then terrorists began to scatter little explosive mines on the sand and in the shallow water. A girl I knew lost her legs. I think that's why my mother finally left and brought me here to the United States."

"Bright woman."

"Was she?" Sharai sighed. "She loved Rafi but she left him anyway."

"Sometimes love isn't enough. You have to be able to live together, too."

My voice must have given me away. Sharai turned quickly, looked at me, then nodded. "He said that you still loved your wife."

"Rafi talks a lot for a man in his line of work," I said in a clipped voice. "And she's my *former* wife."

Sharai smiled sadly. "My husband is dead, but that doesn't change what was between us. It was good, very good. And then it was gone."

The sadness in her face gave way to something much harder: hatred. The expression flashed for only a second but it was unmistakable. Sharai hated as passionately as she once had loved.

"He was Israeli?" I asked quietly.

"Yes." The word was harsh. The sound of it startled her. She closed her eyes for a moment. "Yes," she said again. "After

Mother died, I went to live in Israel with my father. He required it. I was barely sixteen."

"You resented moving?"

"No," she said without hesitation. "But sometimes I wonder how different I would have been had I remained here." She turned and watched the ocean again, concealing the emotion that had drawn her face into strained lines.

"Tell me about it?" I offered quietly.

Ten miles went by before I heard her say, "Not yet."

I would have decided that she meant never but for the fact that her hand crept over just then and rested on my leg. No come-on, just a simple hunger for human warmth. I put my hand over hers. It was a long, silent, yet oddly peaceful drive to Jarvis's San Diego hideaway.

The ranch was in one of the valleys east of Oceanside that divides the coastal lands' rugged, rumpled hills. The ocean and the desert beyond the mountains fought for dominance over the land. The result was chaparral-covered hills that were sun-blistered by day and cooled by sea breezes at night. Coastal orange groves gave way to avocadoes and lemons, and then to the wine grapes of the few remaining vineyards in Southern California. The grapes weren't great and the wine usually reflected that fact, but the ground was gently sandy and the air was clean.

From the looks of the countryside, people had finally caught onto the fact that the land was better for horses and houses than vineyards. Discreet signs along landscaped driveways proclaimed which horse was at stud behind white fences. There were a few thoroughbred farms and more quarterhorses. There were also a few spreads that housed some of the world's most pampered descendants of the oldest domesticated horse, the Arab.

It looked like F. Robert Jarvis owned the biggest ranch of all. It was on a winding little county highway, far enough inland that the desert influence was substantial, yet high enough that the chaparral had given way to oaks and grassland. Since it was summer, the grass was the color of toast. Four very dry months had left the leaves of the black oaks thick with dust. There was still the smell of desert heat in the air, but by now the temperature was in the high seventies, headed down in a hurry. The air was like the silk dress Sharai wore, clean and complex and sensual. She rolled down the window to let wind flow through her short hair.

"Wonderful," she murmured, eyes closed as she drank the sensations of the wind and the land and the moment.

I agreed and silently cursed the fact that I was taking her to a place where we both would have to be wary. Impatience seethed in me, a hungry heat that hadn't left me since I had seen Sharai's first unguarded smile. The thought of her father using her to reconnoiter against Salameh made me both savage and sad. If the Palestinian were here tonight, I'd make damn sure that he didn't get close to Sharai. And vice versa.

Which meant that I had to get my business with Jarvis settled first and fast.

"I have to meet with the Imperial Jarvis at the beginning of the evening," I said. My voice must have been harder than usual, because Sharai's eyes opened and her head snapped around toward me. "He's going to use me as a shill for other league contributions. We're going over my lines to make sure that there's no hitch. Only I'm going to tell him a few things he doesn't want to hear about his eager little students. Then you and I will get the hell out and enjoy the evening somewhere else."

"You aren't really going to give these people any money, are you?" said Sharai.

"I can always stop payment on the check if things don't work out."

"What if he already knows about the league?"

"Then I try other methods of persuasion."

"Such as?"

I looked at her. She looked away.

"No wonder my father likes you," she said in a low voice. "You're rather like him in some ways."

I put the Mazda into a tight curve as we came down a small hill and into a broad, golden valley that was dotted with oaks so green that they looked black in the thick evening light. Across the valley, lights glowed in the shadows around the low-roofed house and outbuildings of the Jarvis ranch.

"If anyone asks," said Sharai, "my name is Anna Papadopoulos."

"Any particular reason?"

"Greek women are such great docile cows that nobody ever pays them any attention."

I laughed at the slander. "It won't be that easy, Sharai. You're very hard to ignore."

Sharai gave me a glance out of great dark cow eyes. She

had done something to her expression that had erased all the subtle tensions of intelligence and vitality. She smiled as slowly as she was breathing. In all, she suddenly looked like she had the IQ of a well-mannered houseplant. Then she winked and spoiled the image.

There was a full squad of guards at the gatehouse beside the highway. Their uniforms were black tie, no tails. A guard checked the invitations of early arrivals as though they expected gate-crashers. The scarlet-bordered set of papers that Calvin's courier had delivered to me earlier were just what the guard had been hoping to see, even if the inexpensive Mazda wasn't.

"Please park next to the ranch house, sir," said the head guard. "And give your name to the guard there. Mr. Jarvis is expecting you. Thank you, and enjoy your evening."

The discreet bulge under the man's left armpit suggested that if I had any arguments or amendments, I'd better keep them to myself. I put the little Mazda in gear and went up the long, lavishly landscaped driveway. Beside me, Sharai laughed softly.

"How big did you say your contribution was going to be?" she asked. "Those men treated you like a pasha."

"Twenty-five grand. Enough to get Jarvis's personal attention but not enough to worry him."

Sharai nibbled on that bit of information like a shy koi. Perhaps Rafi's background report on me hadn't prepared her for the fact that I could write a big check and still pay the rent.

The road to the ranch ran between white fences that enclosed paddocks and pastures the color of money. Rainbird sprinklers shot curtains of pulsing silver water over the pastures, keeping everything green despite the desert climate. Arab brood mares and their colts gathered at the fence, thrusting their small, elegant heads over the rails to watch the passing cars. I tapped the horn once. The horses snorted and pranced and a few of them bolted along the fence.

"It's cruel of you to make them run," said Sharai.

I glanced at the three horses racing the car, running cleanly, heads high and nostrils flared wide to drink the incomparable air. "It's cruel to keep them fenced. They were born to run."

The driveway was exactly a half mile long. During the drive I got a look at the rest of the grounds. There was a lawn the size of a football field falling away from the ranch house. Several large, open-fronted tents had been erected. At first I thought they were circus tents. On closer inspection, however, they proved to be more exotic, straight from Arabia and made of sumptuous, colorful fabrics. The tents sheltered huge tables that were being dressed and stocked by fifty caterers. The smell of beef and lamb roasting over open fires drifted through the car's open window. There was something else in the air, too, a piquant mixture of spices that I didn't recognize.

Below the grassy slope and tents, there was a show ring seventy-five yards long and forty wide. A crew of stable boys, mostly Mexican illegals from their looks, were turning the ring's sandy soil and then raking and smoothing it. In an outdoor corral beyond the ring, a dozen Arab horses were being groomed and saddled. Even in the fading light the tassels and bangles decorating the tack glowed with jewel-pure colors.

We were early, but there were already several dozen cars in the dirt field that orange traffic cones had converted into a makeshift parking lot. As always in California, the cars said a lot about the guest list. Damn few people but Arab princes and show-biz types use stretch limos these days, even on the Gold Coast.

The parking lot attendant was an off-duty San Diego County deputy wearing his Sam Browne belt and a regulation thirty-eight. He tried to point me toward the dirt field but I waved the scarlet-edged invitation at him. Instantly he stepped aside and gestured me up the drive toward the ranch house.

It was a big place, all unexpected angles and windows and redwood siding rambling in careful disarray across the knoll. Several sets of large picture windows broke the dark wood. One of the windows looked out over a thirty-yard-long swimming pool. A massive oak and a sycamore framed the house, aided by a huge eucalyptus that arched like a wave from the backyard. In all, an adequate ten-bedroom weekend retreat.

In the small macadam parking area next to the swimming pool, another black-tie guard inspected the invitation, authenticated it and genially waved me into a slot between a Mercedes and a Rolls. The lights were on around the pool, drawing early moths. The bar was doing some drawing of its own. Checkered kaffiyehs seemed as numerous as balding Anglo pates. There were a few of the solid white or black kaffiyehs worn by Arab royalty, but at the rate Saudi royalty reproduced, the monocolor headdress wasn't much of a distinction.

At the pool gate I presented my invitation yet again. The blond receptionist checked my name against her list, smiled charmingly and handed me off to Maude Gunther, the dry-voiced humorless assistant I'd spoken with on the phone that morning. She seemed surprised I'd been able to find a black-tie outfit. She looked more closely and realized that the tux hadn't come off someone's rental rack. I went up a notch in her estimation, but there was a more substantial reason than vanity for my custom-made clothes. The Detonics in the small of my back looks like an oil derrick beneath a standard cut jacket.

"Mr. Fiddler," she said. "Mr. Jarvis will see you in a few minutes. Let me introduce you and—?" She glanced at the female clinging decoratively to my arm.

"Annie," I said carelessly, leaving off the fictitious last name, all but saying that it didn't matter: Annie or Tawny or Sylkie or Boopsie, they were all the same in the dark.

Ms. Gunther repeated the name and then utterly ignored Sharai. Acting like a bimbo can be the best disguise for an intelligent woman. The men Sharai met took one look, memorized her body and forgot her face entirely. I was introduced to a Saudi prince, a Banque Suisse vice-president in charge of the Los Angeles office, an Aramco executive in a dark suit and two Palestinian ophthalmologists, one from Burbank and one from somewhere out on the desert beyond Palm Springs.

"A pleasure," said the prince, who was sipping champagne from a Baccarat crystal glass.

"How do you do," said the two executives in perfectly matched skepticism.

"Nice to see you," said one of the Palestinians.

"Welcome to the bloodletting," said the other.

I liked the last Palestinian already. His tone matched the one I had adopted for the evening. I accepted a glass of champagne from a passing waiter and chatted with them. Sharai smiled dimly and watched me as though I were a lifetime meal ticket. Ms. Gunther had disappeared after the last introduction left her thin lips.

"How much did you pledge to get into the inner circle?" asked the Palestinian who had welcomed me to the bloodletting. "I'll have to work an extra week to cover mine. I sure hope these crazy kids appreciate it."

"You were once a crazy kid, too, Ali," said the one from Burbank. To me, he said, "We were the first Palestinian students in USC history."

"Yeah," said Ali, "but we had rich parents so we didn't have to go begging for tuition. And we were both smart. The first chance we got, we stayed. There are thousands of these kids now and they're all going back to Kuwait or Dhubai. I can't stand the Middle East myself."

The conversation switched to baseball. Like most immigrant citizens, the former Palestinians knew more about things American than I did. I wondered if they had any idea that their contributions were being used by those "crazy kids" to import a bit of old-country terrorism.

Ms. Gunther appeared. "Mr. Jarvis will have a word with you, if it's not too much trouble."

I allowed myself to be escorted away. Sharai blinked and asked slowly about "the lady's." Ms. Gunther pointed toward a lanai just beyond the pool. Sharai wandered off.

Jarvis's house was custom built, with high ceilings and warm wood paneling on the walls. The art was still American, but Southwestern and Native rather than Eastern. Ms. Gunther left me in the living room. I inspected some Fritz Scholders serigraphs and a big Charles Russell original on the wall above the Arizona sandstone mantel. The Russell intrigued me. It showed a dry, dusty herd trailing out across the Great American Desert with a bunch of cowboys chasing and shagging and fighting their saddle broncs. The painting crackled with vitality.

The facing wall displayed events closer to Jarvis's life. He was a hunter, or had been. The most recent photographs showed him with Remington and Weatherby Magnum bigbore game guns. There were also the obligatory dead elephants and lions. The heads of other dead creatures were mounted on the wall. Various antelopes, a moose, and a noble bighorn ram. Bighorns have always been scarce in California and have been protected for as long as I could remember. The plate on the wooden collar around this one said that Jarvis had shot his sheep in 1959 in the Santa Rosa Mountains. I doubted there were many rams alive today that could rival this one; his massive gray-black horns curled for at least forty inches from base to tip.

I'm not a big-game hunter. I don't understand the impulse, any more than I understand the fascination of making a killing in the stock market. Fish, now, are a different matter. But I have never put any of the salmon or trout I've caught on a wall. What I keep, I eat. The rest I release.

"Isn't he something?" a voice said behind me.

I turned away from the bighorn to face F. Robert Jarvis himself. He was of medium height, more balding than his publicity pictures suggested, and had the bleached look of someone who should have quit smoking twenty years ago, when he was middle-aged. His eyes were faintly bulged, and the skin around them was heavily pouched and wrinkled. He puffed on a cigarette as he crossed the room toward me. Not surprisingly, his voice was hoarse.

"I used to hunt all over the world," he said, "and the trophy that means the most is the one I got closest to home. I shot him a hundred yards from the front porch of the house where I was born, out in the Chocolate Mountains east of the Salton Sea." He smiled professionally at me and extended a hand. "I'm Robb Jarvis." His handshake was firm and dry and very self-assured. "I'm glad you could come tonight."

There was a manner about the man that was hard to define but which made you want, down deep, to like him. He was the distillation of the modern high-powered executive—forceful, attractive, intelligent and completely at ease with his power. He seemed to know exactly what he was doing, exactly what he wanted, with no hesitations and no regrets. That may have been his secret. While other people considered alternatives and shades of gray, Jarvis made a decision and moved on, wrapped in confidence. For the rest of us mere mortals, such decisiveness is fascinating.

There was also a hard glint of humor in Jarvis's eyes, as though he might be laughing at something, perhaps even himself. That prospect was reassuring. Perhaps I could cut a deal with him. Maybe he would be as put off by Salameh's extracurricular extortion as I was. I decided to probe beneath Jarvis's seasoned hardwood exterior for a human reaction—any human reaction.

Jarvis stood looking up at the ram's head, and began talking as though he were thinking aloud. "It's wonderful country, the desert. Everything is reduced to its essence. There's no phony sophistication, no veneer of artificiality. It's all real. That's why I enjoy my dealings with the Muslim desert people so much." He paused and gave me a sympathetic smile. "Tom Calvin tells me you aren't having as much pleasure in that regard."

"Well, it could be just that I'm new at this game, Mr. Jarvis," I said, spacing my words. "I like basic folks, myself, but sometimes 'basic' can also mean 'base,' if you get my drift."

Jarvis tilted his head to the side, as though trying to measure the drift I'd mentioned. "Most cultural differences can be resolved by a combination of education and goodwill."

"And twenty-five grand," I said blandly.

"A tangible expression of goodwill," agreed Jarvis, giving me a smile that was just a trifle hard. He was not budging from the moral high ground he had staked out for himself.

"I assume that tangible expressions of goodwill aren't limited to me?" I asked, letting more of my own natural speech rhythms come through. Sarcasm, too, I'm afraid.

"I don't believe I understand."

"No Arab construction deal, no donation," I said succinctly.

Jarvis's professional smile slipped even farther. "All your league donation entitles you to is personal satisfaction and an exemption on your income tax."

"I'll be satisfied with a few signatures on the dotted line."

He stopped me with one hand, palm out like a traffic cop. "Let me make things perfectly clear to you. This evening is designed to amuse my guests and raise a little money for students who are studying here in the U.S. Now you can be a part of that, and welcome. Or good night. Which will it be?"

Nothing like self-assurance. Without it, power brokers are just pimps, and old F. Robert Jarvis was not a pimp. He was more like a harem master for Khadaffi Duck. The more I thought about that, the less I felt like being polite. That's the problem with being independently well-heeled. You find yourself less and less inclined to be nice to people who figure they should have their ass kissed because they're rich and powerful.

"I'm in," I assured him. "Got my check right here. Now if you'll just tell me where to ante up, we'll get on with the game."

Jarvis shrugged off my attempt to irritate him with plain speaking. He had said his set piece and I'd said I was in. After that there was nothing but social chitchat, and I wasn't a member of his chatting circle.

"That won't be necessary right now," he said. "This isn't a cash-and-carry catalog store."

That was good, because I had decided that I'd write that check about the same day they ice-skated in hell.

He stubbed his burned-out cigarette into a crystal ashtray. "After the horse show I'll make a speech explaining where the money goes and asking for contributions. That's when I want you to get up and announce your donation. You can turn over your check to the executive chairman of the Muslim Student League. The man's name is Mahmoud Faoud."

"A student?"

Jarvis slanted me a look from shrewd eyes. "An employee of IC. Why?"

I suspected that the employee sometimes called himself Salameh. I felt my good ol' Brooks Brothers persona going into the toilet and I really didn't give a damn. I had tried being nice and it hadn't worked. With Jarvis, nice just didn't get it done.

That left nasty to do the job.

"Answer me one thing, Jarvis," I said carelessly.

"What." The word was flat, uninflected. Uninterested.

"Why are you and all these other powerful folks, including the Arab princes, pimping for the Palestinians? I could understand if it were, say, the Libyans whose asses you were kissing. But the Palestinians? Hell, they don't even have a country for you to build sewers in."

"I don't like your language," he said, looking me over slowly, "and I don't like you."

"But my money will spend just the same, right?"

Jarvis kept talking as though I hadn't rudely interrupted. "The Palestinians are a special issue for the rest of the Arab world. They are a homeless people, without wealth and without hope of ever acquiring any. It is for that very reason that the other peoples of the Arab world share everything they have with their less fortunate Muslim brothers."

Except their countries, I thought cynically.

But then, if the population of the refugee camps were absorbed into the rest of the Arab world, a very useful political icon would be lost. Nobody wanted that, least of all the Palestinian government. The only people who would benefit from the end of the camps would be the poor wretches who had been forced to live there, and nobody was asking them for interviews on the ten-o'clock news.

I didn't bother pointing out the obvious to Jarvis. He was well and truly launched into the centerpiece of tonight's fundraising spiel.

"The Palestinians symbolize suffering in the face of world indifference," he said urgently. "They have endured death, disease and poverty, and they have done so with a grace that we in the Western world would do well to imitate. Lacking that grace, the least we can do is contribute to the welfare and education of their students in the United States."

Good corporate noblesse oblige. Change the ethnic origins of the recipients and it could be a speech from the chairman of Chase Manhattan would give to a Black College Fund, or the one Joseph Coors might give to a Latino civil rights convention. I have no quarrel with the sentiments. What bothered me in this case was the naked two-billion dollar self-interest that Jarvis was trying to disguise.

"Yes," I said rather abruptly, "the Palestinians have been badly treated by fate and their fellow man. Is that an adequate justification for terrorism?"

"I don't understand."

"Bombs. In cars. BOOM! Dead folks raining down."

"Who the hell are you? Some Jewish Defense League plant? If you are, you're making a serious mistake. You don't know what's involved."

Well, I had managed to get a human reaction, even if it wasn't very coherent. "I don't work for anybody but myself," I said. "Right now, I'm trying to do a favor for a nice old guy who once held power in Iran. Maybe you remember him— Imbrahim Zahedi."

"I knew there was something wrong with that old shyster introducing you to Tom," said Jarvis coldly.

"The only thing wrong was what led up to it." I waited for Jarvis to light his cigarette because I wanted his full attention. "Want to know what your students do when they aren't in class? They intimidate old men with pistols."

"You're crazy," said Jarvis flatly.

"Wrong. I'm angry. Your poor, oppressed Palestinians are shaking down Jews here in LA to the tune of five grand a month, each. The victims can't complain because they'll be beaten or turned over to INS or both."

I watched Jarvis suck hard on the cigarette, and wondered if it was helping his nerves any.

"Zahedi asked for help, and I ended up with a bomb in my trunk. A PLO trademark bomb, Jarvis. A bona fide terrorist bomb made of dynamite and a Timex watch. Maybe that's how the students work their way through school, or maybe they just get their nuts off bullying old Jews and planting bombs." I shrugged. "Either way, it's something you may want to stop. Otherwise you are likely to start seeing banner headlines in the Los Angeles *Times* like 'International Constructors Underwrites Terrorism.' That would be right beside an even bigger headline, the one that says 'IC Builds Libyan Reactor.' "

All the color had drained from Jarvis's face except for two spots of burning red high on his cheeks. He stared at me with an uncharacteristically puzzled expression. He started to say something, then stopped.

"You are seriously confused, Mr. Fiddler," he finally said.

"It's a confusing world, Jarvis, but I try to keep it as simple as I can. That's why I really don't care about your two-billion-dollar business deals in the Middle East. All I care about is Imbrahim Zahedi and his family. If the Palestinians leave them alone, I'll forget I ever stepped into this cesspool."

Jarvis stood staring at me, the cigarette still smoldering between his fingers. He seemed to be having trouble breathing, but not enough to make either one of us nervous.

"Do you really think you can prove your allegations?"

"You'll be tried by reporters, not lawyers."

"I'll sue."

"The reporters will love that."

"What you're saying is preposterous!"

"Can I quote you on that?"

Jarvis flinched. I waited for him to accept the inevitable with the decisiveness that was supposed to be his trademark. He did.

"I'm sure that no one has made any trouble for Zahedi in the past," said Jarvis coldly. "And I'm very sure that no one will make trouble for him in the future."

In the law business, that's called *nolo contendere*, which means roughly that I didn't do it before and I promise I won't do it ever again. I nodded once, accepting Jarvis's deal.

He drew sharply on his cigarette, coughed, and threw it into the ashtray to smolder and stink. "Now get out, or I'll have you shot as a trespasser."

"You can try, but I'm not as civilized as Zahedi," I said as I glanced at the Bighorn trophy on the wall. "Or as defenseless as he was. I can shoot back. Keep that in mind before you turn your rented cops loose."

10

The cosmopolitan gathering around the swimming pool had grown while I was inside. The heat of the executive pressure cooker was being diluted with scotch and champagne, breaking Muslim taboos. The makeshift parking lot now had more than a hundred cars in it and was overflowing into the field beyond. A small water truck was scurrying up and down the lanes, trying to put down the dusk kicked up by tires and well-shod feet. At the corner of the parking lot stood a group of ten or fifteen uniforms. Chauffeurs, not guards. The drivers stood around laughing and scratching and swapping lies like old friends, which they probably were.

I couldn't see Sharai anywhere.

The Arabian tents were full of people carrying little plates of food or big drinks. Most of the guests seemed to be businessmen and their wives, WASPish and comfortable at these kinds of affairs. I passed through both of the tents, looking for Sharai but didn't see the blue flame of her dress.

Several groups of charitable folks were being entertained by what I assumed were the objects of benefaction, college-aged Middle Easterners in kaffiyehs, doing their best to look exotic and to hide their embarrassment or disdain at being on display. Offhand, the impulse to be publicly charitable is one of the more unappealing that I can think of, for both donor and recipient.

Beside the ring a crowd had gathered to watch the beginning of the horse show. A young Arab in a flowing white abayah flashed into the ring on a gray Arab stallion that galloped like he had springs for hooves. The horse was supple and powerful. The rider was not. He was definitely over-matched.

The kid sawed at the bit and looked worried. Genetic heritage is no substitute for experience. The way he rode, he was a long way from his Bedouin roots. The horse knew it. He reared suddenly and fought the bit, almost dumping the rider on his wallet. Two lackeys darted out and swung from the bridle until the stallion came back down on all four springs.

Sharai was not in the crowd at the show ring nor in "the lady's." I was beginning to worry that I might have misjudged her. Perhaps she had found Salameh and decided to do a little work for father and country—with a gun. I doubted it, but I'd been wrong before, and I hadn't checked her purse for weapons. Then there was always the off chance that one of the Arabs had recognized her as an Israeli diplomat trying to pass for a Greek bimbo.

I headed for the only other building around, grateful that I was armed. I usually don't carry for a social function, but I make exceptions for people who leave bombs as calling cards. The barn was deserted except for a couple of young Mexican stable hands standing in a doorway, smoking cigarettes and watching the fancy folks out front. I asked one of the boys if they had seen a pretty young woman in a blue dress. The boy smiled and looked confused. He was willing but not able. I tried the same question in Spanish. The boy pointed up the slope, away from the tents and the lights, and told me in Spanish that such a woman had walked up the path just a few minutes ago.

I quickstepped over to an oleander hedge. After a moment's hesitation I drew the Detonics and held it down along my left leg where the matte-finish on the weapon would blend right into the black of my clothes. The Detonics isn't a flashy gun, just very, very functional. I paused to let my eyes adjust somewhat to the darkness, and my ears to the sounds of the land rather than to cocktail chatter. I caught a flicker of movement next to a big sycamore, halfway back to the ranch house. I made for the tree, sticking to shadows and keeping my white face down.

Somehow I wasn't surprised when Sharai stepped out from behind the sycamore. Even in the dim light of stars and half moon, I could see the tight, almost desperate expression on her face. Then I saw the black outline of a pistol in her hand. The gun had a short silencer screwed into its barrel.

I hesitated, then holstered the Detonics. Sharai hadn't noticed me yet. She had attention only for the lighted area between the barn and the pool. People walked back and forth there, sipping from champagne glasses that glittered like canary diamonds in the spotlighted yard. Sharai tracked the people with a perfect pistol stance and trembling hands.

Rafi had been right. She wasn't an assassin. But she was trying to be. I spoke her name softly. She jumped and turned, automatically bringing the pistol to bear on me. She had been well trained, but so had I. My right hand closed around hers as I swept her gun up over her head. A hard squeeze numbed her hand, making it impossible for her to pull the trigger even by accident. I took the gun from her, put on the safety, and dropped the deadly little pistol into my pocket. She rubbed her hand and tried to stop shaking.

"Salameh," she whispered.

Her voice was rough, as though fear and adrenaline had dried up every bit of softness in her mouth.

"Salameh is here," she continued, her voice too harsh, her eyes searching the darkness between her and the pool. "I saw him go from the barn to the pool. If he comes back the same way I will kill him."

She repeated it several times as though it were an incantation, then she put her face in her hands and just stood, trembling, her deadly focus finally broken. She had the training and concentration to be a shooter, but not the stomach. Buck fever had gotten her.

"It isn't going to happen, Sharai," I whispered. "Not here and not now." *And not by you,* I added silently. Let Rafi import a real shooter or do the bloody work himself. Not Sharai.

"I could have done it," she said, her voice low and harsh.

"There's the small point of deniability," I said, drawing both of us back against the sycamore, where no one could see and wonder about outlines against the night sky. "The cops would start asking questions about the guests and about who might have a grudge against our friend Salameh. I'd be at the top of their shit list after the talk I just had with Jarvis."

I held Sharai close enough that I could feel her trembling and she could feel that I wasn't. I kept talking, trying to bring her down from the adrenaline high that was pumping through her like a wild chemical storm, making her shake.

"Some homicide investigator would come around to talk to me," I continued softly, "just routine of course. He'd ask if I owned a silenced .22 automatic or if I knew anyone who did, and one thing would lead to another. You can see how unpleasant it would be for both of us."

Sharai let out a deep sigh and sort of sagged against me. I held her until I felt control return in stages to her body.

"You should have let my father come with you tonight," she said finally.

I took a deep breath, trying to ease the rage that was the

natural aftermath of adrenaline. As I breathed in, Sharai's perfume coursed through me like a wave of cocaine, making every one of my senses leap into focus. She felt both soft and strong against me. I tightened my arms around her until I felt her over every inch of my body. There was no hesitation, no fumbling for position. She stood on tiptoe to meet me, and she tasted of champagne and fire.

Adrenaline is the second best aphrodisiac. Mutual desire is the first. We had too much of both. It was all I could do not to take her down to the ground. She wouldn't have fought me. We both knew it. By the time I gathered what was left of my self-control, we were both breathing too hard. I forced myself to let go of her. She swayed slightly, shook herself and looked at me as though she'd never seen a man before in her life.

"Come on," I said. "Let's leave before you change your mind and try to use that little purse pistol on me."

Sharai didn't say a word on the way to the car, just looked at me from time to time out of eyes that were like night, dark and full of shadows. I tucked her into the car, started it and left the parking lot behind. I didn't turn on the lights until we approached the guard who was directing traffic. He inspected the Mazda as though he'd just gotten on APB on a car that exactly matched this one. He probably had, too. Jarvis had been both eager and determined to see me removed from his life. Doubtless he was informed the instant my taillights disappeared down his ranch road.

I drove hard, putting the Mazda out on the breaking edge of its engineering and holding it there, because high-wire driving helps me to think. Right now I was trying to figure out what I could use on Rafi to get him to let go of Sharai. Next time I might not be around to prevent her from becoming a stone killer. If Rafi was too well known to get close to Salameh, surely the Mossad or whoever it was he worked for could import a shooter that Salameh and his cohorts wouldn't recognize on sight.

Sharai was silent beside me on the winding roadway, listening to the tires whine, thinking as hard as I was. The dashboard lights softly illuminated her face, the only gentle thing about her at the moment. Whatever her thoughts, they were deadly enough to have brought her to the point of murder.

Later, as we turned onto the freeway, she touched my arm, sliding her fingers down until they met my skin.

"It's a long story," she said, pitching her voice above the

sound of the engine, "and at this rate we'll be back at your home before I finish telling you."

I let up on the accelerator a bit, enough that the rotary engine quit screaming. Sharai sank back in the seat and drew a deep breath. I watched out of the corner of my eye as she tried to compose herself. She looked at her fingers resting on my hand, then folded both of her hands firmly in her lap.

"Where to begin . . . How to begin."

She spoke so softly that I could barely make out the words.

"The beginning, maybe?" I suggested dryly, backing off a touch more on the accelerator.

Sharai gave me a sideways glance.

"The beginning?" she said, with a trace of irony, "That was a thousand years ago, or two or three. So long ago no one knows where or when or even how. But my part in this began in 1972 . . ." Her voice trailed off again. Her eyes were unfocused, looking inward, lost in memories more personal than historic.

"I remember 1972 very well," she began again after a moment. "That was the year I was married. God, it seems so long ago. Nearly all I can remember, now, is how strong Arye was. Is it odd that I remember that?" Her eyes gleamed briefly, then she closed them as though willing herself not to cry. She pressed her fingertips against her forehead until the blood was driven from beneath her fingernails.

"Arye and I lived in Tel Aviv," she continued, speaking quickly now, getting it over with. "Rafi and I had almost made our peace. He was in the security service then, and it was a terrible time, hijackings all over Europe and endless reprisals against the Palestinians who were responsible. I remember that he came to see us one night and fell asleep between words. He had been awake for five days."

Sharai released the pressure on her forehead. Lacing her fingers together, she put her hands once again in her lap. She looked out the window but her eyes saw only the past. She didn't even blink when headlights from oncoming cars flared harshly over her.

"My father was appointed to oversee the security of Israel's Olympic team."

An image from 1972 flashed through my mind, a television picture of a thin, slightly stooped young Arab standing on a sterile concrete balcony overlooking Connollystrasse in the Olympic village. There was a strange hood covering his head, like a ski mask with a topknot, and the eyeholes were gaping and cadaverous. The image had been frightening and alien, then. It was more familiar now. Family, Terrorist. Genus, Middle East. Species, Palestinian.

"No wonder Rafi turned into Ethan Edwards, Indian killer," I said, remembering Olympic carnage.

The silence in the car was suddenly claustrophobic. Sharai felt it pressing against her and tried to push it away with words.

"I was in Israel but we watched it all, over and over, like the rest of the world," she said harshly, "until I couldn't bear it anymore and—"

I remembered what it had been like, staring at the television and trying to understand the unspeakable. I wondered what Rafi's memories were. Unlike the rest of us, he hadn't had the option of turning a knob and making it all go away.

Sharai's voice came to me, speaking in counterpoint to my thoughts.

"My father was there, in the tower, watching the airport and listening to the Germans argue and debate and temporize and worry and then begin all over again, talking talking talking. They tried, but they were so worried about appearing uncivilized to the rest of the world, about strengthening the myth of superefficient Nazi killers."

Sharai's voice was like that of a narrator describing the flickering incidents in an old newsreel. There was emotion but no true passion, certainly not enough to drive her to a shooting stance under an old sycamore. I waited, listening, wondering why I was hearing only Rafi, not Sharai.

"So many times my father said to me: 'They did everything but shoot straight.' Did you know that one of the German sharpshooters had never fired at anything except paper targets? He had never shot at a living thing, not even a deer. His target was the Arab who stayed with the second helicopter, the one who had the grenade, the one who lived to blow it all to hell." She took a fast breath and continued, words coming more quickly now, racing toward some finish line only she could see. "The Germans said their sharpshooter just missed his target. My father says the shooter never fired at all." Then, very quietly, she added, "Like me."

There was a difference in her voice now, resonances of both old and new passions. She wasn't describing images on a television screen any longer, with reality suspended for commercial breaks. Death and terrorism and reprisal and death were the textures of her father's life, just as the textures of the lives of Ethan Edwards and Martin Pauly and Lewis Wetzel had been killing Indians and being killed by them, back when there was something worth fighting for, even if it was only your own life and the existence of your own kind. That was Rafi, epitaph for an Old Testament warrior. I didn't want it to be Sharai's epitaph, too.

"Would turning you into a killer change what happened in Munich?" I asked.

There was a long silence. When Sharai spoke, it wasn't to answer my question, at least not directly. "We Israelis see the world differently. We must in order to survive. Those who kill Israelis must die. There can be no compromise."

Rafi again. I could hear him in every implacable syllable.

"After the shooting stopped, three terrorists were still alive," continued Sharai, her voice dry. "The Germans arrested them. A few months later Black September hijacked a Lufthansa airliner and demanded the release of the three Palestinian terrorists who had survived Munich. The Palestinians went free."

Sharai turned and faced me. Her face was no longer calm; it was radiant with rage. Her voice was husky, caught between the distant past and the recent past when she had waited for a terrorist to show over the barrel of her pistol.

"One of the terrorists was Salameh. He was the one the Germans found hiding behind the bodies of the four Israelis he had murdered with his grenade and his AK-47. They were tied in their seats, helpless, when Salameh killed them. *And then he hid behind their bodies so he wouldn't be hurt.*"

A shudder went through Sharai. Her nails were leaving crimson arcs in her palms but I doubted that she noticed. The events she was recalling couldn't have been more real to her if she had been in the helicopter herself, felt the bullets tearing through her own body.

"Mahmoud Faoud wasn't known as Salameh then," she continued, her voice husky with hate. "That name belonged to his infamous cousin, the one who called himself the Red Prince, the man who planned Munich. We killed that Salameh in Beirut in 1979. It was then that Mahmoud took the name."

She drew a deep breath, steadying herself against the hatred that vibrated through her. "After they were freed by the Germans, Mahmoud and his comrades were flown to Yugoslavia. He disappeared for a time, finally surfacing in the

United States. He finished his education here, probably with the help of a scholarship from someone like Jarvis."

"How did Israel find him?" I asked.

"One of our operatives was making an inquiry into the Al-Makr project and Mahmoud Faoud's name came up," she said. "We had one of our engineers inside International Constructors get his fingerprints out of the personnel office there."

"You have agents everywhere, it seems," I said.

"This one was a Jew, not an agent. He did it for a dream that was already old when his ancestors walked out of Egypt."

"What about the other two terrorists who survived?"

"Dead."

I didn't ask how and where because it didn't matter. I didn't have to ask who, either. I knew. "Rafi."

It wasn't a question. It didn't get an answer.

"That's a long time to hunt someone," I said.

"Israel worked more than twenty years to get Eichmann," said Sharai quietly. "What are those years measured against the thousands of years of our history?" She drew another deep breath. "Symbols are important to us, Fiddler. They were all we had to hold us together during the Diaspora."

"So execute Salameh symbolically in the press. Expose him so that no legitimate corporation would touch him. Burn down his little house of cards. Surely you have some 'assets' among American reporters who could handle the character assassination for you."

"No," she said. "That might be good enough for Israel's dainty new politicians but it isn't good enough for me." Her voice changed, husky again, vibrating with passion. "Arye was one of the men who was tied up and blown to pieces at Fürstenfeldbruck. It was my husband's body Salameh hid behind. For that, Salameh will die."

Christ. No wonder she had waited in ambush for Salameh.

"Fine," I said harshly. "Let Rafi kill him."

"It's not that easy. My father isn't young anymore."

"So what? How young do you have to be to put a few ounces of pressure on a goddamn trigger?"

Silently, she shook her head. "What is it that football players shoot into their knees to take away the pain? Without that drug, Rafi is crippled. And the longer he uses it, the worse his knee becomes."

"Then why the hell hasn't Mossad put him behind a desk?"

Sharai said nothing. It was as though I hadn't spoken. I

swore viciously, feeling her slip through my fingers like the night itself. History, Rafi and her own passions had done their work well. Maybe she had been born to hate and to kill after all.

Yet Rafi had said that it was life, not death, that had drawn Sharai to me.

I drove hard again, but there was no sport to it on the broad freeway, no relief from the devils pursuing me and Sharai. I had no illusions about the capacity of women to kill; they are fierce fighters when pushed to it. They give no quarter and they take no prisoners. Ever. It's as though once pushed that far, they have little left to lose. It's not that way with men. Men kill more easily than women. I don't know why that's true, but I've seen it time and again. The difference may be physical, emotional, chemical or cultural, or some deadly mix of all four—I don't know. All I know is that for women the cost of killing is always higher than it is for men. It would cost Sharai whatever she had left of life. Rafi knew it. I knew it. Sharai suspected it, and reached for me.

"You've never killed," I said.

She was so still that I thought I had already lost her. After too long a time she let out a deep sigh.

"No, I've never killed." She shrugged. "I'd never slept with a man, either. Until Arye."

"Making love is a hell of a lot different from killing someone."

"Yes," she agreed sardonically. "Making love requires more skill."

I got a better grip on the steering wheel and my temper. "Have you thought about how you'll feel afterward?"

"No. I've thought about how I feel *now*, knowing that Arye's murderer lives and laughs and kills and no one cares but my father and me!"

She was silent for a long time, staring out the windshield, her eyes reflecting back the darkness of the road ahead. Then she stirred and turned, watching me instead of the night. In the wan light she gave me a sad, tired smile, asking for understanding or warmth or . . . something.

I looked at her strained face and wished to Christ that I knew more about the care and nourishment of a woman's soul. I ran the back of my index finger over her cheek, then took her hand. Her fingers were still for a moment before they curled around mine.

As the miles went by, her body slowly relaxed into the seat. She kept her fingers laced with mine. When she spoke, her voice was normal again, husky, intimate, the voice of one of the most intriguing women I'd ever known.

"This wasn't supposed to happen," she said. "Everything was complicated enough as it was. I didn't need this."

"Maybe. And maybe this is exactly what you needed. You're human, Sharai. So am I. There's nothing complicated or new in that."

But it felt new with her fingers laced through mine.

We were an hour from home and neither one of us felt like talking. Sharai found a classical station on the radio. Soon the strains of Beethoven's Violin Concerto shivered through the car. Pinchas Zukerman played the concerto with a purity of sound and purpose that I deeply envied. Sharai listened with her eyes closed, her lips moving slightly as she whisper-sang the familiar notes. I looked at her and tried to find an assassin. I could not. I looked at the future and tried to find a way out for her.

I was still trying when I turned off into Crystal Cove. The radio told us it was just past ten of yet another day in paradise. Sharai stirred and stretched.

"I have to drive back tonight."

"Why?" I asked, shutting off the ignition and lights.

She hesitated. "I'm not saying I won't make love with you."

"What are you saying, then?" I asked, watching her, sensing a tension that had nothing to do with sex.

"I haven't slept with anyone since Arye."

I didn't bother to hide my shock. Sharai laughed.

"There have been men, Fiddler. I've used them but I've never slept with them. Do you understand?"

I nodded. "Waking up with someone in the morning can be a hell of a lot more intimate than screwing in the dark."

"Yes," she whispered.

"No problem. There's more than one bed in the place. You can do whatever you like, Sharai. Except drive back. Adrenaline takes everything out of you in the long run that it gives you in the short. You've been fighting to stay awake for the last ten miles."

"Feed me first," she said huskily. "Then we'll see."

Neither one of us was up to Luz's sizzling cuisine, so I

threw together some cheese omelettes, fried a potato with
onions and opened a bottle of Gamay Beaujolais. We sat elbow-
to-elbow at the little breakfast bar and demolished the food.
Sharai was quiet most of the time. When we did talk it was
about Israeli wines, North American Indian art and the feel of
Southern California sand between your toes.

I dumped the plates in the sink, snagged the bottle of
wine and glasses in one hand and Sharai in the other and settled
her in the living room where the old picture window overlooked the sea. I didn't bother to turn on the lights. There was
a half moon in the west. Its thin silver light outlined Catalina
Island's rugged spine, skated over dark ocean troughs and tangled in the breaking waves. With every breath I took I could
smell Sharai's elusive perfume. She was close but very careful
not to touch me. It wasn't coyness or teasing on her part. At
some level she was deeply wary of me. We sat silently for a
long time, enjoying the night and the warmth of another human
being.

"Can you swim out there?" she finally asked, her voice
like a shadow in the darkness.

"Yes, but it's damned cold."

"How cold?"

"Last I heard it was in the middle sixties," I said. "I'll
wait until August. It might hit seventy by then."

"I won't be here in August."

Sharai stood up in a sudden, lithe movement that reminded me that she was graced with a strength and flexibility
that I found sexier than an overstuffed bra.

"Do you have a swimsuit I could wear?" asked Sharai.

I shook my head. The only odds and ends of women's
clothes in this house were Fiora's, who was about seven inches
shorter than Sharai.

She shrugged and stretched. "Then I hope I don't scrape
anything on a rock."

I relented and went to my bedroom. I rummaged until I
found a handful of black patches and strings that Fiora insisted
was a bathing suit. String was string. Maybe it would stretch
to cover Sharai. And then again, maybe it wouldn't. The thought
made me smile. The thought of that cold ocean made the smile
fade. I really didn't want to go swimming tonight.

"You don't have to swim with me," Sharai said from the
bedroom doorway.

"What are you, a mind reader?" I asked.

She smiled and walked into the pool of moonlight on the floor by my bed.

"If it's just exercise you want—" I began hopefully.

She laughed and shook her head. I draped the handful of string over her fingers. She cocked her head to one side, looking dubiously at the bikini.

"Am I expected to knit it myself?" she asked whimsically.

"Best I could do, unless you want to swim in one of my T-shirts."

Sharai shook her head again and left the room. The swimsuit dangled from her hand like a few shreds of night. I cursed quietly and began pulling off my dress clothes. I put on a pair of cutoff jeans and a heavy cotton rugby shirt. I'd swim if I had to, but I wasn't going to get all undressed for the occasion. I grabbed my bathrobe off the bed. The material was black, thick and warm.

When I came out of the bedroom, Sharai stood in the middle of the living room. At first I thought she'd given up on the bathing suit and opted for skinny dipping. Then I realized that it wasn't lacy shadows covering her breasts and the apex of her thighs, it was the spider webbing of the bikini. There was just enough of the material to cover most of the vitals, most of the time. I found myself holding my breath for the between times.

"You're staring," she said.

"You're worth staring at."

"The suit is a little small," she admitted, adjusting the top in a way that made me decide to give up breathing altogether. "I'll have to be careful."

"Not on my account."

I would have sworn that Sharai blushed. With a curse I held out the bathrobe and stopped acting like a teenager. She was a grown woman. If she wanted me, she knew where I was.

"Here," I said, holding out the robe. "No point in freezing on the way down to the water."

She put on the robe quickly and followed me out the side door to the path that led down to the beach. I sent Nkrumah back home when he tried to join us. We quietly descended the stairs to the sand. Overhead the moon rode low in a sky empty of clouds. The beach was empty, too. The tide was out, slack, ready to turn, the waves so indolent that they almost couldn't be bothered to dissolve into foam. The beach near the water was packed hard and burnished with reflected light. The sand changed color around our feet as we walked, as though our weight squeezed out moonlight, leaving darkness behind.

A wave curled over and sighed, lapping coldly around our feet. I'd been too optimistic. It felt more like sixty than sixty-five. But then, I hate cold water. Something about growing up in Montana, I guess. The damned lakes never got warm there but we swam anyway, fools that we were.

"The ocean is peace," Sharai said softly.

I sighed and began pulling off my shirt, knowing that she wasn't going to give up just because the waves were cold.

"No," she said, putting her hand on my arm. "I won't be long."

"You shouldn't swim alone."

"I always do." She put her fingers across my mouth as I started to object. "Please."

I sensed that being alone in the water was important to her, so I nodded. "Stay in the moon trail," I said. "There are rocks to the right and a kelp bed about fifty yards beyond the breakers."

She slipped off the black robe and handed it to me. I watched her in the moonlight as she walked to the water's edge and into a small shore-breaking wave. The wave tumbled and foamed and rose to her hips. She could have been wearing only the silver light and velvet shadows as she walked gracefully into the cold sea. She didn't hesitate or look back at me but simply dove into the new black wave that was building before her. I caught a pale flash of her skin as she surfaced and swam toward the elusive brilliance of the moon.

The first few strokes told me that Sharai was very much at home in the water. There was ease and unhurried strength in her movements. She swam into the center of the moon's radiant pathway and stayed there despite the currents I knew would be trying to tug her to one side. Once beyond the breakers she turned over on her back and floated. She remained in the water for several minutes, holding station skillfully, awash in a midnight ocean, alone as she had wanted to be. I wondered what she was thinking, what ghosts whispered to her out there, what questions she might be asking them. And I wondered if she heard any answers.

Waves rose blackly, broke into pale washes of foam and retreated back into the ebony body of the ocean. I ignored the cold water licking up my ankles, knowing it must be far colder for Sharai. Suddenly, as though she had been released, she turned over in a single strong motion and began to swim back down the silver shaft of moonlight toward me. The tide was running with her now, dark water pushing her toward shore. She rode the breaking edge of a wave, body-surfing with the same grace that she walked.

Sharai rose out of the sea, slicked back her hair with both hands and began coming toward me up the gently slanting beach. The moonlight was behind her, blinding me to all but the feminine silhouette. I held the robe open. She walked into it, turned away and looked over her shoulder at me. Light gathered in water drops on her skin, trembling each time she breathed. She tightened the robe, turned her head away and there was only darkness. If it hadn't been for the feel of her shoulders beneath my palms, I would have thought that she had vanished. I stepped away from her. Her head came up suddenly and she looked over her shoulder at me again. The movement made water shimmer on her wet skin, on her eyelashes, on her parted lips.

"I'm cold," she said, her voice husky. "Warm me, Fiddler."

I looked at her for a long moment before I put my hands on her hips and slowly pulled her back against me. She smelled like the sea and the night. With a long sigh she leaned against me, pulling my arms around her. I held her until my warmth sank into her and she stopped shivering. She drew a slow breath and moved my hands inside the robe until her breasts rose against my palms, filling them to overflowing. Her hands stayed on top of mine, telling me wordlessly what she wanted.

Beneath the wet top her nipples were hard with cold. My thumbs found the straps of the swimsuit and slipped them past the points of her shoulders, down over her arms. I moved my hands slowly, savoring flesh that was both firm and soft. Even after her skin was warm again, her nipples stayed hard, pressed against my palms. I bent to lick water drops from her neck and felt her heartbeat race. She arched herself against my touch, moving her body in rhythms as slow and sensual and ancient as the sea itself. When my hand slipped down over her ribs and grazed her taut, arched belly, she shuddered deep in her body. Her hand guided mine to the warmth we both were seeking. She groaned softly, deep in her throat. I knew what she meant. I was beginning to hurt with wanting her.

Sharai turned slowly in my arms. I slipped my hands inside the robe and drew her to me, wanting to feel her resilience and heat stretched along mine when I kissed her. Her lips opened and her hips moved against me. I was hard and full and her body felt it, was drawn to it, as we buried ourselves in the first deep kiss of two people whose hungers and discoveries mated smoothly.

I seldom get weak in the knees since puberty, but it happens once in a while, and it happened now. To both of us. I lifted my mouth and began to seek the source of perfume along her hairline and behind her ears, biting gently the whole way. She clung to me as though her knees had turned to sand. I brushed her nipples with my thumbs to hear her gasp with pleasure and because it was incredible to touch such responsive flesh.

"Look," I said, my voice as husky as hers and a hell of a lot deeper. "Unless you've always wanted to make love in wet sand, we'd better get upstairs. Real soon. Now."

"But I'll be cold without you," she said softly in my ear.

There was nothing cold about her tongue teasing my ear.

"Once we're upstairs," I said, "I promise to make you warm again. And again. And again."

I felt her shudder, the instant response of her body seeking mine. She came all the way up on tiptoe, molding herself against me as she pulled my head down to her mouth. It was a long time before I broke away, and even then it was to find and hold the tip of her breast, learning her textures with my tongue. She made small, wild sounds and I both blessed and cursed the brutal history that had brought a woman like her into my arms. I didn't know what she wanted from me beyond this moment, nor did I know if I could give her what she sought.

"You shouldn't waste your life, Sharai," I said against her soft skin.

"I won't be wasting it tonight with you," she said in a husky voice, "no matter what else happens. Let's go upstairs," she said, running the tip of her tongue around my lips. "Tonight I want—everything. And then I want to fall asleep hearing your heartbeat beneath my cheek. I want—" She stopped, smiled hesitantly. "I want too much, but I'll have tonight. All of it."

Sharai was chilled again by the time we reached the top of the stairs. I took her to the outdoor shower in the lee of the redwood deck. She luxuriated in the pouring warmth for a long moment, then her hand snaked out, her fingers found a belt loop on my jeans and she tugged. Pulling off my soaked rugby shirt was a tussle that reduced us both to laughter. Somewhere along the way, laughter went down the drain, along with patience. The bikini strings were knotted. They snapped like rotten thread in my hands.

She was magnificent, both elegant and taut, hungry for me. She wasn't afraid of her body—or mine. When she began to pour over me like warm water I decided that the bed would have to wait for the second time. Or the third. Then she slipped from my arms and ran to the house. Both of us were wet when I pulled her onto the bed but we didn't care. She opened her arms and her body to me without hesitation. We fitted together completely, as easily as holding hands, easier, and infinitely more sweet. We lay motionless for a long moment, almost afraid to spoil the unbelievable feeling by moving.

And then the hunger and the nearly painful desire overtook us like a hot, breaking wave and we began to move, riding the wave and each other until there was no past or future, only now.

11

The phone's first summons dragged me out of the depths of sleep. On the second ring, I opened my eyes. False dawn had begun to shimmer over the ocean and Sharai was a long, sweet warmth next to my naked skin. Her head was on my chest as though she were listening to my heartbeat even in her sleep. By the third ring I had figured out that it wasn't my alarm. Normally I'm not that slow, but there had been nothing normal about the last twenty-four hours. I'd been asleep for maybe an hour when the phone went off.

Only trouble calls come before dawn. I didn't want trouble. I wanted to watch Sharai wake up in my arms. I cursed the fourth ring and then gave in.

"Yes," I said curtly into the receiver.

"Thank God you're there! They've taken Father!"

It took me an instant to recognize Shahpour's voice, for there was nothing left of the cosmopolitan banker. My first thought was that Salameh was a poor loser and had turned in the Zahedi family. "Immigration?"

"Arabs," he said, his voice rising and thinning. "Three men broke into the house with guns and took Father away!"

"*Shit*."

"He thought we would be safe in America, that—" Shahpour's voice broke. "Is there no place in this world to escape madness?"

The only answer I knew wouldn't have comforted him, so I asked a question instead. "Did you recognize them?"

"Yes! They were Arabs and they had guns! What the hell else do you need to know? What—"

"Shahpour, listen to me," I said, making my voice hard and cold, cutting through his fear. "When this is over you can cuss me out and welcome to it, but right now yelling won't help your father."

I heard a few ragged breaths at the other end of the phone and then an equally ragged apology.

"Forget it," I said. "Were you there when it happened?"

"No. Just—my mother."

I thought of the self-effacing, white-haired old lady dealing with Salameh's playmates and wanted to commit a little old-fashioned violence myself. "I understand," I said, squeezing the phone until my hand ached. "I'm sorry, but I've got to ask questions and keep asking them until something shakes loose. Is your mother with you?"

"Yes."

"Can you translate for us?"

I could hear Shahpour gulp air, slowing down, fighting for control. He drew a few more broken breaths and then one good clean one. I heard a burst of foreign syllables, then Mrs. Zahedi's soft-voiced answer.

"Arabs," said Shahpour into the phone. "Mother said they were Arabs, young men in their twenties. Maybe Palestinians. She didn't know. They didn't tell her."

"Did they say anything, give any indication why they were taking Imbrahim?"

The Farsi conversation resumed. Her reply was so soft it was all but inaudible.

"They struck him in the face when he tried to protect her," said Shahpour.

"Those miserable little shits." My words echoed on the line, telling me I'd spoken too loudly.

"They told her not to call the police, that we would receive instructions later," he continued. "They want half a million dollars in cash. You must deliver it to them. You, Fiddler. They said it would be a lesson in humility."

I remembered Salameh's eyes and decided that he'd rather have me dead than humble, but he wouldn't mind beating on me for a while—if he had someone to hold me down.

Sharai's hand touched my back, making both of us aware of how rigid my body had become. I tried a few of the breathing exercises I've learned but it wasn't enough. I knew I wouldn't really relax until I had Salameh's neck between my hands. Sharai slid her fingers into my clenched fist, gently prying it apart. Her skin was warm and smooth and very much alive. I hoped Imbrahim still was, too.

My hand relaxed and curled around Sharai's. "It's nice to know your work is appreciated, even by extortionists," I said sardonically. "You said they were armed. What kind of weapons did they have, and how many?"

I could hear him question his mother. His voice was almost calm now. After a few moments he came back on the line.

"Mother said two had small guns and one carried a big gun with a curved magazine, like the Revolutionary Guards in Teheran."

I almost wished I hadn't asked. Kalashnikov AK-47s are hard to come by in the United States. These guys were loaded for bear. The only hopeful sign so far was that they hadn't used the damned thing on Imbrahim. They were probably saving it for me.

"Did they say when they would make contact again?"

"No, only that they would call here," said Shahpour. "They did say that you would need the money and a good car with plenty of gas before you could carry out their instructions."

Maybe they intended to run me all over the landscape to make sure I was not being tailed by the cops. The Arabs weren't cherries in the kidnap game. They knew that the exchange point was their only vulnerability, and they knew how to limit that vulnerability by scraping off tails.

"You call it, Shahpour. Cops or me or any combination you like."

"*No police!*" His voice started high and kept going.

"Then understand this, Shahpour. Salameh plans on dumping both me and Imbrahim as soon as the ransom changes hands."

"You won't do it?" Shahpour asked, surprise and despair mingled in his voice.

"You aren't listening," I snapped. "I'm trying to tell you that right now you have a choice. You can call in the official trouble hounds, but the chance of them pulling your father out of the line of fire isn't real good. Frankly, neither is mine. Take your pick."

"You. I trust you."

Great. Just great. But I kept it to myself. The choice was Shahpour's, for now. That might change with the next phone call. If I thought a squad of eager SWAT types would get it done better, I'd be the first man on the phone dialing 911. Unfortunately, Salameh wasn't your average barricaded druggie on a bad trip or bungling felon caught in the act. The instant Salameh felt a trap, he'd start shooting and everyone within range would start dying.

I wondered how much Jarvis knew about his not-so-tame Arab. I dismissed the thought because right now it didn't matter. If Jarvis didn't know, there was nothing he could do to help after I told him. If he did know, I'd catch up to him later—if there was a later. Right now, I needed men who had been under fire before, men who were hunters and shooters, men who wouldn't be going up against terrorists for the first time.

I needed men like Rafi.

"Can you gather up the ransom money without setting off any alarms?" I asked Shahpour.

"It will take time," he said. "Banks usually don't keep that much currency on hand. I'll have to go through the Federal Reserve Bank in Los Angeles. There will be a lot of paper work. If I rush too much they'll get suspicious."

"If Salameh calls before I get to your parents' house, I want you to be ready with a list of bureaucratic woes. Tell them you can be fast or secret but you can't be both," I said. "Say it will take at least twenty-four hours to round up that much cash, maybe longer. And demand that you get to speak to your father, too."

Shahpour hesitated. "I'm in no position to demand anything," he said unhappily.

"Bullshit. This is a business deal, Shahpour, the kind you make every day. They have something we want. We have something they want. As long as that holds, we have some power to set the terms."

After a moment he replied, "You're a pragmatic man, Fiddler. I see now why my father trusts you so much."

"I'm sure it's a great comfort to him," I said sarcastically, angry at myself that I hadn't foreseen Salameh's reaction to my prodding of Jarvis. "If you think your father has a better chance any other way, tell me now. A few minutes from now may be too late."

I'll give Shahpour this: when it came to the crunch, he didn't whine or dither.

"All right," he said. "I'll stall if they call again before you get here."

"I'll be there within two hours—and I'll have some help with me."

I hung up. Outside the window there was neither darkness nor color, simply an amorphous gray light. The early-morning clouds generated by the cold ocean had absorbed the stars. Out on the water, just north of the cove, a single light gleamed weakly, moving very slowly toward the horizon. Probably a dory fisherman headed out from Newport to lower his baited hooks into the cold sea. I wished both of us luck.

"Where is Rafi?" I asked, not looking away from the window.

Covers shifted and whispered as Sharai sat up.

"Why?" she asked.

"He has something I want. I have something he wants." I looked at Sharai and tried not to be angry. It wasn't her fault that Imbrahim might die of a scorpion's sting.

"I don't understand," she whispered.

"Rafi will."

Sharai said nothing. She didn't have to. Her hurt at not being trusted was in every line of her body.

"Sharai," I said, leaning over her, pulling her close. "I want you out of this. All the way out."

After we let go of each other, she picked up the phone. As she dialed I stared out the window, arranging and re-arranging the facts in my head as though they were notes to a symphony I was trying to score. Hell of a symphony. Not one lyric passage in the whole mess.

"When you get him," I said, "tell him that I've decided to try his way of dealing with scorpions and frogs."

She stopped dialing and reached out to touch the faint cleft on my chin, one of the few distinguishing marks that came to me via genetics rather than mayhem. In the dim light of the digital clock, I could see her faint smile.

"So he told you that horrible story," she murmured.

I kissed the palm of her hand. "Tell Rafi we'll need some extra 'assets.' Consulate guys with big boots who don't mind stomping on deadly insects."

Her whole body tightened for an instant. Slowly she withdrew her hand from mine. Her finger held down the disconnect button on the phone, ending the incomplete call. "That will be impossible," she said, her voice deep with regret.

"What do you mean, impossible?" I said. My voice was more harsh than I intended, but I wasn't feeling very gentle. "Don't tell me you don't have a few tough boys on the consulate staff because I don't believe it."

"There will be no help from the consulate, Fiddler," she said. There was no doubt in her words or her voice. Her eyes were watching me.

"Why not?"

She turned away and began dialing all over again.

"Why not?" I demanded, pulling her around, forcing her to face me.

"There are things you don't know, things I can't tell you Rafi's secrets, not mine."

"Fuck Rafi," I snarled. "There's an old man out there wh trusts me and he's going to die unless I get some help. I don want an army. Just three or four hard cases. Hell, I'll settl for two!"

"Hire them."

"You can't hire the kind of men I need on short notice. I watched the expressions change on Sharai's beautiful face Nothing I saw encouraged me. "What's wrong? Why won't Raf help me? We're finally on the same side, nothing held bac and no regrets."

Sharai closed her dark eyes. "There are two places calle Al-Makr. Only one is in Libya, a little nothing of an oasis o the way to Chad."

She hesitated, as though waiting for me to understan what she hadn't yet said. An unbidden mental image flashe through my mind—Jarvis and I standing side by side in fron of a funhouse mirror, both mumbling the name "Al-Makr, and both wondering what the hell the other guy was talkin about.

This time I was going to be sure.

"Give it to me, Sharai," I said softly. "Where is the oth Al-Makr?"

"Israel," she said slowly, unwillingly. "That's the Al-Mak where Jarvis is building the nuclear plant. In Israel. That's wh the Israeli government wants to avoid embarrassing Interna tional Constructors. Jarvis is a very important man to us at th moment." Her fingertips touched my lips lightly before slidin away. "I'm sorry," she whispered.

For a moment I was stunned, both by my own stupidit and by Jarvis's cast-iron balls. He was trying to sleep with th Arabs and the Israelis on the same night, in the same bed. H couldn't afford to alienate his long-time but no longer high spending customers in Abu Dhabi and Riyadh, so he kep Salameh and his pals on the payroll. Neither could Jarvis affor to turn down the $2 billion the Israelis were paying him fo Al-Makr. He must have damn near swallowed his cigarett when I made my smart-ass reference to the nuclear plant a Al-Makr, Libya.

I was beginning to understand how much of a fool I ha made of myself, or rather how much of a fool I had let Raf and Sharai make of me. I grabbed her shoulders, wanting to shake her until the truth fell out.

"How much of the rest of it has been lies, too?" I snarled.

"We haven't lied to you," she said urgently. "We just haven't told you the whole truth. You assumed I was an agent. I'm not. I spent several years in the Israeli army, but I really am just a cultural attaché, nothing more." She looked in my eyes and found nothing to comfort her. "I haven't lied to you, Fiddler! Arye died bound hand and foot like a beast and it was Salameh who murdered him!" She drew a sharp, painful breath. "The rest is truth, too. Last night, my feelings for you—"

"What about Rafi?" I interrupted harshly, not wanting to remember last night until I had more answers from Sharai, because if I started remembering I might forget which questions to ask. "Is he Mossad?"

"Yes."

There was a hesitation in her manner that said this was one more ticking half-truth that might explode in my hands. Fragments of my patio conversation with Rafi burst through my mind like images from a wilderness of mirrors. Suddenly I could guess what Rafi's secrets might be, but guesses weren't good enough, not with Imbrahim's life at stake. And mine.

"The truth, Sharai," I said coldly. "All of it."

Sharai's composure finally cracked. "Jarvis is frightened that Salameh's death might anger his Arab customers. He has demanded that the Mossad leave the Palestinian alone."

"Did Israel agree?"

She looked at me without expression. "The highest levels of the government have decided that Al-Makr is more important than Salameh. He is not to be touched."

I loosened my grip on her shoulders. "Then I take it that Rafi is on an unsanctioned mission."

Sharai looked at me, pride and anger suddenly clear in her eyes. "Rafi and I are both acting without sanction," she said. "A few others, in the Mossad and elsewhere, agree Salameh should not be allowed to go free. They've been helping us by providing us with intelligence. But they've done all they can. Now it's up to us."

I shook my head. "And Rafi accused *me* of being too direct."

She studied my face for a moment. "You and he are very much alike," she said softly.

It wasn't a comforting observation. Being like Rafi wasn't one of my life's ambitions. Unfortunately, handling violence seemed to be a skill that came naturally, most of the time. The rest of the time I picked up odd scars, little physical reminders like Rafi's knee: those who live by the sword sooner or later get cut to the bone.

"When Rafi's vacation is over, will the Mossad take him back?" I asked.

"Oh yes. He'll have a desk and a title and a lot of memories. He'll be honored."

I grimaced. No wonder Rafi shot his knee full of dope and crawled around in the dark hunting scorpions with his bare hands.

The phone began to wail, telling us that we had kept the receiver off the hook too long and for no good reason.

"Call Rafi," I said. "Tell him to meet me in the restaurant at the top of the Holiday Inn on Sunset Boulevard. Ninety minutes."

I let go of Sharai and went to take a shower. Nothing like a faceful of cold water at dawn to get your blood moving. Problem was, I couldn't get the water cold enough. I was still steamed when I came out of the shower and got dressed. Being end run by Salameh and the Israelis—and the beautiful Sharai—had raised my temperature too high.

Sharai was just hanging up the phone. "He'll be there in ninety minutes," she said quietly.

She watched me out of the corner of her eye as she dressed. I put on some clothes without paying much attention to details of color or fabric. Finally Sharai walked over and stood in front of me.

"I'm sorry I couldn't tell you the whole story last night, Fiddler." There was a roughness to her voice. "I told you everything I could, more than my father wanted me to tell you."

"Just out of curiosity," I said, yanking open my dresser drawer where the cold comfort of the Detonics waited. "Was screwing me your idea or Rafi's?"

She didn't say anything. She didn't have to. The look she gave me made me feel about an inch long and half an inch high. I swore and jammed the pistol into place in the holster at the small of my back. Sharai wasn't looking at me anymore. She was looking out the window at the ocean where waves turned over and came apart. I went up and stood behind her.

"I'm sorry," I said. "Last night happened, period. I'll settle for that."

"You must understand one thing," she said softly, watching a gull float in the thin, watery light. "Israel is very important to me, but it is Rafi's whole life. And what we're doing is, technically, betraying the interests of Israel. That is how important killing Salameh is to us."

Then she turned and faced me, watching me with eyes that didn't waver. "As for last night, it wasn't supposed to happen." She reached up with one soft hand and touched my cheek. "I swim to feel close to Arye," she said. "I swam out last night, thinking somehow that the water and his presence would turn you into one more man I could use and then forget. But I didn't feel Arye's presence." Her smile was sad and soft and luminous. "At least I didn't feel his disapproval. All I could feel was the anticipation of having you inside me, of holding you next to me. If that was wrong, then—"

I kissed Sharai to shut her up. I kissed her again, more softly, to tell her that it was all right. Then I kissed her because I wanted her and she wanted me. Then we both quit because it was the wrong time, the wrong world, the wrong everything. I held her in my arms for a moment anyway, trying to give her something, reminding her that life held more for her than the execution of her husband's murderer.

"We'll do what we have to do, Sharai," I said into her hair. "Then we'll see what's left."

Her eyes were shadowed, as though she were seeing from one side of history to the other. "Whatever happens—forgive me, remember me. As I will forgive and remember you."

Sharai's smile was as sad as her eyes. Even as I dialed the phone, I heard her car pull out of the driveway and onto the narrow road leading to the rest of the world. I would follow quickly, but I wouldn't catch up. Sharai and I weren't going to the same place.

Benny answered the phone after one ring. It didn't surprise me that he had been awake. He once said that the hour before dawn was the worst for pain, whether physical or mental. I talked to him for less than fifteen seconds and hung up.

The equipment I needed was more than would comfortably fit into the trunk of the Cobra, so I threw the twelve-gauge onto the passenger seat beside me. Newport Beach is a nice place, and real quiet at five-thirty in the morning, but it's not the place to leave a twelve-gauge unattended in an open car. I slung the weapon over my shoulder and headed for the front door.

"Dove season doesn't open until September," Benny said when he opened the front door and saw the pump gun on the sling. "Besides, that bloody short barrel is going to throw too wide a pattern. You won't be able to hit shit on the wing."

The idea of shit on the wing was more than I could handle at this hour. I just shook my head and took the coffee he was holding out to me.

"What's up, mate?" he asked as I shut the door.

I told him everything, including Al-Makr.

"Well, that explains it," said Benny, drumming his strong fingers on the arm of the wheelchair. "One of my old friends ran every data base he could think of at Langley and we couldn't come up with a hit. Then he dug out some old maps. There's an Al-Makr in Libya—one muddy well and three camels. Near as he could tell from recent satellite recon stuff, nothing has changed there since Christ. We finally found a mention of Al-Makr on a map that had been made up for Patton's Second Army. They still called the place Palestine, and we both thought there was some mistake." He looked at me sharply. "That's Israel today, boyo, in case you've forgotten your geography."

"Yeah and amen," I said. "International Constructors is probably running their project through a Swiss subsidiary or something, just to keep its Arab customers in the dark. Whatever, it's clearly a two-billion dollar applecart that neither Jarvis nor the Israelis are willing to upset at the moment."

"What are you going to do?"

I shrugged. "Frankly, my dear, I don't give a damn what's built, where it's built or who builds it. I'm going to get Imbrahim back, and then I'm going to—what's the modern buzz word? neutralize?—yeah, I'm going to neutralize Salameh's ass."

"We used to do that in Vietnam," Benny said, "only we called it terminating with extreme prejudice."

"Me? Prejudiced? Never."

Benny smiled. It wasn't a civilized smile, but then sometimes he isn't very civilized. "What do you need from me?"

"What do you have for killing scorpions?"

Benny always has odd bits of lethal and nonlethal technology around the workshop, most of it too fancy to do a Neanderthal like me any good. We did a turn around the place. I spotted a couple of radios I liked. He showed me a night-vision device from Lytton that he was going to reverse-engineer someday so that a friend of his could copy the design. The device was a hand-held monocular unit that weighed about half a pound and magnified starlight beautifully.

"It's a honey, too," said the King with his usual enthusiasm for high-tech toys. "There's a lady up the strand who likes to sneak out about midnight and skinny-dip in the ocean. She has the most incredible—"

"I don't need to hear about your prurient nocturnal activities," I interrupted.

"She was bloody fascinated when I told her about them," he retorted. "Now she calls me before she goes out, just so I won't miss her. Then she comes over here to borrow a towel. She thinks I have cute wheels."

I handed the monocular back to him. "I'd hate to deprive you of a toy," I said.

"Take it," he said generously. "She's on vacation this week. Just remember that the batteries have a short life. No more than a halfhour of full use before the power pack starts to fade a bit."

"I'll tell the Palestinians to hurry," I said. "What else do you have lying around?"

He wheeled over to a drawer, opened it and brought out a box of grenades.

"They're rather hard on hostages," I pointed out.

"Not these. Magnesium concussion grenades, known to illiterates as flash-bangs," he said. "Pull the pin and four seconds later there's a flash that blinds you and a bang that will knock you on your bum. Of course, you've got your eyes shut and your target picked before you set off the bugger. SAS loves them in hostage situations. Lets their sharpshooters pick off the guys with the guns before the hostages get killed."

"How long will a flash-bang put someone out of commission?"

"Two seconds. Maybe five. Long enough, boyo, if you know what's coming and they don't. Unless the grenade lands on top of someone. Then it's rather permanent. Concussion isn't good for the brain."

"I'll be sure not to drop it in Zahedi's pocket," I said, scooping up four of the flash-bangs and putting them with my other loot. "I'll need some barbecue starter, too."

"Barbecue? Oh . . . C-4."

Benny watched in silence while I stuffed bricks of the plastic explosive into a bag.

"Hell of a roast you're planning," he said.

I didn't argue.

"You still have those special nine-millimeter loads I gave you?" he asked.

Benny had presented me with a handful of pistol rounds some time ago, leftovers from a special order that had been placed by the CIA. The bullets were hard-steel balls that wouldn't take ballistics marks and therefore were untraceable. Unfortunately, that time I'd had to settle for a belt-buckle knife which would escape a pat-down search.

"They're still in the clip," I said.

"They're bloody great under three meters. After that, you'd do better throwing rocks," he warned. "What do you have in the twelve-gauge?"

"Double-aught," I said. "That doesn't take barrel marks either."

"Get a box of deer slugs, too, if you can," he said. "Better range. Or are you doing close work?"

I shook my head. "Wish to hell I knew. They said I'd need a car with plenty of gas. I imagine they'll run me around the barn six or eight times to make sure I'm not the leader of a pack."

"Wait."

The Ice Cream King wheeled swiftly down his workshop and then rolled back just as fast. In his lap he had two items. One was a small electronics unit with a grid screen. The other was a little metal box.

"Bumper beacon," he said. "A little magnetized transmitter to go on your car, and a short-range RDF receiver for whoever wants to keep track of you."

I smiled. "I like it."

"You want some more backup? I'm all right as long as I can wheel."

I hesitated, knowing how good Benny was in a fight. If he had ever flinched, it was so long ago that even God had forgotten. "I wish I could, Benny, but I've got a hunch this one won't go down on city streets."

"Suit yourself, mate," he said cheerfully. "Just remember that these folks have got lots of ways to kill you and you've only got one way to die."

Comforting man, Benny. But then, I hadn't come to him for comfort.

I made good time on the freeways, having started an hour or more before the leading edge of northbound commuter traffic. Rafi was sitting at a table by the window of the fifteenth-floor restaurant, looking down on the slowly congealing traffic headed south down the San Diego Freeway. Rafi was alone at the table but he didn't appear to be lonely. When he turned toward me his face showed the leashed eagerness of a hunter on a fresh trail. His eyes were like a starless winter night—clear, black, bleak. If I had only one avenging Jewish angel on my side, I was glad it was Rafi Yermiya. There wasn't a flinch left in him, either.

Silently he saluted me with his coffee cup. I simply nodded, sat down and told the waitress what I wanted for breakfast. I ordered enough for two men my size because I suspected that it would be a while before I bellied up to another decent meal. A few scraps of steak and eggs in front of Rafi told me that he'd had the same idea.

"I'm glad you realized that we're on the same side," Rafi said.

"Maybe. Maybe not."

He shrugged. "We both want Salameh dead."

"That's number three on my list. Number one is Imbrahim alive. I know you have strong views about Jews and sacrifice, but that old man's not going to die if I can help it."

Rafi watched me with his desolate winter eyes. "I have no problem with that," he said finally, finishing his coffee with the same swift motion that some men use to finish a shot of neat liquor. "But I can't guarantee Imbrahim's safety, either."

"Nobody's safety is guaranteed—not yours, not mine, not his. I'm talking about what the lawyers call 'best-faith efforts.' Give me your word that Imbrahim's life comes before Salameh's death."

"And if I don't?"

"You stay home."

"And you die."

"My problem, not yours. Yours is getting close enough to Salameh to kill him." I watched Rafi, trying to guess what decision he would make and how completely he would abide by that decision. "Look," I said finally, "you can't bring back the eleven Israelis who died in Fürstenfeldbruck. I have a decent chance of bringing another Jew back alive, and that's what I'm interested in."

"Are you sure that's all you're interested in?" Rafi asked sardonically. "Imbrahim is number one on your list. Salameh is number three. Who's number two?"

I studied him for a moment, wondering how to phrase my answer.

"I know where my daughter spent the night," Rafi said. "I also know of her feelings for you. I heard it in her voice when she talked to me this morning."

I drank the orange juice that had been put in front of me and set the glass down gently. "I don't want Sharai to be an executioner." My voice was soft but my determination wasn't. Rafi knew it.

"Would you make a better assassin?" he asked.

I just looked at him.

After a long time he sighed and said, "I wish you had been in Germany twelve years ago. Five police sharpshooters, and none of them had ever fired at a man." He rubbed his hands tiredly through hair that had more gray than black. "All right. If it comes to a choice between saving the old man and killing Salameh, I'll save the old man."

It was hard not to show my relief. I must not have been entirely successful, because Rafi's smile was both sad and savage.

"As for the rest," he said, "it's beyond your control. Sharai is coming with us because she is good and we need someone good."

"She's never killed," I said tightly.

There was a long silence and then Rafi spoke softly, the measured phrases and rhythms of Ecclesiastes rising like the tide between us.

" 'The thing that hath been, it is that which shall be; and that which is done is that which shall be done: *and there is no new thing under the sun.*' " The smile came again, sad and savage as the words themselves. "I sometimes believe all the wisdom of the Jews, the Muslims and the Christians can be found in Ecclesiastes. What a pity we had to destroy that clarity with prophets and messiahs." Rafi leaned forward suddenly, his eyes narrowed, intense. "I'll help you save that timid old Jew," he said coldly, "and then I'm going to kill Salameh if I have to shoot through you to do it."

I looked at Rafi and didn't doubt it. Then I saw his expression change as he looked over my shoulder. I turned and saw Sharai walking toward us. I started to get up, to tell her to go back, that we didn't need her. Rafi's hand clamped around my wrist, holding me in place.

"It's her choice, Fiddler. Hers, not yours!"

Pain shot up my arm but it was nothing compared to the agony of watching Sharai walk across the room toward us and hearing again the words she had spoken this morning: *Forgive me, remember me.*

Sharai looked at me. I said nothing because there was nothing left to say. Whatever I had given her last night hadn't been enough. Rafi was right. It was Sharai's choice and she had chosen death.

12

Imbrahim's house made me angry all over again. I looked at the elegant Korans in their cases, beauty and religion enshrined even though it wasn't Imbrahim's art or faith. Imbrahim had devoted his life to accommodating his world to that of the larger world around him. He had wanted nothing but a reciprocal tolerance—and he had gotten Salameh instead.

Shahpour ushered us through the living room to the kitchen, where his mother was shuffling about in a housecoat and slippers, cooking. When she saw us, tears began to well again in her red, swollen eyes. Shahpour introduced Rafi and Sharai as my friends. Sharai immediately spoke to the old woman in Hebrew. Within moments the two women were talking comfortably.

After a time Sharai turned to me and said, "She recalls that one of the men had a scar on the back of his hand."

Salameh himself. Arrogant as always.

The two women continued to talk. Sharai spoke calmly and reassuringly to the older woman. Shahpour hesitated, then led Rafi and me into his father's office.

"They called over an hour ago," Shahpour said in a low voice. "The man spoke English. He repeated the demand for a half million dollars in small, nonsequential currency. He said Father would be killed very slowly if we didn't follow the instructions." Shahpour looked drawn but controlled. He was puffing on a cigarette, the first I had ever seen him smoke.

"Did you demand to speak with your father?" I asked.

Shahpour nodded. "The man on the phone said that would be impossible until they reached their destination. They would call us then."

"What time did the call come in?"

"Six o'clock, almost exactly."

"And what time was your father taken?"

"Just before five o'clock," he replied.

"I'd guess they took off for wherever they were going immediately," I said to Rafi.

He nodded absently as he began thinking aloud, a man

158

who had dealt with situations like this for most of his adult life. "They would drive carefully, obeying every speed limit to avoid being stopped by the police. At freeway speeds, with time out to call, say an average of fifty miles per hour. Off the freeway—" Rafi shrugged.

"Could you tell anything from the call itself? Was it long distance?" I asked Shahpour.

"I—it's impossible to say. It was a good connection."

"Was there any kind of background noise?" asked Rafi. "Traffic or machinery, airplanes?"

Shahpour shook his head.

"What about the money? You told him there would be a delay, didn't you?" I asked.

"He was very angry when I told him I couldn't get the money right away," Shahpour said. "But you were right. When I explained what I would have to do, he calmed down. I asked for twenty-four hours, and he didn't say no. He said he would discuss that with you when he called back." Shahpour sighed and stubbed out his half-smoked cigarette, only to light another immediately. "I spoke to a friend at the Federal Reserve Bank," he continued. "Our bank itself is liquid enough that I can arrange the currency transfer without special efforts. The Fed will be open at nine. I should be able to pick up the money by eleven."

Sharai and Mrs. Zahedi brought us coffee. We waited in the small office, drinking coffee and watching the phone as though our thoughts would make it ring. I looked more closely at the instrument. It was a business phone with two lines and the usual lighted hold buttons. Nothing new.

Something was nibbling at the edges of my mind, some forgotten phrase trying to work itself into the score. I shut out the rest of the room, the muttered noises and small movements, the silent phone and the old woman's silent tears, and I waited for the thought to surface.

The phone rang first. Eight-oh-three, exactly.

"Answer it," I said to Shahpour, coming out of my chair in a rush. "Keep him on the line as long as you can. Use up time. Say that I'm in the other room and you'll have to get me. Then put the phone on hold and walk away. Got it?"

Shahpour nodded.

The phone rang again. He picked it up. Rafi was right beside me in the hallway. We both listened as the banker answered the phone. Shahpour was a quick study, stumbling and stammering as though he were nervous, making the caller repeat everything twice, using up time.

"He's not here right now," said Shahpour. "You'll have to wait." He paused. "No, no, no. He's nearby. You must just wait a minute. Please." A pause, then Shahpour said almost frantically, "He's in the bathroom! Please, it will just take a minute for—"

Shahpour grimaced and held the phone slightly away from his ear. I tried not to laugh out loud as I thought of Salameh standing on one foot and then the other waiting for me to get out of the can.

"Yes. I'll hurry," said Shahpour. "He'll be here in a minute."

Shahpour punched the hold button and listened to make sure that the line was dead. Then he gave me a thin smile. Nothing like a small sense of control to make a victim feel better.

"It sounds like he's calling long distance now," he said.

"Let's just hope that it's from a phone booth," I said. "Get ready, Rafi. If we wait much longer he'll think we've got a trace on."

Perhaps sixty seconds after the first ring. Rafi was in place at a second extension. I called out "Three, two, one, *go*." We both picked up our receivers.

"If the delay is to allow the police extra time to trace the call, the old man will die, Fiddler."

"Hello, Salameh. Relax about the cops," I said carelessly, speaking at about two-thirds normal speed, slowing things down as much as I could without being obvious about it. "Shahpour didn't understand your instructions or I would have answered the phone myself. There won't be any cops."

"A trace wouldn't do you any good," Salameh continued, "because if I see any police the old Jew will live just long enough to pray for his own death."

Nice man, Salameh. A real prince.

I was listening hard to the background, as well as to Salameh's voice. There was the distinctive hollowness of long distance on the line, but in this day of microwave and satellite relay, it was impossible to tell if it was the long distance of Beirut or Bellflower.

"I did you a favor last night," I said cheerfully. "I prevented somebody from blowing your head off. I should have done the world a favor instead."

He made a sound that could have been either a chuckle or a snarl. Both, probably.

"You sure Jarvis won't be pissed about your latest league fund-raiser?" I continued.

"Mr. Jarvis and I had a conversation, yes," said Salameh. "He told me that for the greater good of Islam, I must withdraw from the league and take my men with me. Unfortunately, we had been counting on league funds to pay for a small lesson in humility to the Israeli government."

"Yeah, sure, I'll just bet you had a real biggie planned," I said, disbelief in every syllable, trying to make Salameh mad enough to be indiscreet. It didn't work. He was all business.

"Do you have the money?" he asked coldly.

"The banks aren't even open yet. It's going to take time. I thought that was explained to you. Besides, nothing happens until I know Zahedi is still alive."

I heard a scuffling sound and then a noise I couldn't place at first. The second time it came I recognized the grunting sound of sudden exertion, then a human groan of deep pain. I held that phone hard enough to leave permanent fingerprints. From a long, long way off, I felt Sharai's hand on my arm, trying to soothe me.

"Do not come! They will kill me anyway! Do not give them money to kill other Jews!"

It was Imbrahim's voice, barely recognizable. There was another sound of pain and then something else, traffic noise. I had a mental image of Salameh opening and closing the phone booth door for Imbrahim's frail, struggling body. I shut down my emotions and listened carefully, filtering out the sounds of human agony. I heard what could have been a diesel tractor laboring through low gears, as though it were moving from a dead stop.

Salameh came back on the line. He sounded just a bit breathless. Without further civilities, he began rapping out instructions.

It was too soon. The operator hadn't come on the line yet to demand more money. I started talking fast and hard, overriding Salameh's words as though I were a man in the grip of nearly uncontrollable rage. It was a convincing gambit, because it wasn't all that far from the truth.

"Listen, you prick. You're a real terror with old men and people tied to chairs. How are you one on one? Did you feel like God and Muhammad all in one when you shot eleven

helpless men to bloody shreds? When was the last time you
went up against someone who was armed? Never, right? You're
chickenshit all the way to the bone. If you aren't hiding behind
dead bodies in Germany you're hiding behind dumb grad students in Los Angeles. Mahmoud Chickenshit Faoud."

"So you know about Munich. You've been a pawn of the
Israelis all along," he said tightly.

"Wrong. I'm a free agent. I do what pleases me, and right
now nothing would please me more than to scrape you off my
boots."

"Surrender in the face of overwhelming odds is honor-
able," said Salameh angrily. "As you say in the West, I lived
to fight another day."

"If I'd been a German cop, they'd still be finding pieces
of you drilled into the pavement cracks."

Sharai's fingers dug into my arm. I took a silent breath
and got a better grip on the tiger of rage that I was riding. I
didn't mind threatening Salameh, getting him off balance, but
I didn't want him cutting and running, leaving Imbrahim dead.

"Are you forgetting that I hold a man's life in my hands?"
asked Salameh softly.

"Not for a second. You'll get your money. As long as
Zahedi is alive and well, you don't have to worry about me.
I'm just a courier."

I kept Salameh talking longer than I'd expected to, but
the phone company wasn't cooperating. Normally, Mabel the
Mechanical Operator comes on as soon as your first three minutes are up. No such luck so far, although it felt like Salameh
and I had been jacking one another around for about three
hours.

Just as Salameh started to say something, I heard the
mechanical beep and the wire sounds as a human operator
cut in.

"Your time is up, sir," she said. "If you wish to continue
your conversation—"

I shut up while she discussed coins with Salameh. I held
my breath for a minute, fearing that she would cut us both off.
Then I heard Salameh mutter and begin to feed more money
into the phone. I gave Rafi a thumbs-up signal and counted.
One, two, three, four, five quarters. It wouldn't be a precise
locator, but it could be the difference between Imbrahim's
death or his freedom.

"You have three hours to get the money," said Salameh. His voice held no emotion. He was under control again.

"No way. I need more time."

"Take all the time you wish," Salameh said softly. "Just be in a town called Indian Wells at five o'clock this afternoon. Don't bother to get there sooner, or with friends. Indian Wells isn't your real destination, merely a place where we will check you for lice."

Indian Wells. The low desert east of Palm Springs. I had been reminded of a place like that recently. When? Who? Under what circumstances? And did it matter now?

"I don't like it," I told him.

Salameh laughed.

"All right," I said flatly, "I'll be there and I'll have the money with me, but it will be wired to enough C-4 to put the case into geosynchronous orbit. If Indian Wells is a trap, all you'll see of that money is a flash when it's blown to confetti."

Salameh stopped laughing. "That's not acceptable."

"Welcome to the big time, asshole. Where in Indian Wells?"

There was a long silence before Salameh gave in. "Check in at the Smoke Tree Hotel," he said. "It's on the main highway. You'll be called there. Bring a vehicle that can take rough treatment. If you break down, Zahedi dies. Five o'clock. No later. And, Fiddler—you better be able to open that case!"

Salameh hung up.

I jabbed the disconnect button with my finger and stood there for a moment, letting my mind run free.

Indian Wells. Desert. Rough roads. Mountains. Rocks. Something hung below the reach of my associations, irritating me like a flat note when the score called for a natural.

Rafi appeared at the door. He had a thoughtful look on his face, as though he were trying to find patterns, too.

"I got a dollar-and-a-quarter phone call and some truck noise," I said. "Did you pick up anything else?"

"He intends to kill you."

I shrugged. "Everybody's got to die of something," I said. "But I don't plan on dying of a scorpion's sting."

I lifted my finger and dialed the Ice Cream King. He answered on the second ring.

"Listen," I said, "you still have friends at the phone company?"

"Nope, just people who owe me favors."

"That's even better. I'm at a phone in Encino. I just got a call from a pay station that cost a dollar and a quarter for three minutes. I'm assuming the call came from somewhere south and east of here, since Salameh is running me out toward Palm Springs. Do you think your friend can do anything with that?"

"It isn't very much," said Benny bluntly. "Anything else that might help?"

"Truck noise, like eighteen-wheelers winding up in first gear from a dead stop, but that could be a lot of places," I said. "The phone company involved is still using human operators on their toll lines."

Benny made a skeptical sound. "I'll do what I can."

I gave him the number in Encino and hung up. Shahpour had come back into the room and was looking at me anxiously.

"Your father is alive and okay," I said, only half a lie. "They'll keep him that way for the time being."

Shahpour let out a long breath and a phrase in Farsi and lit a cigarette with hands that trembled. "Now what do we do?"

"First, you and Rafi go to the Fed and pick up a half million bucks. While you're out, make a cash draw against my personal account. Ten grand. It could be an expensive day."

"I won't take your money," said Shahpour.

I started to argue and found myself talking to Shahpour's back. Rafi gave me a hard smile and went after the rich Iranian. Sharai and I looked at each other. Silently she lifted her hand from my arm and went back to the kitchen to talk to Mrs. Zahedi.

The Ice Cream King didn't call back for almost forty-five minutes. By that time I'd had three more cups of coffee and exchanged six words with Sharai, as well as a hug that made me feel better and worse at the same time.

I nailed the phone before the first ring was finished.

"I'm a sodding genius, mate, even if I get no recognition for it."

"I'll hang a sign from the Goodyear blimp," I said, and felt adrenaline slide into my veins. Benny never brags unless he's brought home the bacon and the rest of the butcher shop, too. "What did you get?"

"The bloody American phone system is pretty simple," he said. "All the rates are established by zones. The guy I called is in the security department at Pacific, and he told me right off the top of his head that a dollar and a quarter's worth of distance from Encino at that time of the day put the call beyond Palm Springs."

"Cut to the chase, Benny. I've got a lot of ground to cover."

"This *is* the chase, boyo. Listen up. That whole area is served by Desert Telephone Company in Indio, and you were right, they're pretty old-fashioned. My security contact called their security man, and their man walked down the hall to the room where their toll operators sit. There were only five on duty at that moment, and one of them remembered placing the call to Encino."

"Jesus Christ," I muttered in disbelief.

"Not really," said Benny modestly. "*I* roll on water. *He* walked. Anyway, the operator told the security man that the call was placed from a booth at a rest stop in Chiriaco Summit. That's about forty miles east of Indio, out at the edge of the Chocolate Mountains."

Chiriaco Summit. Chocolate Mountains. Hunting. Big-horn sheep.

Jarvis.

"Benny, you're a sodding genius," I agreed, "and now I need one more technological miracle."

"No gigs on water please," he said sardonically, "my wheelchair gets too rusty."

"No water. Just computers. A data-base search. Didn't you tell me that somebody had put the property-tax rolls from all fifty-eight counties in California on a single tape?"

"It's called Tax-Text. Kind of expensive—maybe fifty bucks an hour of sign-on time, for those poor sods who don't know any better."

"And you, of course, do."

"Dead right, mate," he said cheerfully. "Tax-Text didn't pay for their information. It was all public record. Therefore, I don't feel bad about stealing their data. Besides, they don't have much of a security system. What am I looking for?"

"A piece of property in Riverside County that's owned by F. Robert Jarvis."

"Call you back in a minute."

He lied. It was almost five minutes.

"Sorry, Fiddler," he said as soon as I picked up the phone. "Nothing for Jarvis himself. International Constructors has an office building in the city of Riverside, if that helps."

"No good. Jarvis himself told me he still has the family homestead out in the Chocolates. He was born there."

The line went dead. I hung up. Two minutes later the phone rang.

"Yeah?" I said.

"Yeah," said Benny. "You've just been treated to a working demonstration of the First Law of Computers: Computers do what you tell them to do, not what you *want* them to do. So I told the little bugger to list any tax bills, no matter the name of the owner, that were sent to F. Robert Jarvis or IC."

"And?" I demanded, hearing the rustle of paper as Benny tore off a print-out.

"Mr. Jarvis himself receives the tax bill on a parcel of land in Grid E, Range 29, Township 73, of Riverside County," Benny said. "You'll be pleased to know that the owner of record is a nonprofit corporation called the Muslim Student League."

Bingo.

There's always a paper trail, somewhere. It's just a matter of asking the right questions in the right places.

"How far is that from Chiriaco Summit?" I asked.

"Figured that would be your next question. My Triple-A sodding-perfect motel and campground guide for interior Southern California"—sound of pages being turned—"tells me that it's about twelve miles, but looking at the map, I'd guess that the roadside rest at Chiriaco is the closest telephone to the old Jarvis homestead."

"I owe you, Benny."

"Like bloody hell you do. Stay alive, mate."

He hung up before I could respond. I remembered a night a long time ago, when he had told me about the hour before dawn and all the varieties of human pain. He'd also told me that I was one of the few people on earth who looked at him and didn't see a wheelchair.

I hung up very softly.

"Fiddler?" asked Sharai.

"It's on," I said without looking at her. "I'm going to see if that chickenshit scorpion can swim." I turned my head and smiled at her. She stepped back just a bit, silently telling me it wasn't one of my most comforting smiles. I looked back at the phone but I was seeing a scorpion going down beneath the green waters of the Nile. "Jarvis has a ranch out on the desert east of Palm Springs. I'm betting that Salameh is there."

For an instant her eyes reminded me of Rafi's. She grabbed

my hand and gave it a quick, hard kiss, as though I'd just granted her an extraordinary favor. I slid my fingers into her hair, rubbing along her scalp until she closed her eyes and arched against me like a cat.

"Rafi and I will leave as soon as he gets back with the money," I said matter-of-factly.

"I'm going with you."

"I don't have time to take care of you. Neither does Rafi."

Sharai laughed, a combination of anger and real amusement. "You sound like an Arab. You forget that I was raised in Israel. I have more training for this kind of thing than you do. You're not going to deprive me of—"

"Of what, Sharai?" I said, cutting across her words. "Of a chance to keep the war going? Of a chance to kill somebody? I wouldn't think that would be much of a loss."

She looked at me and I knew she was remembering last night and the pistol trembling in her hands.

"Let Rafi do it," I said. "Or me, if it comes to that. Both of us have already paid what it would cost you."

"I can kill my own scorpions," she said. Her voice was cold, certain, like Rafi's.

"Sharai, this isn't the Middle East," I said. "This isn't even Fürstenfeldbruck. This is sunny Southern California. Remember? The land of surfers and safe beaches? This is paradise, not a battle zone. You don't have to go to war unless you want to."

She watched me for a moment before she smiled a thin, amused smile. "This from the man who disarmed a bomb in his trunk," she said. "This from the man who handled my pistol as though he had been born with it in his palm. This from the man who has some very interesting scars on his body. Southern California must be very *peaceful* for you to have learned so much, Fiddler."

I started to change the subject. She wouldn't let me. She just kept on talking.

"The world has become a very small place, or the Middle East has become a very big place. It's here, now, and talking about paradise won't make hell go away," she said, her voice both husky and strangely hard. "I won't go away, either. You need me. The gun I carry doesn't care whether I'm male or female, experienced or not. I've had enough training. Now it's time that I take my place under fire. Even Rafi agrees."

"You don't know the cost," I said tightly.

"Others have paid it. Am I so weak and stupid and lifeless that you—"

"No," I said fiercely, pulling her into my arms. "No, that's not it. It's your strength and intelligence and vitality that worry me. Weak people, stupid people, lifeless people, can kill and walk away without knowing what they've done. It's not that easy for the rest of us. I don't think it will be that easy for you."

Sharai wrapped her arms around me and hung on. "I know," she whispered. "Thank you for caring, Fiddler. Thank you for last night."

The only answer I had to that would have hurt both of us and changed nothing, so I simply held her, praying that she wouldn't see anything worth shooting at—and knowing that she would.

Finally I released her and called an old friend. And I mean old. Back to the days of Uncle Jake. Ernie was still in the same business, running a legitimate air taxi service nine to five and running marijuana the rest of the time. I'd saved his ass a long time ago. He hadn't forgotten it. Whenever I needed a pilot who wouldn't talk, Ernie was only too delighted to have me fly his illicit skies.

I told Sharai to stay with Mrs. Zahedi. I had a bit of shopping to do before I would be fully dressed for Salameh's ball. The Sherman Oaks Galeria yielded several suitcases that would conceal the twelve-gauge and the rest of my gear. A sporting goods store sold me a box of single-slug shotgun shells and a complete set of USGS section maps for the low desert.

Shahpour and Rafi were back before eleven. I had forgotten how bulky a half million bucks worth of currency is, until Shahpour dropped the leather suitcase on his father's desk and popped the latches. The used bills, orderly in their thousand-dollar bundles, filled half the case.

"Any problems?" I asked.

"None that couldn't be handled by pledging all the assets of my family's bank."

"With any luck, this loan will be called in before dark," I said. I looked at Rafi. "Ready?"

He nodded. I threw everything into the trunk of Shahpour's Mercedes and headed for the Santa Monica Airport. We had a six-hour cushion, and I had no intention of wasting any of it. Ernie had a Cessna twin waiting for us. I didn't know the pilot, but he took the ten one hundred-dollar bills I peeled off and stuffed them into his pocket like the professional mule he was. He didn't say a damn thing as we loaded luggage. Rafi's suitcase weighed enough for a small arsenal. When it hit the floor with a gun-metal clatter, the pilot didn't even flinch. He gave Sharai a long look; but then, she was worth it, no matter what business you were in.

We popped up through the summer marine layer and the grunge of commuter effluvium. From above the clouds had a clean, fluffy, white look, and the air was crisp. Smog was camped over the inland parts of the city, creating a knife-edge delineation between pollution and sanity.

Rafi and I studied the survey maps. Armed with the map references that I had gotten from Benny, it was easy to find the piece of desert that F. Robert paid taxes on in the name of international relations. The homestead was in rough country between the Salton Sea and Interstate 10, right at the fringe of a big chunk of rocky terrain whose only real function seemed to be as a target for air force, navy and marine bombs. The USGS map was marvelously detailed, right down to a spot in a blind canyon at the end of a small side road. The spot was labeled "Ranch—Abandoned."

I tapped the pilot on the shoulder and pointed at the map.

"You suppose you could find that ranch and give it a quick flyover?"

The pilot studied the map for a minute. "No sweat," he said. "Wait a minute. Cancel that, because it will be a lot of sweat. It's probably a hundred and fifteen out there today. How close a look you want?"

"Low but legal for the first pass."

"And then?"

I shrugged. "Whatever it takes."

The pilot grinned. I knew then that he was Ernie's mule for more than the money. Flyboy was hooked on adrenaline.

For half an hour we flew above the smog line, looking down through the brownish air at the brownish ground. Where we were, the sky was clear and smooth and hot. The pilot used visual flight rules, following the freeway. I sat up front next to him. Sharai sat beside Rafi in one of the backseats and dozed. Her face was troubled, with little sharp lines etched between her eyebrows like permanent scars. Father and daughter had talked quietly in Hebrew for a few moments after we took off. Whatever they had said obviously hadn't been much comfort to her.

While Sharai slept, Rafi studied the map again, as though he were trying to burn its contour lines into his brain. He was wearing rough clothes—tan khaki the color of the desert—and his jacket gapped open just enough to reveal the butt of a Browning nine-millimeter looped to his belt. He wore the pistol high and reversed. Like Rafi, the weapon was worn, competent and hard.

We left the eastern edge of the Los Angeles metroplex behind us at San Bernardino. The landscape pitched up and began to rumble a bit. The mountains on either side pinched in, rising to peaks so high only rock could survive. Between the mountains was the flat fault zone known as the San Gorgonio Pass. Civilization began to thin; subdivisions became scattered houses which, in turn, yielded to open country with an occasional ranch and small blot of roadside development. The inhabited areas were a startling green, like emeralds thrown onto sand. This wasn't real desert. Not yet. But soon. I began to sweat as the sun and the temperature climbed.

The true desert began east of Banning, where chaparral gave way to scrub cedar and then, suddenly, to creosote and paloverde and cholla. The heat of the desert rose, creating clear-air turbulence. The Cessna was batted around without warning. Sharai woke with a start and for a moment looked lost. I reached back to touch her hand, anchoring her in the present. She gave me an uncertain smile, as though she had just awakened from a bad dream and wasn't sure that reality was much better.

In the hard light of the low desert sun, the land changed. Except for the garish primaries of the cars on the freeway, colors bleached to dry browns and grays and tans. The ground itself seemed gnarled and twisted by the heat. The center of the cabin of the airplane was cool from the air conditioning, but sunlight beat in through the thick Plexiglas until the windows radiated warmth like heat lamps.

As Rafi watched the ground beneath us change, he changed too. He sat without moving, shut down like a desert animal, spending no effort on movement unrelated to survival. I sensed the same changes taking place in myself, but to a much smaller degree. I'm comfortable in the desert, but Rafi was born to it.

He looked up from the map opened across his thighs. "Your country is so extravagant," he murmured, pointing to the map. "If my country had had maps like this, we would have won every war for the last forty years." He shook his head slightly. "And the maps, if they existed, would be guarded like the military secrets they are!"

The pilot checked over his left shoulder, keeping an eye on the interstate just off the left wing. The divided road looked like a striped gray snake curving across the brown landscape. Every five or ten miles a side road branched off and headed into the mountains or out onto the sandy flats. Some roads were paved at the beginning, but quickly faded to dirt tracks that lost themselves in the rock hills and mountains that thrust up from the desert floor.

Off the right side of the plane, the straightedge streets and palm-lined boulevards of Palm Springs grew out of the base of Mount San Jacinto. A jetliner rose up from the airport runway at the east edge of town. The commercial development along California 111 at the base of the Santa Rosas appeared as a narrow green stripe painted on either side of the highway. Beyond the green was rock and sand and saltbush. The desert was flat, broken only by sudden upthrustings of wind-gnawed rock and a scraggly coating of brush. The farther east we went, the thinner the veneer of living plants became.

Fifteen minutes east of Palm Springs, Indio sprawled over the sand. The town was surrounded by a few thousand acres of vineyards, grapefruit groves and irrigated alfalfa fields. Agriculture existed because of the Coachella Canal, a man-made ditch that dragged irrigation water a hundred miles across the desert from the Colorado River. The canal ran past the north edge of the Salton Sea, which was no more than a great brackish lake left behind eighty years ago when the Colorado leaped its banks in a magnificent flood. Over the years the sun had shrunk the sea to the point that the water had gone from fresh to too salty even for striped bass and corbina. The game fish were dying out, leaving their bones to drift down to the muddy, lifeless bottom of a sea that was itself dying.

"Salameh should be comfortable down there," I said to Rafi, pointing at the checkerboard of irrigated fields and untouched desert. "One of those little towns is called Mecca."

Rafi's mouth shifted in what could have been a smile. "I wonder if he prayed today."

The airplane had been losing altitude slowly since we left Indio behind. The pilot was following the Coachella Canal, skirting the edge of the rock hills that humped up a few thousand feet above the sand. There was a scattering of houses and a palm grove or two along the eastern edge of the Salton Sea, but otherwise the desert showed no man-made scars.

"Have him fly this course," Rafi said.

His blunt finger traced a railroad line that cut inland between two small mountain ranges. Once the railroad had supplied Eagle Mountain Mine, before Kaiser Steel had gone down under a wave of domestic labor demands and imported steel. The map showed an unimproved road running through the crease between the two mountain ranges and directly past the mouth of the canyon that held the Jarvis ranch.

I showed the pilot the course we wanted and said, "Stay at five thousand until I tell you different."

He changed heading and maintained altitude without a word. Below, the black-and-gray granite of the Orocopias Mountains pushed up to just over two thousand feet. If we stayed high, we'd look like any other small plane bound for Phoenix.

The Orocopias were five miles across and barren. At this altitude the only sign of human activity was the spill of dark red mine tailings on a steep gray slope. The binoculars brought up enough detail to see the open mouth of an abandoned, unsealed mine, but only God Himself knows what might have been dug out of that hole. It was a remnant of the grubstake and jackass days. I saw no sign of a road anywhere. Like the Orocopias and the desert itself, the mine was a monument to loneliness and perseverance.

I wondered how the hell Jarvis's parents had found enough to survive on, much less raise kids.

Ahead, the Chocolate Mountains rose to more than four thousand feet, every inch as barren as a fistful of rock. The map showed the old ranch in a crease between the two ranges, but from a distance it didn't look as though there was a break in the mountains for fifty miles.

As we approached, the Orocopias fell away and revealed a flat, boulder-strewn dry wash that snaked between the two ranges. The wash was wide enough to accommodate a single strand of railroad tracks and, beside it, a dirt road. The rail line was an old spur that ran from the Southern Pacific main line at the edge of the Salton Sea to the Eagle Mountain Mine. The road was called the Bradshaw Trail. It ran twenty miles from the brackish sea through the wash to Interstate 10.

There wasn't one damned sign that anyone had been in

he area since Jarvis left fifty years ago. I combed the desert
with the binoculars, looking for something, anything, to tell
me that I hadn't guessed wrong, that Imbrahim was down there
somewhere, that I had even one chance in hell of pulling him
out alive.

I didn't see anything but the shadow of the airplane raking
over the unforgiving land.

13

Rafi's hand closed hard around my arm.

"There," he said, pointing without lowering his binoculars.

Even with his coaching I almost missed the faint dirt track that took a tangent off the trail, headed across the railroad track, and vanished into a lateral canyon.

"Follow that," I said to the pilot, pointing to the vague, pale line.

Like Rafi, the pilot was experienced at reading the desert from the air. We were too far up to see whether the road had been used recently. The wind can be fierce back in those canyons. After a few weeks nothing is left to mark a vehicle's passage except dead plants and scars on rocks.

"Come on, come on," I muttered to the distant trail, feeling time slipping away from me as surely as windblown sand. "Get wherever you're going."

I found the corral without glasses, but I almost missed the house and outbuilding. They were huddled among freight-car-sized boulders, and the structures had been built of the same water-rounded granite stones that littered the dry wash. The house was as good a demonstration of natural camouflage as I'd ever seen.

It also looked as uninhabited as a handful of sand. I began to sweat from more than the heat pouring through the windows. If Zahedi and the Arabs weren't here, I was fresh out of bright ideas for saving the life of the man who had been foolish enough to trust me.

Then I saw it.

"There's a car in the shadow at the back of the house," I said, staring through the glasses, hearing the relief in my voice and not giving a damn.

"There's another car under cover in the rocks at the mouth of the canyon," Rafi said. "They have sentries out."

I stared for several moments before I saw sunlight glinting off a windshield through holes in camouflage netting. The flash of light was perhaps four hundred yards from the house, at the

174

mouth of the lateral canyon. The car was small, a dune buggy or the like. No one moved near it.

"They're probably up in the rocks, out of the sun, watching traffic coming up the wash," Rafi said as though he had been reading my mind. "Arabs post two men together, to keep one another awake. They hate to sit watch alone."

The pilot gave Rafi a quick, speculative glance out of the corner of his eye but said nothing. Any friend of Ernie's friend was a friend of his, too.

We were almost directly over the house and outbuilding at the end of the canyon. The place looked deserted except for the green Firebird that was tucked among the boulders. Despite the lack of movement, there was no doubt that the place was inhabited, or at least cared for. The pole corral was intact and the roof of the house and rock-walled shed were solid.

The rocky massif behind the house rose up and blanked out our view.

"You want me to go around again?" the pilot asked.

I looked at Rafi. No use having experts if you don't use them.

"Hold this heading for a few minutes, go up to eight thousand and swing around to fly the canyon north to south," Rafi said. Then, in a low voice to me, "We'll look like another aircraft."

The pilot didn't need the explanation. He knew how the "change your profile" game was played. He flew us east and north, gaining altitude.

"That's Chiriaco Summit," said the pilot. The rest stop straddled the interstate on the shoulder of a rising plain eight miles away. "There's a pretty good strip there, if you want to get down on the ground."

"How about at the other end of the wash?" I said. "Maybe something with a Hertz counter."

"Well, there's the North Shore Airport," he said. "I don't know if there's a Hertz, but Ernie's got a few contacts around here if you need wheels and aren't fussy."

"The closer the better," I said, hearing minutes whisper away like sand. It was one o'clock. One way or another, I had to appear at Indian Wells by five.

The pilot was good—but then, the ones who survive tend to be. The rest end up pranged on a rocky summit with a load

of weed for a funeral pyre. Flyboy got on the radio while we
flew the north-south leg, down the gut of the big canyon between the two mountain ranges. I saw two vehicles winding
along, both moving quickly enough to raise small rooster tails
of dust, a good indication that the road was in decent shape.
The south end of the rift opened up in an alluvial fan that was
cut by the canal and transversed by the road and the rail line.
There were a few houses scattered across the fan, and more
down at the shore of the sea. Other than a car or two, there
was no sign of life. Man, like the other desert creatures, had
gone underground and pulled the hole in after him to escape
the searing sun.

We passed over the Jarvis ranch at eight thousand feet.
From where I sat I could see three other small aircraft at various
altitudes.

"Lot of air traffic through here?" I asked the pilot.

"All the time, man. This is the Phoenix route."

"Many people make low passes?"

He laughed. "Are you kidding? Half the assholes in the
air are frustrated jet jockeys. They go down on the deck and
count jackrabbits just for kicks."

I looked over at Rafi. He nodded.

"You like counting jackrabbits?" I asked the pilot, pulling
two hundred-dollar bills out of my wallet.

There was a two-beat pause while flyboy counted zeroes.
The bills vanished. The plane dove. We were down on the
deck so fast I saw spots.

He held the plane just under a hundred feet for a northbound pass up the big canyon, following the serpentine wash
like a coyote running down a rabbit. Below us, the sound must
have been brutal when it bounced off the rocks. As we passed
the mouth of the small lateral canyon that held the Jarvis ranch,
two young Arabs popped out of the shade like rabbits out of a
hole.

We were so low that I felt like I should lean back from
the Plexiglas to avoid being recognized by the graduate physics
student I had trailed to the USC campus. Mrs. Zahedi had
been right: both Arabs carried Kalashnikov assault rifles, but
they seemed more curious and amused than belligerent. They
watched the Cessna with open mouths, flinching when the
sound of the twin engines hammered off the canyon walls.

I looked over at the pilot. He was smiling, utterly focused

in the screaming instant of speed. I hadn't seen a smile like that since I let a friendly enemy drive my Cobra.

A mile up the wash, the pilot sent us into a sweeping loop, twisted over and pulled a few gees, and was ready to make a run up the lateral canyon and over the ranch house. The scream of the engines preceded us up the narrow canyon. As we came by, three men stood in the shadow of the porch, watching us. Rafi got his glasses up long enough to identify them.

"Salameh," he said quietly.

Sharai twisted in her seat as though she would see her husband's murderer face-to-face, but it was too late. The house and the small canyon were gone, blurred into the desert by the speed of the Cessna's passage. Sharai was gone, too. It was there in her eyes as she looked down the long tunnel of the past, time blurring into one endless soul-destroying war.

"Take us down where we can rent a car," I said harshly.

For a moment it was as though the pilot hadn't heard me. Then he shook his head, throwing off the trance of speed and adrenaline and skill. No one said anything until we were on the ground again.

It was like landing in hell. Heat began to build the instant we touched the sun-bleached strip at the North Shore Airport. Sunlight drilled through the windows and welled up from the tarmac. The plane's air conditioner couldn't do any more than take off the top ten degrees. We were all sweating by the time we coasted to a stop on the shores of California's version of the Dead Sea.

There wasn't a Hertz outlet, but the guy who ran the airport knew someone who knew someone who knew Ernie. Thirty minutes later I had rented a four-wheel drive Bronco, two hundred dollars and no names asked or given. I didn't even have to sign a waiver for additional collision coverage. The Bronco had already acquired its full allotment of dings and dents.

We loaded three people and three suitcases into the Bronco's rolling oven. First stop was a fisherman's store. There we bought three Lister Bags, which we filled with water, and some light-colored adjustable baseball caps. With our dusty, scruffy clothes and idiot hats, we looked just like all the other suburban explorers driving a four-by-four into the boonies.

It was one-thirty when we left the highway and headed up the dusty road that paralleled the Coachella Canal.

"I counted five," I said.

It was Rafi who sat beside me, and Rafi who answered. Sharai was present in body but not in mind. She had been that way since she had heard Salameh's name.

"At least six," said Rafi matter-of-factly. "At all times they'll have a man sitting in the room with the hostage. At the first sign of an attack, the hostage dies."

I recalled the kidnapping of the NATO general, Dozier, in Italy. "Sounds like the Red Brigades."

"Terrorists attend the same schools," Rafi said. "I've read their textbooks."

"And written a few of your own?"

Rafi didn't answer.

The two lane dirt road was wide and well graded until it crossed over the canal. The waterway was cement-lined, straight, rough as double-coarse sandpaper. There was nothing to disturb the flow of water. It slid by like a freight train in the thirty-foot-wide ditch. The surface looked cool, smooth and inviting. I knew better. That unfenced canal was the most dangerous predator in the desert, including the rattlesnake.

Sharai watched the slick blue-black water as we crossed the narrow bridge.

"A miracle, all that water in the desert," she said slowly.

"It's also a killer," I said. "Those canal walls are slick with algae and the current is going like hell. Get in and you won't get out until somebody throws you a rope or fishes you out with a grappling hook. The locals know, but every year they lose a few Mexican field hands who never saw a river they couldn't wade."

"Stupidity is a capital crime in any desert," said Rafi.

"How about ignorance?" I retorted.

"In the desert there's no difference."

The road narrowed and began picking its way across the alluvial fan. The outwash had carried sand and talus from the two mountain ranges onto the flats. The smallest rocks were carried the greatest distance by the intermittent floods, which meant the rocks got bigger as we came up from the valley floor to the mouth of the big canyon between the two mountain ranges.

When we entered the wash, the mountains on either side pinched the dirt road and the abandoned railroad line together. The two began to run side by side. The sun had just passed zenith but the temperature climbed. The rocky walls of the wash radiated heat into the covered Bronco. I guessed the temperature was near a hundred and twenty, but neither Rafi nor Sharai seemed bothered by it. Despite the heat and dust and wind pouring through the open windows, Sharai looked almost cool in her khaki shirt and shorts. The deeper into the searing desert canyon we went, the more abbreviated the conversation became.

"How far?" asked Sharai.

"On the map, nine miles to the mouth of the lateral canyon," I answered.

"There was an oasis at about eight miles," said Rafi. "The way the land lies, the sound of the motor will carry to the ranch if we get much closer than that."

As he spoke, he was watching the road and the canyon walls and squinting a bit from the sun.

"What do you have in mind?" I asked.

He looked sideways at me. "Our course is fairly obvious, isn't it?"

I waited for him to tell me the obvious so we could compare notes. Then we could have a tug-of-war over who did what and with which and to whom—if it came to that. I was hoping it wouldn't come to that.

"I will tell you exactly what will happen," said Rafi in a clipped voice, as though he were lecturing a class of recruits. "Having lured you and a half million dollars out into the desert, the Arabs will grab the money, walk you and Zahedi up into the rocks, kill you and leave your bones to be scattered by scavengers."

I nodded. So far, Rafi and I were in absolute agreement.

"The terrorists have only one vulnerable moment," continued Rafi as though he were reading from a textbook. "That will be when you, Zahedi, the money and Salameh are all together in one place. That will come at the ranch house in the small canyon."

I nodded again. So far, so good—or bad, if it went down according to terrorist textbook numbers.

"That's why you're going to take me in as close as you can," continued Rafi. "I'll climb the mountain and come in behind the ranch house."

"Your knee."

It was all I said. It was enough. Rafi slanted a hard look over his shoulder at Sharai for telling me. She gave him back the same look.

"It's not a difficult climb and there are several hours before dark," Rafi said coolly.

"I'll go," said Sharai quietly.

"Like hell you will!" Rafi and I said at once. Then he continued and I shut up. "I trained you for close work," he said coolly, "and that's how you will be used. If you object to that, get out now. Fiddler will pick you up on the way back out."

"But your knee—" she began.

"Stop the car!" ordered Rafi.

I let off on the accelerator. Instantly Sharai shut up. She wasn't dealing with her father anymore. She was dealing with a professional soldier, spy and assassin who would not bend at all. Just the man to take on Salameh, if she would only admit it and if Rafi's knee would only hold out.

I fed gas again. There were no more objections.

"When you arrive with the money," continued Rafi as though nothing had happened, "and when the moment is right, I'll take my best shot at the man guarding Zahedi. After that, it's everyone to his target of opportunity. There won't be much you can do but grab the old man and take cover."

"Why?"

Rafi looked at me as though I were unbelievably stupid. "You won't be armed."

"Don't bet on it."

He sighed and began to lecture me as he had undoubtedly lectured other frogs who wanted to be scorpions.

"Salameh will have you and the car searched thoroughly before you're allowed close to him. Their whole purpose is 'to eliminate the chance of any rude surprises,' as one of their textbooks puts it."

"Fair enough," I said, not looking up from the driving, which had gotten a bit tricky now. "I haven't had the advantage of advanced graduate study in Cuba or Lebanon, but I spent that time on the phone with Salameh doing more than waiting for the operator to wake up. I established a definite pattern, that of a proud man who will cooperate only as long as he considers the risks to be rational."

"What do you mean?" asked Sharai.

"Delivery of the ransom is rational only if I'm sure Imbrahim is alive, so I made sure he was alive. Being wary but not terrified of Salameh is rational, but wandering unarmed into the back country with a half million in cash definitely is

THE FROG AND THE SCORPION

ot. I won't do it. Salameh will piss and moan but in the end
e'll give in because he expects me to be so badly outgunned
hat the only thing I could carry to make a difference would
e a Sherman tank."

Rafi was watching me carefully. "So you did it on pur-
ose," he said, fishing a cigarette out of his pocket. "I thought
ou were just strutting for Sharai." He cupped the match against
he wind, ducked his head quickly, lifted it and blew out a
ong stream of smoke. Then he laughed softly. "If you pull it
ff, you'll be a footnote in my textbook."

"Thanks, but I'd rather be alive."

Rafi's smile thinned. "Wouldn't we all?" Then his face
ecame even harder as he drew on his cigarette and thought
uickly. "You might bully them into letting you keep a small
istol, since you'll be alone."

"Alone!" exploded Sharai from the back seat. "And just
what in hell am I going to do—walk home?"

With a single look Rafi silenced her. "You're a woman,"
e said calmly. "As far as the Arabs are concerned, Fiddler is
lone when he is with you."

I remembered Sharai's fear and determination as she waited
or Salameh to turn her into an assassin. She may have been
nexperienced but she wasn't someone to be ignored. I knew
t and was damn glad the Arabs didn't.

"Don't be surprised if I come out of the car with more
han a pistol," I said.

"If you manage that, I'll give you a whole chapter," Rafi
said dryly. "These people cut their teeth on Kalashnikovs and
RPG-7s. No matter how you break down an automatic weapon,
hey'll recognize the pieces."

He said no more, settling back in the seat, smoking in
silence, inspecting the canyon walls and his own thoughts.

The oasis had fallen on hard times. Some budding arsonist
had repeatedly set fire to the beards of the palm trees until
he green fronds of the topknots were scorched and all but
dead. The ground beneath the palms was littered with beer
cans and polyurethane containers. Neither the aluminum nor
the plastic would degrade this side of the Second Coming. I
found a spot of shade beneath a rock overhang where the
Bronco was concealed from the road.

Rafi opened his suitcase. He had come prepared both for
the desert and for action. He pulled out a pair of mini-Uzis
and ten thirty-two-round clips.

"Uncle Jake would have loved you," I said, shaking my head.

"Oh?"

"Yeah. He was a smuggler. Like you."

Rafi smiled swiftly, looking almost human for an instant. "I didn't smuggle these into the country. I bought them at a surplus store in Santa Monica. They were legal semi-automatics—until I made some adjustments." He picked up one of the weapons, hefting it gently. "Now they work as well as anything in the Israeli armory."

I dragged out my own suitcase and produced the twelve-gauge, which I had broken down for travel.

"You interested in diversifying your holdings?" I asked.

Rafi took the pump gun and looked it over. I showed him the mixed box of buckshot and shotgun slugs I had put together.

"Oh, but these are both outlawed by the Geneva Convention," he said mockingly.

"No shit. Want to trade? One of your Uzis might work better for what I have in mind."

"And what is that?" asked Rafi.

It was more of a demand, actually, but I didn't let it get to me. I liked the looks of Rafi's Uzi.

"Weed, guns or blue jeans, it's all the same to a smuggler," I said.

"Like your Uncle Jake," said Rafi sardonically.

"And me, sometimes. Like now."

Rafi hesitated over the trade until I threw in the night scope that the Ice Cream King had loaned me. If the Arab jerked us around until dark, the scope would be worth its weight in diamonds. That, plus the night sight on the shotgun, persuaded Rafi to give up one of his nasty little Uzis. He smiled over the luminous bead on the shotgun barrel, handed me an Uzi and four clips and took the pump gun.

"You ever used an Uzi before?" he asked.

I was too busy checking out the gun to answer. It worked very sweetly, fast and positive, like the gearshift on a race car. As I put the weapon aside, I looked up in time to find Rafi watching with an odd expression on his face. I guess my smile was a shade wolfish, because he smiled back like the manhunter he was and began rummaging in my suitcase for other items to fill his backpack.

One of the ultra-small radios that the Ice Cream King had provided disappeared, along with an earphone and the mixed box of shells for the shotgun. The rest of the clips for his Uzi followed. He picked up the receiver for the bumper beeper unit and, without comment, tucked it into his backpack. Obviously he had seen and used such tracking devices before. When he came to the flash-bangs, he smiled.

"Grenades?" he asked. "How unsporting." He laughed softly and took two of the four for himself.

"Flash-bangs," I corrected. I began to explain, but Rafi's next words told me to save my breath.

"Too bad they aren't fragmentation. But flash-bangs are better than nothing, especially if you drop them down someone's throat." Rafi tied one of the Lister Bags to the bottom of the pack and then slung and reslung the submachine gun and the shotgun on his shoulders until they rode without knocking against one another. He took the Browning from the holster on his belt and handed the pistol to Sharai. Then he calmly rolled up his left pant leg, pulled out a hypodermic kit and shoved the steel needle deep beneath his kneecap. Sweat stood out on his face from pain, but he didn't rush the job. He shot up that knee as thoroughly as a team doctor working over high-priced meat just before the Super Bowl.

When Rafi was finished, I moved away ten or fifteen yards to let father and daughter speak in private. I saw Sharai give Rafi a hard hug. He hesitated, then put his arms around her and held her as though she were a little girl. When Sharai came back to me there were tears in her eyes.

"Walk with me for a way," Rafi called to me.

Sharai stayed in the shade of the overhang, watching the suitcase with the ransom money in it, as Rafi and I moved down the Bradshaw Trail on foot. The air was hot, clean, as dry as stone. Sweat evaporated almost as quickly as it formed. The canyon was silent except for the click of rocks dislodged by our boots and the distant, muted drone of a small plane high overhead. I looked up for a moment, caught by the image of the people wrapped in their own worlds, their own worries, their own pleasures.

"If there were a way for me to trade places with you, I would," Rafi said, following my glance to the plane.

I shrugged. I wouldn't have traded with him anyway, and he knew it. Imbrahim was my responsibility.

We walked on a few minutes more, feeling sunlight sliding like knives through our clothes. Rafi no more limped than I did.

"What was the name of that beer we drank?" he asked.

"Corona."

"Yes. Corona. And the food?"

"Chiles rellenos, tamales, frijoles refritos."

"Tell Luz I enjoyed her cooking."

"She comes every Thursday. Tell her yourself."

Rafi just smiled.

I knew how he felt. Here on the searing desert, backpack loaded with death, next Thursday was at the other end of the universe, untouchable, unthinkable.

We approached a point where the rough road curved around one of the large boulders that littered the floor of the wash. With a gesture, Rafi signaled me to wait. Staying on the shadowed side of the huge rock, he took out his field glasses and found a cleft close to the ground where he could look up the wash from concealment. Thirty seconds on his belly in the sand, and he had finished inspecting the desert canyon. Then he waved me over.

Even in the shade of the rock the sand was warm. Rafi's big glasses brought up incredible detail, including the nose of the dune buggy partially concealed beneath netting at the mouth of the canyon. It took me a moment to find the two Arab sentries. They had changed positions, following the shade around the boulders. Both men were wearing the checkered headdresses that I had seen at the Jarvis party.

"America has made them sloppy," said Rafi. "Their sentry post is exposed to fire."

"They aren't expecting anything."

"Yes," said Rafi, satisfaction in his hard face. "Men die that way—not expecting anything. I was in Menachem Begin's Irgun, back before Israel got its freedom. We fought the first Salameh. He was killed in a desert like this, trying to capture some wells at a place called Ras el-Ein outside Jerusalem." Rafi shifted his body, moving the glasses to a new quarter. His boots made subtle grating sounds against the sand. "Assume that they'll inspect you again at the mouth of the small canyon, even if they've inspected you every meter of the way before."

"Damn. That won't give me much time to dig out and assemble the Uzi."

"Too bad Sharai has to drive. She can put together an Uzi blindfolded in less time than I can. Very quick hands." He touched my sleeve, silently urging me to withdraw from our position.

"How do you expect to go in?" I asked when we were both back up the wash, out of sight and sound of the guards.

Rafi pointed toward a ridgeline that ran perpendicular to the main body of the canyon between us and the sentry post. "In a little while the shadows will lengthen but the sun will still be in the sentries' eyes. When we flew over the second time, I saw what looked like a path through the rocks and over to the lateral canyon where the ranch house is. The climb will be fairly easy, and I have plenty of time. I'll be in position before Salameh contacts you in Indian Wells." He turned and looked at me with eyes blacker than Sharai's. "Any questions?"

"I'm going to try to stall as much as possible on the way in," I said. "Darkness will be to our advantage."

For an instant Rafi looked surprised. "You've done this before, haven't you?"

"Not very often," I said. Then, softly, "Too often."

If Rafi heard, he didn't say anything. "I won't turn on the radio until six o'clock, in order to save the batteries," he said. "It won't have much range in these rocks anyway." He shouldered the pack and the two weapons and adjusted the baseball cap on his head. The cap's neutral brown melted into the colors of the desert like the rest of his clothes.

He turned to go, then looked back at me. "Don't worry about Sharai. She won't flinch. Treat her as you would a man."

I clamped down on the rage that ripped through me, but it showed in my voice. "I'm going to have to," I said tightly. "But Christ! If it comes to a choice between her life and Imbrahim's—"

"She volunteered," interrupted Rafi curtly. "Zahedi didn't. If someone dies because you didn't trust Sharai, blame yourself, not her." He watched me with black eyes. "There is a time for every purpose under heaven," he said, echoing Ecclesiastes. "This is Sharai's time, my time. Don't get in our way, Fiddler."

My hand shot out and wrapped around Rafi's arm hard enough to feel the bone beneath the flesh. "Remember," I said. "Zahedi's life comes first. Killing Salameh comes second."

"And you remember: one shot for the hostage guard and my promise to you is kept."

I looked into Rafi's bleak, patient eyes and saw Ethan Edwards all over again. I lifted my hand. Rafi turned and moved off through the boulders, keeping heavy cover between himself and the sentry post. Despite the forty or fifty pounds of gear on his back and a game knee, he didn't limp. He moved with a rolling gait that looked slow but wasn't. It wasn't noisy, either. Quick, silent, lethal, Rafi was like a primitive force loosed upon an equally primitive land.

And a time for every purpose under heaven. Or above hell, for that matter.

I turned and walked back to the oasis where the Indian killer's daughter waited. Sharai was sitting alone in the driver's seat of the Bronco. She handed me the second Lister Bag as I climbed in. While I drank she started the engine. The canvas bag was porous and had sweated enough that the water inside was almost cool. It tasted better than wine.

Sharai didn't drive like a cultural attaché. She drove like the professional her father had trained her to be. What she lacked in strength she made up for in timing. As Rafi had noted, she had very quick hands. She held the Bronco to a fast pace on the rutted, sand-drifted road. The twin lines between her eyes could have been concentration or something else. Thoughts as bleak as Ecclesiastes, perhaps.

I considered trying to argue her out of coming back with me, but even as the thought came I knew it would be a waste of my time and her mental energy. Neither of us had any to waste. And I needed her. I settled back in my seat and did the only useful thing I could. I slept, storing up energy for what was to come.

I woke up in time to see the pilot come strolling out of the shadows of one of the small hangars, wiping his hands on a grease rag as we pulled up on the apron near his plane. He didn't ask about Rafi as we loaded suitcases into the Cessna. After two hours in the sun, the plane was hot enough to cook pizzas. I left Sharai watching the money and went to call the Palm Springs Airport.

When I came back the pilot had the engine and the air conditioner at full max. Twenty minutes after we took off we landed at Palm Springs and taxied over to the general aviation flight line. A Latino kid was sitting on the hood of a new Toyota Land Cruiser waiting for us, just like the Hertz operator on the 800 number had promised he would be. The name and driver's license I gave Hertz was from one of the spare IDs I always carry, but the money I handed the kid was real. He took off, contract and cash clutched in hand.

"You want me to wait around?" asked the pilot as he landed down the last suitcase.

I considered the possibilities. "Ernie schedule you tonight?"

"Nope. I'm yours till death or the narcs do us part," he said cheerfully.

I handed over another two hundred. "Have dinner on me. Then go to the North Shore strip and kill some time. If someone doesn't come by midnight, leave."

He gave me a thumbs-up, slammed the plane door behind him, locked a brake and spun back onto the taxiway. He was airborne before Sharai and I settled into the Toyota. I flipped her the keys and pulled a suitcase onto my lap. I broke down the Uzi and put its pieces and ammo clips back into the case along with everything else Benny had given me. Then I told Sharai to stop at the J. C. Penney's on Tahquitz-McCallum Way. I bought five packages of plain cotton dishtowels and pointed Sharai in the direction of Highway 111.

Cathedral City has a nice, tony sound to it, until you hear the locals refer to it as "Cat City." As usual, the locals know more than the maps. If you can't afford the action in Palm Springs, there's always the shopworn pleasures of Cat City nearby. I spotted a garage a half-block off the highway. It took me two minutes and a hundred-dollar bill to convince the guy in charge of the tire shop that he needed to take a half-hour beer break at the tavern across the street.

Sharai watched with both amusement and amazement as I went underneath the Land Cruiser, jerked the spare tire and put it on the tire machine. I pulled the pin valve in the stem and air began hissing out.

"What are you doing?" she asked finally.

"Just what it looks like." Then, before she could speak, "We had a flat on the way here, remember?"

"No."

"Start remembering it. If the Arabs want to know why the spare isn't on the rack underneath, our stories better match," I said. "Get the Uzi and wrap the pieces real tight in the towels I bought. Clips, radio, beeper and flash-bangs, too. Turn on the beeper before you wrap it."

Sharai was fast. By the time I had slipped the heavy breaker tool under the bead of the tire and peeled it halfway around, she had everything ready. I stuffed the cloth-wrapped pieces into the tire one by one. The Uzi was a bastard going in Coming out would be worse. I thought of that short, bumpy road up the lateral canyon to the house and cursed as I threw in the bumper beacon.

I used the tire tool to pop the tire back onto the rim. Then I looked around the shop for a sharp piece of trash. There was a wide selection to choose from because the place hadn't been swept since Muhammad was born. I chose a two-inch rusty nail and hammered it between the treads of the spare. I reinstalled the needle valve in the stem, partially reinflated the tire and pulled it off the machine. I bounced the tire hard a few times on the concrete floor of the shop, and heard nothing I shouldn't have—like metal banging against metal, for instance. The tire was heavier now, but I doubted anyone would notice. Offroad tires are heavier than the civilized kind anyway.

"I'd hate to drive too far on it, even without the nail," I said as I tossed the wheel and tire onto the back deck of the enclosed Land Cruiser. "Uncle Jake tried that once, smuggling bricks of grass out of Mexicali. He almost shook his old Buick apart. A loaded tire doesn't balance worth shit."

I drove this time. By four o'clock, we were in Indian Wells

14

The low desert has a unique charm, but don't look for it in the block-wide strip of inhabited land on either side of Highway 111. The Ali Baba Motel offended me. Maybe it was just the coyly salacious come-on lettered across the front of the four-hundred-room two-story tan stucco flophouse. The desert wind had stolen some of the letters, but enough remained that you could read: "X-rated Movies in Your Own Harem for the Night—$22.50 plus tax."

Indian Wells was a little more pricey. Even in the off season, the Indian Wells Inn was not afraid to ask for $150 a night, double occupancy. The ornate rosewood front desk was staffed by bilingual dark-skinned young men with the obligatory hawklike profiles, and the register was printed in Arabic and English. This was probably where International Constructors brought their Arab princes to relax from the agonizing strain of representing the House of Saud in the decadent West.

As we checked in, one of the polite young men at the desk said, "Ah, Mr. Fiddler. Yes, sir, your room has already been taken care of. But we had expected you to be alone," he added, glancing at Sharai.

"Sue me."

He blinked. "There's an urgent message for you at the concierge's desk."

A bellboy appeared and reached for my only bag—the one with a half million in cash. I gave him a look that made him back off in a hurry. Money case in hand, Sharai and I crossed the lobby. The concierge was a blonde, pretty enough, even by Palm Springs standards.

"I understand you have a message for me," I said.

The concierge gave me a professionally efficient smile and handed over a hotel envelope.

"Who delivered this?" I asked.

"One of the room clerks," said the concierge. "He told me you'd be in before five."

I took the smooth linen hotel envelope and cracked the seal. Inside was a single sheet of hotel stationery, folded once.

189

It said: *Five-thirty, exactly, in your room.* There was no signature. None was needed. It was obvious that Salameh had this hotel wired to his terminal.

My prepaid room was on the second story. It was furnished with better woods and softer fabrics than most homes, and the Sony wasn't bolted in place. I crossed to the sliding glass door that opened onto a small balcony. There was a view of the pool's flickering blue water and the improbable green of the golf course. Behind me the bellboy showed Sharai how to operate the air conditioning and inquired as to her heart's desires. I came back inside and gave him two bucks to get rid of him. Sharai started to say something as he closed the door. I leaned down and put my mouth over hers. That shocked her into silence. I turned my head until I could breathe into her ear.

"Wired."

She nodded to show that she understood. She came up on tiptoe and whispered into my ear. To anyone watching we looked like lovers. To anyone listening, we weren't there.

"How long?" she asked, her voice wonderfully husky.

"Five-thirty."

A tremor moved over her body.

"It'll be okay," I said very softly.

She nodded but the trembling didn't diminish. When her fingers touched my cheek I realized that she was chilled from nerves or the pernicious air conditioning, or both. I shut off the unit, opened the balcony door and drew her outside with me. The sudden flare of desert heat poured life through us. Slowly she relaxed, leaning against me, her arms around my hips.

"I could almost feel Salameh in there," she whispered finally. "Like death. Cold. I'm sorry."

I kissed her gently and stroked the sun-warmed, fire-touched darkness of her hair. All the pragmatic things I'd told myself on the way down out of the canyon evaporated in the shared heat of the sun and our bodies.

"What are you going to do afterward?" I asked, only it wasn't really a question. It was more of a demand.

She looked at me. The intense light of the desert had drawn her pupils into black pinheads. Her eyes were very dark, very brown, like crystal in the sun. "Not now," she said, her voice soft. "Right now I want to concentrate on what will happen soon. Like you're doing."

"In a few hours it will be over, win, lose or draw," I said, ignoring her attempt to deflect me. "Then what? What will you use to fill that big hole in your life where revenge and hatred were? What will you use to balance what you'll become?"

Abruptly Sharai tried to move away, to put some distance between us, to deny what I was saying. I didn't let her.

"Your father is different," I said softly, relentlessly. "The boundaries of his world are secure. If Salameh dies, Rafi will have other Arabs to hunt and kill."

"He's not merely a killer!" she hissed.

"I know. He's a hunter, too. I have nothing against him. He's a good man, and a hard one." Sharai's confusion was clear in her beautiful dark eyes. "There's a place and a time for men like Rafi," I said. "Always."

Sharai gave me a doubtful look.

"Listen," I whispered, pulling her hard against me, "Everyone draws the line somewhere. I've known men I'd trade for a head of cabbage and then eat the cabbage. But that's me. Lots of people profess their devout reverence for life, then go home and eat a beefsteak without batting an eye. Hell, some people even take it seriously and refuse meat, but they'd be horrified to listen to the sounds that plant cells give out when you harvest Durham wheat or cut into iceberg lettuce. Plants are alive, too. We're all in it together. Life eats. Other life dies. That's the way it is. What we make of that fact is all that matters."

Sharai shuddered, telling me that the comfort I was offering her was as cold as death and as terrifying as life itself.

"Killing isn't as unnatural as everyone wants to believe," I said, holding her head against my chest, whispering against her soft hair. "But I'm talking about hating, Sharai, about the cold flame that has been burning in you since Arye was murdered."

For a moment she refused to either look at me or speak. Finally she said, "I learned the day Arye died that the future is always different from what we imagine, and that fine words about love and brotherhood are just that. Words. Salameh has killed more than Arye, more than the other athletes at Munich. Salameh's life revolves around the death of Jews. Men, women, children. He doesn't care. They are alive and then they are dead and Salameh goes on to the next school, the next bus, the next embassy. Civilians, Fiddler. Always civilians. People like Zahedi who believe that civilization is more enduring than war."

Sharai looked up at me unflinchingly. "Besides, who knows whether either of us will be alive to ask or answer questions tomorrow? Do you know?"

I shook my head. I didn't know.

"Which only leaves one thing," she whispered, her voice softening. "To live now."

She fitted herself against me and kissed me as though she had been told she would die if she didn't get close enough. Heat burst through me that had nothing to do with the sun-drenched balcony. I kissed her back, hard and deep and aching, because part of me knew that she might well be the last woman I ever touched, just as she knew that I might be her last man.

"Are you sure?" I asked harshly. "Remember, we probably aren't alone in there."

"Then Salameh will have to listen to the sounds of life for once, not death."

The sheets were cool, passive, an intense contrast to the woman I took even as she took me. The sweat and heat focused us, fused us together, and we forgot the listeners, the room, the desert and time.

It didn't last, of course. It never does. But while it did, we were fully alive.

"I'm glad," Sharai whispered finally, biting my ear gently between words, "that you threw away your violin. It would have kept you from what you were born for."

"Bed?" I suggested, smiling and pulling her more closely against me.

"Living. Helping other people to live. You have a gift for it."

I thought of all the scars my "gift" had left on me and others. As though she were reading my mind, Sharai continued whispering in her husky, wonderful voice.

"Death is part of living," she said. "So is being hurt. So is being healed. You're good at that. Healing."

No woman but Fiora has ever said anything like that to me. I buried my face in Sharai's hair and prayed that she was right about helping and healing people, because I knew too well just how good I was at hurting them. In the long silence my watch marked the half hour with a discreet sound. Sharai stirred, kissed me and slipped from my arms.

"Do you want me here when you're contacted?" she asked in a normal voice as she stood up.

"No."

I didn't explain. I didn't have to. If it was Salameh himself, I didn't trust Sharai not to give away the game. Neither did she. She picked up her shoulder purse and rummaged for a moment. The leather sack was big enough to serve as an overnight bag, and apparently she used it as one. She took out a blue swimsuit that exactly matched her lapis ring.

And then I realized that she wasn't wearing her ring today, had not been wearing it since she came out of the midnight sea in front of my house. Had she left the ring behind in a silent offering to a god long dead, or had she simply been unable to bear looking any longer into its blank, all-seeing eye?

"I'll be in the pool," she said and closed the door softly behind her.

I got up and showered, letting the water wash away unanswerable questions and sweat, reviving me. I hadn't bothered with a change of clothes. I pulled on my jeans, a Safari shirt, thick socks and a pair of rough country boots that came three quarters of the way up my calf. A slim Gerber folding knife with a five-inch locking blade slipped into the concealed sheath inside the left boot.

I clipped the pistol holster into place on my jeans, nestled into the small of my back, and tested the draw. The Detonics came easily into my hand, neither hanging up nor dragging. I went over and stood to one side of the sliding glass door, watching Sharai swim. She was beautiful in the water, fluid and strong, reminding me of the way her body had felt when we held each other and forgot time.

At three minutes to five there was a knock at the door. I remembered what Rafi had said about Salameh never doing exactly what was expected of him. I drew the Detonics and went to the peephole. Salameh stood in the hallway looking as casual as a businessman coming for cocktails. He carried a folded newspaper. He was alone.

I was surprised to see Salameh himself. After all, a hostage for a hostage is the oldest form of ransom in the Middle East. I opened the door and stepped aside, keeping the door between me and Salameh. As I closed the door behind me the blunt eye of the Detonics was focused on Salameh. His glance flicked over the pistol like a snake's tongue.

"It will not do you any good," he said bluntly. "My men are everywhere. If I do not leave this room, alone, within ten minutes, Zahedi dies. So do you. So does that woman in the pool."

I nodded.

"The money," he said curtly. "I will see that it is as I ordered."

He was trying to show me how unimpressed he was by the Detonics. I knew better. A gun always leaves an impression on the person who doesn't have one.

"If you're planning a rip-off, you'll be the first one to die," I said conversationally.

"What is a rip-off?" he asked, giving me a deadly smile.

"It's an idiom from the late sixties, usually associated with the dope trade. It means to take somebody's money without delivering the merchandise."

"I and my men have a higher purpose than greed, if that is what you mean. We are fighting for our homeland, the homeland that was stolen from us by people like Zahedi."

"People like Zahedi only want to live in peace. That's why he moved to America," I retorted. Rafi was another can of worms entirely, one that I wasn't planning on opening just yet. "You kidnapped the wrong man, Salameh."

" 'If he is not part of the solution, he is part of the problem.' " Salameh used the same intonations of the last activist I'd heard on the six-o'clock news.

I grimaced, preferring the biting rhythms of Ecclesiastes to the graceless slogans of the modern age.

Salameh glanced again at the bed. The sour expression on his face told me that he wasn't looking at the money case but at the royally rumpled sheets. His reaction confirmed that the room was indeed wired for sound. Normally the thought of aural voyeurism at my expense would have angered me. This time I smiled, remembering what Sharai had said: the sounds of life, not death. I hoped they had burned like acid in what passed for Salameh's soul.

I opened the money case, carefully working the combination lock so that Salameh didn't see the sequence. I stepped back and gestured him closer with the Detonics.

A half million dollars didn't quite fill the suitcase, but the C-4 in the lid made up the difference nicely. Salameh gave the booby trap a long look. I let him, knowing what he would see. Rafi had wired the case front, back and side. Unless you knew the five-digit combination for the lock, it looked like there was no way to get into that puppy without blowing the nearest quarter acre to hell. Salameh's mouth tightened into a flat line.

"That's right," I said softly. "Zahedi better be alive, because that's the only way you'll see this case open again!"

What I didn't say was that one of the crucial wires was a dud. Salameh accepted the case at face value. Carrying live bombs on rough roads was the kind of suicidal risk he took—and took for granted.

He selected a bundle of money at random and thumbed through it, checking that the serial numbers weren't in sequence and that everything was really U.S. currency. Sorting through the contents of the case, he thumbed through several more bundles almost caressingly, stroking the money, watching denominations on the bills dance.

"Go ahead," I offered. "Count it."

"That is not necessary," he said, but he continued to look at the money as though it were a lover undressing for him.

"Funny," I said softly. "I thought OPEC and Khadaffi kept you guys in dollars."

"Their money comes with—how do you say it?—wires?"

"Strings. As in puppets."

For an instant true anger transformed Salameh's face, making him look more dangerous than ever, the way a burning fuse is more dangerous than an unlighted one. Salameh didn't like hearing the truth.

"Like what you see?" I asked as his eyes returned to the seduction of heaped money.

Without looking at me, Salameh said, "Money is not important. Power is."

"Haven't you heard? Money *is* power. The new Golden Rule is simple: The one with the gold makes the rules."

Salameh ignored me.

"No, I suppose that wouldn't be your motto," I continued, watching Salameh. "You'd go along with the terrorist slogan: Power comes out of the end of a gun."

He looked at me without expression. "It is not the terrorist's motto. It is the politician's motto."

"Is that what you call yourself? A politician?" I snapped the case closed. "You've seen the money. Bring on Zahedi."

"You'll have to go to him."

"No way, politician. I'm not going one foot farther until I know he's alive."

Salameh reached into the breast pocket of his shirt and pulled out a white square. He held it out to me. It was a Polaroid picture. I turned it over.

Imbrahim Zahedi stared stoically out from a dark background. He held a folded newspaper on his chest like a prisoner's number in a mug shot. His face showed faint shadows on one side that could have been bruises. Surprisingly, his eyes were clear, focused, and purpose burned in them like black fire. Imbrahim had spent his life fleeing the world of the frog and the scorpion but had been trapped anyway. Being a hostage had changed him. I remembered him shouting into the phone that I should not bring money, that they would kill him anyway and then take the money to kill more Jews.

"As you can see," said Salameh, picking up the newspaper from the bed, "this is the paper he is holding. It is today's Indio *Daily News*. It was not printed or sold until midafternoon today."

I glanced at the front page. Above the fold, the President was talking to a Chinese diplomat in the Rose Garden and the Israelis were retaliating for a border raid. Below the fold, the Planning Commission had approved a new trailer park and the Bank of America had been robbed of $1,116 at 10:10 this morning.

I dropped the paper onto the bed. "You could have killed him before the Polaroid developed."

Salameh's shrug told me take it or leave it. I took it, knowing it was the only offer I'd get. He was doing this by the numbers in a pattern long established in the Middle East.

"At six o'clock," said Salameh, "you will receive a call. You will follow the instructions you are given. Be prepared to drive some distance. We want to make sure you are not followed. Bring the money. Leave the gun and your woman here."

"Wrong," I said.

He watched me but didn't say anything. I had done my preparation well. He was expecting to have to bargain with me.

"The woman comes with me," I said. "She'll drive. I'll hold the gun and keep the money from bouncing around too much." I gave him a smile with a lot of teeth. "What the hell, baby; I'm bringing the money. One out of three ain't bad."

"As you wish," said Salameh. "She is of no consequence."

I sincerely hoped he believed that.

"As for your pistol," he added. "That, too, is of no consequence. A half dozen weapons will be trained on you during the exchange. One small pistol buys you no real advantage."

I couldn't have agreed more, but there was no point in letting him know. "I'll see Zahedi alive before I open this case again."

He shrugged. "Of course." And then he smiled.

He pulled a sheet of twenty-two-cent stamps out of his breast pocket and began licking with meticulous strokes of his tongue. When the sheet was suitably soggy, he slapped it diagonally over the opening of the case and held everything in place until the glue was dry. There was no way I could get into that case again without leaving tracks.

"I would not want any, er, surprises to be in with the money when you deliver it," said Salameh.

Salameh didn't miss many tricks; but then, careless terrorists die young. Salameh let himself out, closing the door softly behind him.

By the time Sharai came in from the pool, I had ordered a light dinner for us. The fruit salads came with yogurt dressing, big slices of date bread and sweet butter and a large jug of unsweetened iced tea. Sharai showered, pulled a pair of black cotton pants out of her bag and put them on with the khaki blouse.

At six o'clock exactly, the phone rang. I picked it up after the third ring. The clarity of the line suggested that the caller was in the hotel.

"Drive on Highway 111 for four miles east, to Jefferson Avenue. Turn right and travel exactly seven point two miles. Then turn around and retrace your route four miles to Airport Avenue. At that corner there is a gasoline station. Go to the pay phone and wait. You will be contacted. You are to make no phone calls, to speak with no one. Do you understand?"

I repeated the instructions, right down to the officious intonations of the man on the phone. He hung up as the last word came back to him.

The green Firebird was parked behind a Shakey's Pizza Parlor across the street from the hotel. I could feel the driver watching us the minute we left the lobby and walked to the Land Cruiser. I gave him a demonstration of love and the brotherhood of man by checking out the Toyota as though I

expected to find a bomb attached somewhere. Considering that
one of those bastards had recently done just that, I doubted
that the watchers would find my suspicion unreasonable. Besides, it used up a little time, got the sun just a bit farther
down in the sky, gave a man with a game leg just a few more
minutes to climb a rocky desert ridge and crawl down on his
stomach close enough to kill something.

When I had stalled enough to make the watchers restless
but not suspicious, I gestured for Sharai to open up the doors,
letting out a searing blast of air that was almost too hot to
breathe. I made Sharai wait out on the pavement while I showed
her another desert trick Uncle Jake had taught me. I splashed
most of the contents of a Lister Bag onto the two front seats
and poured the rest on the steering wheel. The wheel was so
hot that the water evaporated even as I poured, leaving the
black plastic cool enough to handle. The water on the seats
would be gone in five minutes.

We climbed into our poor man's sauna and left the parking
lot. Sharai drove and I watched. The Firebird fell in a quarter
mile behind us and followed us toward Indio. We made the
right onto Jefferson and headed south through grapefruit and
date groves. I took one look at the map to confirm the Firebird's
tactics. The course he had laid ran out onto a desert road that
dead-ended against the Santa Rosas. Anybody following me—
like maybe a plainclothes cop or an FBI agent—would be
burned right to the ground. It was a good basic tactic to flush
surveillance vehicles.

It was also a pretty good tactic if the Arabs were going to
ambush us and take the money, C-4 and wires notwithstanding.
I had put the Ice Cream King's special, short-range loads in
the pistol for the stay in the motel. In an ambush, short range
wouldn't be good enough. I switched clips to conventional
hollow points.

The Firebird disappeared after about three miles. I assumed he had dropped off to watch the traffic behind us. That
probably meant there was another tail car on us. For the next
few miles I spent my time trying to choose between the tan
C-J6 Jeep and the gray Ford Grenada that seemed to be going
the same direction we were.

I let out a long, relieved breath when I saw that the dead
end was too open to provide cover for an ambush. This had
been strictly an exercise in burning tails. Sharai wrestled the
Land Cruiser into a U-turn and we headed back toward town.

The tan Jeep was tucked into the shade of a smoke tree where the pavement took over from the dirt side road. Neither of the men in the open Jeep was Salameh. As they fell in behind us, I watched in the side-view mirror. The passenger was talking into a hand radio.

The gas station had no shade and no enclosed telephone booth. Sharai pulled in beside the unsheltered public phone. While I waited she refilled the Lister Bag. Even though the sun was well past zenith, its rays were punishing. I sat and sweated until the phone rang. It was one of the longest quarter hours of my life.

This time the instructions ran us back to the highway and into downtown Indio. The contact point was a phone booth at the edge of the Date Festival parking lot, a five-acre slab of sun-softened macadam. Heat rose from it in transparent, distorting waves. Nothing else moved, not even the wind. Especially not the wind. We sat and poached in our own sweat for ten minutes before the phone rang.

The game went on for the next forty-five minutes, through three more phone booths, each one farther down the highway. Salameh was nothing if not meticulous. The chances of randomly picking five booths with working phones was remote. He had checked every one and probably had a lieutenant drive every route for time. He had left nothing to chance, except for the irreducible random elements I had introduced with Sharai, the deceptively wired ransom and the pistol in the small of my back.

At a phone booth behind a Wienerschnitzel Drive-in in Mecca, the officious Arab ordered us onto the dirt road beside the canal and told us to keep driving.

"You will be contacted," he said and hung up.

I could see both the Firebird and the Jeep behind us; they were the only other vehicles visible for ten miles in any direction. On our left the canal slid along at breakneck speed, its surface smooth and quiet. On our right the desert sloped off toward the sink filled by the Salton Sea. The dirt road hadn't changed. Sharai made thirty-five miles an hour without effort.

The two vehicles behind us made no attempt to hide. They stayed back just beyond the plume of our dust until we got within a few miles of the spot where the Bradshaw Trail veered off from the canal road. Then they began closing with us. A mile from the Bradshaw turnoff, the Jeep came on hard, pulling abreast of us.

The two young Arabs in the open vehicle were back in their desert element now and had put on their checkered head-dresses to prove it. The man who rode shotgun sat erect, arrogant in his confidence, his Kalashnikov slanting toward the sky as though he were taking aim at the sun. The Jeep pulled past us in a turmoil of dust and grit.

"Let them go," I told Sharai. "They think they're the only ones who know the way, right?"

The tone of my voice was echoed in her small, feral smile.

The Firebird drew up behind us, riding our bumper, chewing our dust. Then the Jeep's taillights flashed, telling us to slow. Boxed between the two vehicles, we approached the single-lane bridge over the canal and into the back country. The Jeep crossed, let us cross and then slammed on the brakes.

The canal water looked impossible, like ice cubes in hell. Close up you could see small whorls and boils as the water slid over the concrete liner like a runaway train. Thirty yards downstream from the bridge, the canal was drawn down suddenly and disappeared into a siphon that was three hundred yards long. A long chunk of greasewood came floating by, black against the green water, spinning in the current faster than a man could walk. At the edge of the siphon the branch caught for a moment on the concrete berm while the water foamed and sucked greedily. Between one instant and the next the branch vanished. It would never reappear on the other side. Before the three hundred yards had been traveled, the current would shred the sinuous wood to matchsticks against the siphon's harsh concrete walls.

The man with the Kalashnikov vaulted out of the Jeep and brought the weapon to bear on us. I wondered whether Salameh had decided to risk opening the money case without my help. There wasn't enough time to get the Uzi unwrapped. I took the safety off the Detonics.

"Be ready," I said to Sharai. The Toyota's metal body wouldn't stop slugs from a Kalashnikov, but it might slow them down. "If anything goes wrong, pull the knife out of my left boot and get the Uzi."

Sharai nodded tightly.

The man driving the Firebird rolled it onto the bridge, parked, pulled the keys and stuffed them in his pocket. The car was now a great green cork stuck into the narrow mouth of the bridge, blocking the only route back to civilization. Without looking at us, the Arab walked between the Toyota and the bridge railing. He swung into the back of the Jeep with a flourish. The man with the Kalashnikov leaped into the passenger seat. Instantly the Jeep leaped forward.

Sharai and I started breathing normally again. I looked over at her. She was pale but otherwise in control. She let out the clutch and followed the Jeep, staying far enough behind that we didn't choke on the dust.

"See how much room they'll give us," I said.

She began slacking off on the gas gradually. The Jeep let us have a little over two hundred yards, then got nervous and slowed. We gradually speeded up. They speeded up. We slowed. We played that game a few times more, never hanging back far enough for them to get worried, but never quite keeping up, either.

The closer we got to the sentry post, the more I itched to unwrap that Uzi and come out firing. All that prevented me was the gut knowledge that a careful man like Salameh would be expecting a signal from the sentry post. If it didn't come, Zahedi was dead. So I settled for buying as much road as I could now in order to have enough time to get to the Uzi later.

When the Jeep reached the sentry post at the mouth of the small lateral canyon, Sharai was three hundred yards behind. The Jeep pulled up in a cloud of sand and gravel. The Arab from the Firebird jumped out and came back to us. In his hand was a big Colt .45, cocked and ready to go.

"Out of the car," he said.

It was the officious Arab from the long string of public phones. I stepped out to face him, suitcase in my right hand and gun in my left. The Detonics was aimed right at his belt buckle. He glanced at the pistol, then looked again, as though he were interested in buying it, or maybe stealing it off my dead body later.

"We will search your vehicle," he said.

Sharai and I stood together just off the road while two of the Arabs rummaged inside the Toyota, the third stood guard, and two more lounged in the shadow of a big boulder. The sun was an hour from setting, but the land had barely begun to cool.

Out of the corner of my eye, I saw an Arab crawling around under the hood of the Toyota, checking the wheel well and the area beneath the chassis. The second Arab, the one who had driven the Firebird, was inside the Toyota, looking under the dashboard and the seats and inspecting the glove compartment. I knew without seeing that he was also checking the door panels and upholstery for signs of recent tampering. They would have made good narcs or customs agents.

And then the Arab came to the spare tire in the back of the Land Cruiser. He flipped over the tire to look at the opposite side. The motion was quick and hard enough to make the tire bounce if it had been fully inflated. The tire wobbled, sagged and flopped back into its original position. He bounced it one more time, his head cocked to one side as though he were listening. Then he turned the tire slowly. He was three quarters of the way around before he found the nail. He pried at it with his fingers, got nowhere and turned to me.

"Why is this tire not where it belongs?"

"You can see the nail," I said. "We'll have to have it fixed."

He dropped the tire and turned his attention to the floorboards.

Hide in plain sight, just like Uncle Jake used to say. And wrap well with towels. All it takes to be a good smuggler is good nerves. Sharai had them, too. She said nothing, not even when one of the Arabs came over, demanded her purse and pawed through it. He let out a yelp of excitement when he found the Browning. The Arabs huddled before the officious one tucked the Browning into his belt and confronted me.

"One gun," he said. "Not two guns." He held out his hand. "Suitcase."

I turned it so that he could see the stamps. He hesitated, waiting for me to hand it over. Then he realized that I wasn't going to release it. He bent toward the case, ignoring the Detonics six inches from his nose. The stamps were intact. He grunted and straightened.

"Now we will search you."

He patted me down with the kind of cool, thorough expertise that comes from practice. If he noticed the Detonics following every motion, he didn't say anything. I damn well know that he was aware of my gun when he went over Sharai, though. I had it screwed right underneath his jaw. He was very careful not to play touchy-feely while he searched her. Satisfied, he motioned to the two sentries. One cranked up a radio and spoke into it.

I turned to the Arab from the Firebird. "Tell Salameh that if Zahedi isn't in the front yard—alive—when I drive in, all you'll see of the ransom money is smoke."

He paused, showing anger for the first time. He sent a

stream of Arabic at the sentry. The sentry spoke into the radio, listened and called out in Arabic.

"It is done," snarled the Arab. "And you will stand in front of the hostage, open the case and remove the explosives." He shoved us into the Toyota and started to climb in after.

Like hell he was going to ride with us. I put the Detonics right into his face this time.

"Out," I snarled. "You're not getting any closer to that money until I see the hostage alive."

I could see him think about it. If anything, he was even more dangerous than Salameh. He looked down the barrel of the Detonics with the coolness of a man who has seen death before and is not all that impressed.

"Let me put it to you this way," I said. "Salameh might not miss you, but he sure would miss that money if I blew it to hell."

The Arab slammed the Toyota door and leaped into the Jeep, which took off like a racer out of the blocks. Sharai waited until a good cloud of dust built up from the speeding vehicle before she followed.

"Come on, come on, quit looking at us," I said beneath my breath.

Grit boiled over the hood, coating the windshield. Scenery raced by on either side, moving too fast, distance and time running out.

15

As soon as the Arab looked away, I pulled the Gerber out of my boot and dove into the back of the bucking Toyota. The knife's blade took care of the tire's valve stem in a single pass. Air rushed out with a whistling shudder, bringing with it a rubbery, already-used smell. I jammed the point of the knife through the sidewall and opened a cut from the rim to the tread face before the blade ground against the steel fibers lying beneath the tread. The Toyota hit a rut that banged my head against the roof and yanked the knife out of the slit. I ignored Sharai's terse apology and the pain in my skull. A few friendly lumps would be the least of my problems if I didn't get the Uzi and all the rest out before we got to the ranch house.

Rather than fighting the steel fibers with a knife that kept slipping against my sweaty palm, I stabbed through the existing slit, turned the blade and hacked along the sidewall for half the circumference of the tire before slicing back down to the rim. I dropped the knife and began dragging out pieces of towel-wrapped metal as the Toyota bucked and skidded on the lousy road up the small canyon.

Braced between the wheel well and the passenger seat, trusting that a few hundred yards and the dust cloud would cover my movements, I unwrapped each piece like a kid frantic to find out what Santa brought for Christmas. Flash-bangs and sections of the Uzi collected in my lap.

"Halfway there." Sharai's voice was a lot calmer than I felt.

I assembled the Uzi, snapping the barrel and collapsed stock into place and slapping home a clip. Other clips went into my jeans pockets. The bolt worked as sweetly and positively as I had remembered. I felt a lot less naked as I crawled back into the passenger seat, Uzi in one hand, radio in the other and flash-bangs in my shirt pockets. I laid the Uzi across my lap, jerked the Detonics out of its holster and put the weapon on the seat between Sharai's legs. An extra magazine followed.

As I reached for the radio, she positioned the gun for a

fast grab. I snapped on the radio, hunching over to keep it below the line of the dashboard. I didn't have much hope of getting through to Rafi. The solid rock of the canyon walls would soak up all but line-of-sight signals. The rattle and banging of the Land Cruiser on the rough road nearly drowned out the radio's sound even with the volume cranked up to high.

"Rafi, can you read? Over."

About the eighth time I tried, an answer came. It wasn't a voice but a thumping sound.

"He's tapping the microphone with his finger," Sharai said. "It's an ambush technique they teach in the army. One is 'no,' and two is 'yes.' He must be so close to the cabin that they might hear him if he spoke."

Great. And lousy. I had to know where he was.

"Can you see us?"

Two thumps wrapped in a lot of static.

I closed my eyes for a second, re-creating in my mind the terrain around the ranch house as seen from the air. There had been several spots in the jumbled rocks that Rafi might have chosen for sniping sites.

"Are you in the position you want to use?" I asked.

Two thumps.

"Is the hostage in the front yard?"

One thump.

So much for Salameh's promise. "Can you get a flash-bang into Zahedi's room?"

One thump.

Shit! Now I'd have trust that Salameh was so worried about the money and the C-4 that he would at least have Zahedi in sight when I pulled up.

"Are you closer to the house or the rock shed? One for the house, two for the shed."

Two thumps.

I thought fast, time running out, the ranch house growing up from the dusty road ahead.

"There was a rock hognose that extended down almost to the edge of the corral. Is that close to your position?"

One thump.

"Then you must be on the opposite side of the corral, probably in that jumble of rocks on the south side of the canyon."

Two thumps, a break, then two more thumps.

"I understand you to be in those rocks," I said.

Two thumps.

"I've got everything I packed. Sharai has my pistol. She's driving. We'll come in slow, then turn and go like hell for the rocks. If Zahedi is in sight, I'll drop a flash-bang as soon as we cut for the rocks. Sharai will hit the lights at the same time I drop the grenade. Close your eyes, count four and take out the man guarding the hostage. Then you and Sharai can cover me while I pick up Zahedi. Got it?"

Two thumps.

"If Zahedi's still in the house, I'll demand to see him outside. While we're arguing, you can come in close and heave a flash-bang through the window. Okay?"

Two thumps. Then silence.

Dust was thick in the air. I could taste the grit on my teeth and feel it in my eyes. I dug tissues out of a pocket, tore off two wads and gave them to Sharai for earplugs. I took two more for myself.

The ranch house was nearly on top of us.

"If anybody tries to stop us now, run over him," I said.

Sharai nodded once. The Jeep ahead veered aside. I leaned forward, straining to see through the haze. The ranch house was slightly to the right, the corral off to the left. The yard was dead ahead. Imbrahim Zahedi was being dragged down the stone steps by an Arab who had his gun jammed into the old man's ear. The rocks where Rafi was positioned were just across the corral, about a hundred feet away from the house. Partway between the two was a stone shed. Rafi couldn't get a clean shot at Imbrahim's captor; the angle was wrong.

"Take out the corral fence and whatever else gets between us and that pile of rocks," I said, pointing to the corral. "We want to set up there. Whatever you do, *don't look toward Zahedi.*"

I slung the Uzi on my shoulder, pulled the pin on a flash-bang and held the spoon down with my palm. Nothing would go off until four seconds after I let go. I prayed to God that Salameh would wait that long before killing Imbrahim.

The Jeep's brake lights flashed on, burning like embers in the dust, stopping almost directly in front of the house. Men started piling out before the tires stopped turning. I lowered my arm out of the window.

"Hit the lights!" I snapped.

Sharai flashed the lights once as I lobbed the concussion grenade with an underhand throw. By the time the flash-bang was gone, she had downshifted, stabbed the accelerator and

erked the Toyota into a hard skid. Dirt, sand and gravel spewed
rom beneath the spinning wheels. As I started counting sec-
nds, time slowed down the way it does when your body goes
nto adrenaline overdrive.

One one-thousand: We smashed through the pole barrier
of the corral fence. The wood snapped and ricocheted dryly.

Two one-thousand: Sharai slammed the accelerator down
flat and held it there while the Toyota bucked and skidded in
the corral's soft ground.

Three one-thousand: I saw the Jeep turn to follow while
a man scrambled back in, legs and arms and gun barrel going
n different directions. I saw a man rush out onto the porch,
then saw him leap back inside as someone shouted instructions
from the house. I saw the gleam of a gun barrel behind an
uncurtained window and knew that would be where Salameh
was hiding.

Four one-thousand: I saw the haze of grit glittering like
gold dust in the slanting afternoon sun, and the silver trail of
sweat shining on Sharai's cheek as she fought the Toyota in
the soft sand. And then I closed my eyes and covered my ears
against the eye searing, mind-numbing explosion as the flash-
bang blew apart in the middle of the ranch house yard. Shock
waves of thunder hammered through the canyon, stunning,
deafening, overwhelming men who had expected nothing more
than the impudent report of a pistol.

The Toyota burst through the other side of the corral in
a shower of wood. I rolled out of the door and came to my feet
while running in zigzags toward the yard, wishing to Christ I
could hear more than the ringing of overloaded auditory nerves.

Imbrahim was down. So was the Arab who had held a gun
to his ear. There was blood on the old man, but it could have
been the Arab's. He didn't have a head.

Bullets kicked dirt around me. I could see a muzzle flash
in the darkened house. Salameh must have guessed what was
happening and closed his eyes in time to save his vision from
the searing light of the magnesium grenade. I sent a line of
bullets stitching at waist level through the glass, then dove to
cover Imbrahim's body as he began thrashing around in the
dust.

The Jeep had skidded to a stop as its blinded and deafened
driver held his hands over his eyes. The passenger was no
better off for the moment. Slugs poured out of the house. I
grabbed Imbrahim and started rolling us over and over toward

the shelter of the stalled Jeep. It was hard on the old man,
but not as hard as dying. There was no way to reassure him
because he was as blind and deaf as the Arabs. He had been
closer to the grenade than anyone except the guard Rafi had
killed.

My few seconds of grace were up. Men in the house began
firing at me, trying to pick me off. They were protected from
Rafi's return fire by the angle and by the rock-walled house
Salameh hid behind. The Detonics rang out, sounding clean
and hard amid the slurred barrage of automatic weapons. The
men in the house took cover.

I came up on the far side of the Jeep, ready to kill the
stunned occupants. Somebody had saved me the trouble. Rafi,
possibly. Sharai, probably.

Three down, at least four to go. I propped Imbrahim
against the front tire, out of the line of fire from the house,
and checked him over. The gore all over his head and shoulders
wasn't his own. He blinked his watering eyes, trying to focus.

Sharai burst from the rocks as Rafi laid down a pattern of
automatic fire that turned hunks of ranch house stone into dust.
She dove behind the rock wall of the shed and prepared to
cover Rafi's advance. The Detonics is good, but not that good.
He would need more help than a pistol gave him. I slapped
the Uzi's barrel onto the Jeep's bumper and emptied the clip
into the house. Rafi didn't need a second invitation. He was
out of the rocks and into the shed's shelter before I lifted my
finger.

And he was limping badly.

I heard some of my shots ricochet and then Imbrahim
groaned and I knew that the effects of the flash-bang were
wearing off. I'd bought enough time to get Imbrahim some
cover, but not enough to guarantee his life. Bullets whined
over the Jeep. Rafi's Uzi poured out an answer.

For an instant there was silence. I snapped out the spent
clip, slapped another one into place, and chambered a round.
The sound was unmistakable, like the racking of a shotgun. I
hoped Salameh could hear it. I bent over the old man.

"Imbrahim—*Imbrahim*!—can you hear me? It's Fiddler."

Dark eyes opened and tried to focus on me. "My eyes."

"You'll be all right in a minute." The Arabs already were,
but there was no reason to tell Imbrahim that. "Stay put. Don't
move until I come for you. Understand?"

He nodded.

The Jeep driver's weapon was within reach. I grabbed the ck, felt my hand slip on blood, wiped it and tried again. is time the gun stuck to me. I'd never shot a Kalashnikov. was an ungainly bastard. I slipped the safety, aimed at the use and pulled the trigger. A single round spat out. It took e a few seconds to switch to automatic fire.

Rafi darted to the side of the shed where I could see him t where the men in the house couldn't. He held up his hand, owing three fingers, then two, then one. By the end of the untdown, I had the Kalashnikov over the bumper, spraying gs through the black hole in the house where glass had once en.

My heart stopped as I saw Sharai go flying toward the indowless side of the house. Bullets kicked wildly to one side her—but didn't hit her. Apparently the sniper hadn't fully covered his sight or his nerve. The Detonics flashed in the n as she snapped off two shots. There was nothing wrong ith her eyes or nerve. An Arab reeled out from behind the use, clutching his shoulder. Rafi and I brought him down. e stayed down. Sharai caught herself just before she slammed ainst the rock wall of the house. She inched along toward e back, flopped on the ground and looked low around the rner.

Thumbs up. No sniper.

Rafi held up one finger and pointed to himself. I wanted argue the toss but there was no time. I was the only one ho could cover him. I nodded and counted to ten before pptying the Kalashnikov's clip into the front of the house. afi was moving at the first shots, heading for the blind side the house. When he was a few yards away, his leg gave out d he went sprawling against the rocky wall. He got to his et, yanked off his backpack and reached in. He came out ith a flash-bang. He gave it to Sharai and motioned toward e front of the house.

Treat her as you would a man.

I made a dive for the dead passenger's weapon, grabbed and flopped back down in the dirt while bullets whined and at around me. I fired into the window, holding down the igger until there was nothing left, driving the men inside way from the window while Sharai ran down the side of the use. I threw aside the spent weapon and grabbed my Uzi ain. Sharai was already on the porch, her back flat to the n-warmed rocks as she crept toward the window. She tossed

the flash-bang past the splinters of glass hanging in the windo
frame and then spun away with her eyes closed and her ea
covered.

I started running with my eyes closed. Even then I sa
the flash. The concussive force of the explosion sent soun
waves hammering through the tiny canyon again. Before th
first echo came back I was on the porch. I sent a short bur
through the window and leaped in after it, throwing myse
down and to the right, rolling through shards of glass. By th
time Sharai came through the window the only Arab in th
room was dead.

Five down, and none of them Salameh.

Sharai came through the window and rolled to the lef
Rafi was right on her heels and on his feet before she wa
despite the blood running down his left arm and the fact th
his left knee wouldn't take his full weight. He beat me to th
hallway as he sent his second flash-bang rolling toward th
back of the house and then dove back into the front room. Th
explosion went off like a cannon in a stone closet. Even e:
pecting it, I was disoriented, punch-drunk. I staggered towar
the hall again, and again Rafi beat me to it. He brought th
shotgun up suddenly and fired at the floor at the end of th
hall. A pattern of slugs bounced off the floor's stone surfac
and spread like grapeshot. I heard men screaming as my ea
recovered from the initial shock waves of the blast.

Rafi gestured to me. I came into the hall. Sharai followed
Without being told she turned her back to us and covered th
doorway we had just come through. Rafi pointed to the en
of the hall. Rooms opened off to the left and the right. H
held up two fingers and pointed to the left. Then he held u
one finger and pointed toward the right. He pointed to himse
and to the first room, where he thought there might be tw
men. I pulled the last flash-bang out of my pocket and pointe
to myself. He gave me a hard smile, shook his head and too
the concussion grenade. I was too much of a pragmatist t
argue. The next maneuver called for finesse, not speed, an
Rafi knew a hell of a lot more about room-to-room fightin
than I did.

He began easing down the left side of the hallway, sup
porting most of his weight on the wall. The flesh wound o
his arm left an erratic trail of blood on the white plaster. Th
door on the right side of the hallway opened. I snapped o
two shots. The door slammed shut. Rafi never paused. Hi

pression was intent, that of a man utterly focused in this one
oving instant of time. The left-hand door was slightly ajar.
anding well clear of it, Rafi nudged the door open with the
rrel of his gun and rolled in the flash-bang.

Bullets chewed through the plaster by the door, starting
floor level and working their way upward, giving Rafi no
ace to hide. Pummeled by slugs, his body spun around and
ammed against the opposite wall as the world went white
ound us.

The concussion grenade was all that saved Sharai and me
om being chewed to bits by the bullets spewing through the
all. I went to my knees and fought to see, to hear. By the
me I felt my way down the hall to Rafi, he was dead. I squinted
rough my flash-stunned eyes and waited for someone to leap
to the hallway and finish the job. No one came. I felt Sharai's
nd on my arm.

"Rafi's dead," I said harshly.

I felt her go by me to her father. I snagged her arm and
nked her back, pointing her toward the two doors at the end
the hall. She couldn't do her father any good, but she could
ep the two of us from being shot up like paper targets while
y head cleared of the effects of the last grenade.

Treat her as you would a man. You bet, Rafi. And may
e best man survive.

I crawled past Rafi's body. Already a part of me raged that
e would never again drink Corona while talking of frogs and
orpions and hummingbirds. I shoved that thought into a dark
rner of my mind as I emptied the Uzi's clip in a burst of
ind shots at floor level. They penetrated the door, shredding
ything alive in the room. Mourning for Rafi could come later.
rvival came first. Adrenaline bridged the gap.

As I smacked home a fresh clip, Sharai brushed past me
ward the left-hand room. The Uzi she had taken from her
ther's body chattered briefly before she spun back and dove
rough the right-hand door, firing blindly. I dove in after her
nd landed on the body of an Arab. It was the man from the
irebird. His front pocket had been torn out as though some-
ne had been frantic to get at its contents. His checkered
eaddress fanned out around him.

Six.

Sharai crawled to the window while I covered the hall and
e other room. She turned and said something to me. I couldn't
ear her past the ringing in my ears. She shouted.

"The Jeep is gone!"

I could see quite clearly now, and I didn't like what I sav
The ranch yard had three bodies in it. I couldn't tell if one
them was Imbrahim. I went back up the hall, stopping on
long enough to take my shotgun from Rafi's body. I could hea
again. It didn't help much. All I could hear was Sharai's foo
steps and my own breath tearing through my throat. Nothir
moved out front. Nothing moved on either side. Considerir
Salameh's past history of saving his own ass, I guessed he wa
gone. I wasn't going to bet my life on it, though. I tossed Shar
my last clip.

"Cover me," I said, gesturing toward the front door.

Sharai changed to the fresh clip and took up a positic
that gave her a clear view of the yard. At my signal she fire
quickly into the only available sniper cover. Bullets ricochete
among the rocks by the corral and around the Toyota as I dov
into the yard and came up ready to fire. No answering sho
came. I scrambled past bodies to the Toyota. None of the dea
was Imbrahim—which meant that Salameh had taken him.

I knew then why the Arab had had his pocket ripped ou
Salameh had grabbed the keys to the Firebird. I wondere
how long it would take him to get there, turn the car arour
and then kill the hostage he no longer needed.

A gesture brought Sharai out of the house on the run.
covered her but nothing stirred. I reached for the wheel. Shar
pushed me aside.

"Your arm," she said curtly.

I looked down. My right arm was bloody from should
to elbow and the hand was red. It must have been cut whe
I went rolling through glass. Blood oozed rather than pumpe
out, telling me that I hadn't cut anything I couldn't live wit
out. My ability to fire a gun was intact, but a steering whe
would slip like butter out of my hands on the ranch's roug
road.

Sharai pulled keys from her pocket and started up th
Toyota as coolly as though we were going for a Sunday driv
She was running on nerve, but she had plenty of that. Sh
might break into a million pieces after it was over. Right no
she was what she had been thoroughly trained to be. A soldie

She drove that Land Cruiser like a woman possessed. Th
money case knocked and banged around the back as the tir
skidded and found traction and skidded again, spraying sar
and small stones in every direction. She shouldn't have bee

strong enough to hold the car to the road at that speed, but she was. Adrenaline and quick, sure hands. Rafi had raised a hell of a fine soldier. Too bad he hadn't lived long enough to appreciate his work.

Too bad I hadn't been good enough to spare her the killing.

"I'm sorry." I didn't realize I had spoken aloud until I heard my own voice.

Sharai shook her head, denying both my apology and the responsibility implicit in it. "My father expected to die," she said harshly. "The only thing he feared was that Salameh would survive him and that no one would have the dedication to run Salameh to ground again. Now I know that same fear. Israel has been forced to become so *politic*"—she slammed back down into first—"in order to keep America's favor."

I couldn't disagree. As Salameh had noted, other people's money came with puppet wires attached.

The Toyota spun out. Sharai let it drift, then pulled it all together in a wheel-spinning roar that made the car leap forward. Neither one of us spoke. There wasn't anything to say. Either we would catch Salameh at the bridge or we wouldn't. If we lost him, it wouldn't be because Sharai was afraid to risk her life running him to ground on that breakneck road.

She used that Chevy-powered Toyota hard in the next miles, slamming between second and third gears on a road that had been designed for a cautious crawl. The sun was going down with its usual lack of fuss, turning the land deep gold and then bloody orange, cushioning ruts and rocks with shadows. Ahead of us we caught the brief glow of taillights as Salameh braked to avoid an obstacle. Sharai's breath came in sharply and she said something in Hebrew. I didn't ask for a translation.

I leaned over and snapped on the headlights to make Sharai's job easier. There was no element of surprise to give away. Salameh knew we were coming. That certainty was all that was keeping Imbrahim alive.

We shot around a curve and onto the downhill slope toward the canal bridge and the Salton Sea. The water was almost black beneath a purple sky and lights from the shoreline houses looked like sparks twisting up into the night. For the first time we had a clear view of Salameh's Jeep. It was a quarter mile away, parked sideways across the road, its headlights a shaft of pale illumination against the darkening land. The bridge over the canal sloped just beyond.

At first I hoped that Salameh had overestimated his driving skills and ended up in a ditch. Then the Firebird's headlights came on, bathing the Jeep in white light. I braced myself against the door and ceiling, knowing what Sharai was going to do, knowing that it was our only chance of catching Salameh and a damn poor chance at that. She floored the accelerator held it there while the engine screamed an anguished mechanical plea that ended when she finally slammed the stick into fourth. Salameh gunned forward and then backed the Firebird around, trying to line it up with the mouth of the bridge. We came down that last long curve to the canal like the Apocalypse, closing much too fast on the Jeep Salameh had parked across the road to block us.

"Left!" I yelled, spotting rocks off to the right.

Sharai spun the wheel, throwing the Toyota into a skid. Our tail kicked out, barely missing the Jeep, and then we were in the rough. I hung on to everything I could. Sharai hung on to the wheel, pulling us out of the skid, overcorrecting, downshifting, losing it and skidding again, and then clawing back onto the road just as Salameh got the Firebird pointed toward the bridge. We spurted forward, using our greater momentum to ram the Firebird, putting it sideways into the rough again just a few feet short of the canal. The Toyota's headlights illuminated Salameh, Imbrahim and the cloud of grit boiling around the Firebird.

I damn near took the door off the Toyota getting out but Salameh was still too quick. He grabbed Imbrahim by the collar, jammed a gun in his ear and dragged him out of the Firebird into the harsh glare of the Toyota's lights.

"Drop your gun." Salameh directed the order to me. He was crouched behind the old man, using him as a shield.

"No way, baby," I said, holding the Uzi steady and wishing to hell it were my Detonics. Salameh was bigger than Imbrahim. There was almost enough of the Arab showing to chance a shot. Almost, but not quite, especially with the Uzi. I couldn't be sure of not hitting Imbrahim.

"I'll kill him!" yelled Salameh.

"No you won't," I said reasonably, smiling. "I'll give you the money just like we planned and you'll give Zahedi to me. Then you'll go your way and we'll go ours, no hard feelings and no regrets."

I was lying right through my California smile. I planned to dump that son of a bitch in his shiny black shoes the instant

mbrahim was free. Salameh started to speak but the old man
eat him to it.

"No!" said Imbrahim, struggling suddenly, wildly. "If you
t him go he will use that money to kill again and again and
will never stop! Kill him here! *Kill him!*"

The old man was brave, but no match for Salameh. His
rm tightened across Imbrahim's fragile throat. From the cor-
er of my eye I caught movement. Sharai. Cold sweat broke
ver me as I realized what she was going to do.

"Bring the mon—" began Salameh.

I yelled but it was too late. It had been too late a thousand
ears ago.

The Detonic's harsh report shattered the twilight once,
wice, three times, a fusillade of sound echoing over the land.
mbrahim jerked hard and a dark stain began spreading over
is torn white shirt. Salameh screamed as Sharai's first bullet
pun him sideways to meet the next bullets. I grabbed Im-
rahim and took him down to the ground, trying to protect
im while Sharai fired again and again, emptying the Detonics
vhile Salameh jerked and spun like a holy man praying to a
unatic god. His arms flew up and he called out wildly as he
ell into the canal. The water took him without a murmur,
losing over him, tumbling him gently, swiftly, tugging him
own and down into the siphon's endless night from which
othing emerged, ever.

I heard someone swearing viciously and realized it was
ne. I shut up and bent over Imbrahim. The wound in his
houlder was through and through, high enough that I hoped
hat it hadn't nicked his lungs. There was another wound on
is waist, a furrow plowed through his frail flesh. Blood flowed,
ut didn't spurt. His pulse was light, thready. So was his
reathing. He was dazed but conscious. His eyes were focused,
vatching me.

All in all, it was a hell of a fine bit of shooting Sharai had
lone. What enraged me was that she had been willing to shoot
hrough Imbrahim to get to Salameh. I should have forced her
o promise to protect the hostage instead of her father. Rafi
ad trained his daughter all too well.

"Easy, Imbrahim," I said when he tried to speak. "It's all
ver. Salameh's dead. You're safe now."

*Yeah, and you're about an inch from dead, too. Nice
oing, Fiddler.*

"The woman."

His words were more a sigh, but Sharai heard him. Sh
went down on her knees at his side, the empty Detonics flash
ing coldly in the headlights.

"I'm sorry," she said over and over, a futile litany spoke
in a voice that could hardly be recognized as Sharai's. Her eye
were the same. Blank.

"Shut up," I said coldly. "Hold him."

I peeled off my shirt, tore it into strips and began bindin
the old man's wounds. When I had done all I could, I got u
and played car jockey until the Firebird was on the other sid
of the bridge and the Jeep and the Toyota blocked the bridg
artistically. The scene could have passed for a friendly littl
off-road fender-bender, in case anyone should wonder why th
bridge was closed.

"This is going to hurt," I said to Imbrahim.

He smiled. "Do you know," he whispered, "pain is no
. . . as bad as . . . I feared. All my life . . . afraid."

I carried Imbrahim and placed him as gently as I coul
in the Firebird's backseat. Sharai brought the money case an
windbreakers we had left in the Toyota. She put the thin, dar
jackets over his body. I turned and gave her a look that mad
her flinch.

"Get in the backseat," I said, tossing the money case int
the front with me. "Hold him. It's going to be hard on hir
when I hit a bump."

I bit back the rest of what I wanted to say, words as savag
as the moment Sharai had shot through the harmless frog i
order to kill the scorpion. I drove away from that bridge beate
and bruised in ways I couldn't name, feeling as though I'd bee
to another country and died there. I was half right. I'd bee
to another country—the Middle East. I hadn't died, though
I just felt like it. I'd live to swim another day, to take a scorpio
for another ride or to feel my stinger sink into unprotecte
flesh, and to watch a woman I could have loved kill.

It was a long ride back to civilization. There are days whe
I don't think I made it.

Epilogue

Rafi might not have been dearly loved by the political types of Israel, but his name was pure gold with the covert operators. One phone call from Sharai and men came up out of the cracks and converged on the Jarvis ranch.

That's it, boys. Lock the barn up tight. The horse is dead.

I'm told that the Jarvis house is as good as new, except for a few spots where bullets knocked chunks out of the rock-walled exterior. The flimsy interior wallboard has been replaced by real plaster unmarked by gore. The next terrorist who tries to shoot through the bedroom into the hall might have a tougher time. I doubt it, though. They told me that Salameh had used Teflon-coated armor-piercing bullets.

The Israelis took care of Imbrahim, too, giving him the best, most discreet care Cedars-Sinai could provide. According to his medical charts, he recovered nicely from the car smash that had drilled a piece of metal through his shoulder and burned a furrow in his side. Part of his recovery was no doubt due to the very beautiful "granddaughter" who rarely left his side.

My body healed faster than my mind.

Rafi was buried with full military honors in his homeland, hero-victim of one more nameless border clash. It was what he had chosen over being buried alive with his memories.

I think of him at times like this when I'm filling the ever-blooming flower and listening to the urgent vibration of hummingbird wings around me. King David is gone but a new king is in place, iridescent purple rather than scarlet. Nothing else has changed. The hummers still screel and curse and fight with the grace of tiny, fierce angels that haven't learned to combine and conquer. The king still gives potential usurpers just enough nectar to keep them dancing sweet and vicious attendance.

I try not to think of Sharai.

Forgive me. Remember me.

The second part is all too easy. The first part finally drove me to Ecclesiastes, font of all that man needed to know, if Rafi was to be believed. I heard his voice many times, a river running down to the sea and not returning again, leaving the sea unchanged. I heard the rhythms of inevitability and acceptance and endurance beneath the sun. And then I heard the truth and the question that had driven Sharai into my arms.

Two are better than one . . . for if they fall, the one will lift up his fellow; but woe to him that is alone when he falleth; for he hath not another to help him up.

Again, if two lie together, then they have heat: but how can one be warm alone?

I haven't found the answer.

Kinsey Millhone is . . .

"The best new private eye." —The Detroit News

"A tough-cookie with a soft center." —Newsweek

"A stand-out specimen of the new female operatives."
—Philadelphia Inquirer

Sue Grafton is . . .

The Shamus and Anthony Award winning creator of Kinsey Millhone and quite simply one of the hottest new mystery writers around.

Bantam is . . .

The proud publisher of Sue Grafton's Kinsey Millhone mysteries:

☐ 26563 "A" IS FOR ALIBI $3.50
☐ 26061 "B" IS FOR BURGLAR $3.50
☐ 26468 "C" IS FOR CORPSE $3.50